SABERS FROM THE BRAZOS

FIRST OF A TWO-PART SAGA

WE CONQUER
OR DIE

BY

ERMAL WALDEN
WILLIAMSON

Giant Shadow Publishing
Branson, MO

Printed in the United States of America

We Conquer or Die is published by:

Giant Shadow Publishing
Branson, MO 65616
www.ermal.com
An imprint of Seven Locks Press
Santa Ana, CA

Production Credits:

Editors: Jo Mayberry, Paula Cravens, Paul Press, and Pat and
Cheryl Pruett
Design, Layout and Production by: Kira Fulks
Front Cover Photo by: Betty Williamson
Flag Picture: © 2007 by Paula Cravens
Printing: Express Publishing

DEDICATED TO

The brave officers of Terry's Rangers
Colonel Benjamin Franklin Terry
Colonel Thomas Saltus Lubbock
Albert Sidney Johnston
General John Austin Wharton
General Thomas Harrison

And to

My show partner and friend, Paula Cravens
"America's Yodeling Sweetheart"
whose creative insights helped make this book possible.

A disclaimer: This is a historical novel based upon facts and is intended for entertainment without any prejudice or bias.

About the Author

Dr. Ermal Walden Williamson earned his English-Literature and Theater Major from California State University at Los Angeles and also earned his D-Min. from Fuller Theological Seminary. He is an ordained Southern Baptist minister with his Masters from Golden Gate Baptist Theological Seminary, and a second BS degree with a Bible major from Azusa Pacific College in Azusa, California. His interest lied in writing and acting so he became an actor.

Having been selected as the John Wayne look-alike, he later began performing in his own show on the Duke and brought it to Branson, Missouri. He earned the IGCITA Cloney Award in Las Vegas for being the Best Male Impersonator for 2004.

Praise for

WE CONQUER OR DIE

By

Ermal Walden Williamson

"You have done a wonderful job of bringing the men and the events to life. Your sense of dialogue and characterization breathed life into the men. It is as if you connected the dots with dialogue and interaction. I like the involvement of Cleburne as well. Once the Rangers hit the trail, I found it difficult to put the book down.

I also like the way you wove in the Tennessee girl into the story."

Jeffrey Dixon Murrah
None but Texians: A History of Terry's Texas Rangers

In *We Conquer or Die*, Ermal Walden Williamson further highlights his uncanny ability to combine imaginative storytelling with a keen sense of historical perspective and detail. This is the fourth, and easily the best in his "Brazos" series.

-Larry Johns / High Sonoran Style Magazine.

ACKNOWLEDGMENTS

There are perhaps thousands of books and essays written about the American Civil War, or the War Between the States. This is a novel, which is intended to entertain as well as enlighten the reader with a well of knowledge.

Being reared in the South with Negro schoolmates and friends, and having served for a time in the U. S. Marines out of South Carolina, I like to leave the reader with insights about how I believe both sides of the Civil War might have felt towards each side and their separate causes.

I want to specially acknowledge Jeff Murrah for his many suggestions for making my work a true historical novel.

I want to acknowledge my editors, Jo Mayberry, Paula Cravens, Conan Tigard, Pat and Cheryl Pruett, and Paul Press.

I want to give great appreciation to Sidney Bennett of Tennessee, and to Rhonda Stearns of Wyoming for their wonderful help in providing me with the much-needed information for these parts of America.

Acknowledgement goes to a friend, Abe Carson, Civil War Historian, Los Angeles, CA

WE CONQUER OR DIE

PREFACE

T he rugged cowboy is the enigma of God's mind and the soul of His creation. Matt Jorgensen from Bozeman, Montana believed that a greater Being allowed him to become what he would without intervening, until and unless He was asked. He had been taught this from his dad and his dad before him. "Each man comes into this world alone, and he goes out alone," his dad preached to him. "Don't expect special favors and ya won't be disappointed."

When Matt fled Bozeman for fear of being strung up because of a killing he didn't commit, he stuck to the rule. A wayward scoundrel and his brother were killed in a botched-up freight office robbery. A minister was also killed and the townspeople believed the two sons of Wil Anderson were involved, and also the ones who were killed. Matt, however, was not involved in the robbery, but in attempting to save his brother, he fell under the cover of darkness, rolled beneath a walkway and escaped into the night. Some of the townspeople believed a third man was involved, but could not prove it. Since then, Matt had been on the run.

It appeared that it is up to the tough individual to lighten up and talk to His Master. It is then that God penetrates a man's soul with Divine inspiration that can help lead to man's full potential and to his ultimate destiny in life. However, the cowboy has the will to either accept or reject God's divine intervention and go forward, stop or retreat. Such is the story of one cowboy caught up in this philosophy of life and also in the throes of the Civil War in America.

Matt Anderson, now going by the name of Matt Jorgenson, a lean cowboy on the run from the law in Montana, learned that retreat was not an option when he discovered for himself such training and discipline along the pages of life. To pray for God's intervention could be a little unnerving for his character, as he had already experienced that he must face life alone as it is dealt to him. Or, so he supposed, as he did not feel the necessity for Someone to tell him to stop or go forward. He did as he felt was necessary for the moment. Perhaps, though, someone was always watching over him, for he sensed her presence and suspected that her spirit somehow guided and protected him. She was Ginny McBride, the girl he met on the McBride Plantation in Tennessee

Such also is the story of four men from Brazoria County, Texas who dared to change the course of history by leading Confederate horse soldiers into one glorious battle after another in the War Between the States.

A tall man, Benjamin Franklin Terry stood at the edge of the legendary Brazos River and looked at her long robe of flowing waters, seemingly calling him towards his destiny as a predestined warrior. Behind him laid a plantation of over 2,000 acres of land fronting the Brazos River. He had heard of the stories about the Brazos, how the name, *Brazos del Dios* was Spanish for *the Arms of God* He stood dressed in his military attire with his uncle's saber at his side. His hand rested on the saber as if it, too, were speaking to him. He also had heard of the legend that *warriors would rise up from her waters.*

Being a man of intellect, courage and wisdom, Frank, as he liked to be called, knew the need to answer the calling. Like Matt, he only knew that the Being above all heavens would send out His Spirit upon His chosen to lead His people.

It was his time. He closed his eyes, said a quiet prayer and then felt a soft feminine hand gently take his hand and prayed with him. His wife, Mary Lay, spoke softly. "Same dream, Frank?"

Without looking down, he answered her proudly and with grit teeth. "The sharpness of steel cutting through the air and me on my steed charging through an army of devils." He looked into her tearful eyes and said, "The Brazos is calling me, darling. Don't ask me how or why. I know it sounds too bazaar, but I know she's calling me."

"It's a stupid story. You don't have to believe it."

"A legend, Mary. And, yes, I must believe it. I know deep inside that one of the warriors is me. Texas means my whole life, and I'll fight to keep her free."

"Are you sure it's not just the saber barking at you?" she jested. After all, it has a story to tell, too, belonging to your uncle."

She referred to the saber that belonged to Franks' uncle and guardian, Major Benjamin Fort Smith, which was passed down to him.

Frank looked back at the river and stood a little longer. He felt her hand release his and heard her soft steps walk away from him.

Three other men felt the calling that morning along the banks of the Brazos as if the legend were coming true. At this juncture in time, it would appear that there would be no need for such a calling, as times were quiet in Texas except for a rustle of cattle or a man killing another in a brawl; but nothing on a grand scale. Yet all four men felt the calling and prepared themselves to answer it.

Frank ended his prayer with an *Amen!* It seemed to echo across the Brazos and down the banks of the Brazoria County. Unknown to either of the men, a war on the other side of the country was in the making. It was also unknown that their paths would soon cross.

This is the story of four men from Brazoria County who became cavalry leaders in the Confederate Army and rose to the calling of the Brazos. These men are; Benjamin Franklin Terry, Thomas Saltus Lubbock, Albert Sidney Johnston and John Austin Wharton. And this is the story of Terry's Texas Rangers.

Another man stood on the banks across the Brazos in Waco,

Texas; Thomas Harrison. He, too, knew he had to answer the calling. Having fight in his veins and a strong desire to become a political figure, he too looked forward to answering the calling of the Brazos.

And it is the continuing saga of our hero's venture to escape the law in Montana and light some place where he could carve out a life for himself without having to look over his shoulder. It also combines the story of other Texians who become important players in his life, including one deputy, Steve Andrews, and his sister, Brenda. And lastly, it is the story of Matt's one love, Ginny McBride from a plantation in Tennessee, and Matt's relentless search for her upon hearing that she was shot by a Federal horse soldier.

Matt whipped himself in his saddle and spurred Skeeter into a lope. He was joined by his side-kick, Steve Andrews, who had recently jailed Matt only to find that he had the wrong man.

PROLOGUE

A Fast Gun Comes to Nacogdoches

Tuesday 9 April 1861

Usually, nothing much happened in a big way in a small Texas town, but once it did, the story was told by the locals over and over like the ripples in a pond when a stone is skipped across its surface. Such was the story of the shoot-out between Matt Jorgensen, a cowboy from Montana and Sin Crouch, a killer from Tennessee.

"It took three men to kill him?" one of the barber's customer asked, waiting to get his annual hair cut while another sat in the only barber chair with a hot towel wrapped around his face.

"He was the meanest, orneriest varmint that ever come into Nacogdoches," the barber answered. "Why, his looks alone scared my Sammy." He pointed at an empty spot on the floor where his stray mutt had lain by the door. "He ain't been back since. And that's a fact."

Pete the undertaker walked in, removed his hat, hung it on the rack, and sat down. He was there to read the shop's newspaper and chat some, as was his daily custom. He knew today would be a good day as he had witnessed what news had already spread around town.

"You saw it, Pete, didn't cha?" the barber asked.

"Saw what?" Pete answered lazily, scanning the thin newspaper.

"The shootin'?"

"Oh, yeah. Saw the whole thing. My office is at the end of the street, don't cha know. Down by the livery where it all happened. Yep," he drawled, "saw it all."

"Tell it agin' like ya did for the Sheriff."

"Well, Sheriff Potter and me was atalkin' while I was preparin' the gent's new home. I told him what I saw. This mean –lookin' varmint, a six footer." He looked over the top of the paper at the barber and described with his long thin fingers, "I had to use a bigger coffin than usual." Then he went back to perusing the newspaper while he continued his story. "Any how, he come a ridin' real fast down the street when his horse threw a shoe, stumbled, and this cuss falls off it. Didn't hurt him none. Horse hobbled away, though."

"Tell us about the shoot out, Pete," the customer excitedly reminded him.

"Well, I was comin' to it." He turned the paper inside out and neatly creased it. "Our deputy, the young man Potter hired. Nice fella. Well, he and this here lanky stranger, from Tennessee, I heered, if you please." He scratched his balding head and looked at the customer, sitting next to him. "That's a fir piece. He rode all this far to get this guy 'cause he killed some folks in Tennessee, you see. Includin' a marshal."

"Are you goin' to tell us about the shootout, or not?" the barber asked, now impatient.

"Reckon so." He laid the newspaper neatly across his lap. "Well, this Tennessee fella, he was no lawman. Jest a fella evenin' a score, I 'spose. Anyhow, he and the deputy was a chasin' this mean cuss. I heered them call him out. This bad'un got up, then this tall Tennesean run over and grabbed him, fierce like." The story teller reached over and pulled on the customer's vest to emphasize his story.

"This guy was a mean-lookin' cuss," the barber gestured with tight fists, "the one this Tennessean was after."

"The shoot out, Pete," the customer came back again, pulling Pete's hands off of his vest. "Tell us about the shoot out."

"I'm comin' to it. This here tall stranger, not the dead man, but the Tennessean . . . he beat him up real good. He had a lot of hate in him. I could tell. I thought that it was all over for the varmint. But 'twarn't. This ugly hound comes up with a gun in his hand. Never knew where he got it. 'Spect he had it in his shirt or someplace. Anyway, he aims it at the deputy's head. I told myself I better go help him, but when I saw what happened next, I knowed there 'twarn't any use. I heered a shot. T'warn't from their guns. Well, this man grabbed his leg and fell down. I looks over at our smitty, Jesse, and he's a holdin' a rifle. He done shot him."

"That ain't no shoot out," the customer rebuked.

"'Tis more," the storyteller continued. "The deputy, he draws his gun real fast, and shoots this bad man."

"And, and . . ." the customer interrupted.

"Not through. Seems this bad un falls down, but has enough life in him still and ups and shoots at this cowboy, but his shot goes wild. Zing!" He fixed his eyes as if he were seeing what he was describing. "Well, sir. This here Tennessean guy drew faster than greased lightnin' and shoots this bad cuss between the eyes. Yes, sir," he grins, "right between the eyes. Killed him cold." Then Pete picked up his newspaper and buried his head into it.

"Killed him cold." The barber pointed to his eyes. "Right between the eyes."

"Two shots, I heered," the customer added.

"If I'd a blinked, I woulda missed seein' it," Pete continued talking behind the newspaper.

The customer noticed that the man in the chair sat without saying a word. "What d'ya think, mister?" he asked. "You in the chair."

The man in the chair took the towel from his face and handed it to the barber. "It took three shots," he answered. "This here Jesse you talked about got him in the leg, your deputy, Steve, hit him in the chest, and I got him between the eyes."

The barber splashed some toilet water on the man's face and said, "Now you'll smell pretty." Then he smiled into the faces of his bewildered-looking customers.

Matt Jorgensen got out of the chair, paid the barber a few coins, picked up his wide-brim hat and walked out while the rest of the men looked on with their jaws hanging. He was a strapping man in his twenties, six-foot-four, weighed two-hundred pounds, and wore a leathery face with steely blue eyes.

"See," the barber said excitedly, "he's my customer. I shaved him. Knowed he was here all along. Jest wanted to see ya'll's faces when he got up."

"That's him all right," Pete said nonchalantly as he unfolded the newspaper fully and buried his head back into it while the rest stood, staring at Matt as he walked down the street to the general store.

Deputy Steve Andrews was standing outside waiting for him. "Got all cleaned up jest 'cause I'm takin' ya home to meet my sister?" Steve asked as he greeted Matt. "You sure do smell purty." Steve was a six-footer in his early twenties, like Matt, with sandy hair and brown eyes.

"I'm stayin' 'cause you asked me to," Matt said. "And, I don't cotton to no heroes' welcome the town folks are givin' us tonight. But I'll stay, and then I'm headin' back to Tennessee."

"Fair 'nuf," Steve replied, removing his hat and shaking his hair, letting it fall neatly back into place. "Got folks in Tennessee?"

"A gal. Gotta post my letter," Matt said.

Matt looked inside the store and saw a group of people talking amongst themselves, and he knew it was about the shootout.

Two men walked out and grabbed Matt's hand and shook it until it felt to Matt like it was going to fall off. "I want to tell you, mister that was some mighty fine shootin'. We're proud to know someone who can stand up to killers like you and Steve here."

"Yep," the other chimed in. "We didn't know about him bein' a killer and all 'til the deputy told us how he killed some people up in Tennessee. How many, four or five?"

"Yes, sir," Matt responded. "Thank you, but I've gotta post this here letter."

"I'll do it for you, mister," another man said, taking it and going back inside.

"I heered the dead man killed a woman," a woman said as she and others huddled in back of their men, wanting to see the heroes. "Why," she gasped, "he coulda murdered some of us."

"Let's go, chum," Steve said, putting his hat back on his head, "before we get mobbed." The two men meandered over to the jail where their horses were tied to the hitching rail, mounted up and rode at a slow pace out to a farm house on the edge of town.

Matt thought about the letter the man had taken to mail for him as they rode. It was addressed to his girl in Tennessee, Ginny McBride. In it, he had written,

Dear Ginny. Today, I sent Sin Crouch to his Maker. I'm not proud of it. Just grateful it was him, and not me. I'll be on my way home by the time you read this. Watch for me, my darling. Matt.

She would understand the circumstances behind the killing. She had been beaten by Sin Crouch just before he murdered her house nigger and, later, a marshal.

Steve's sister, Brenda was a pretty twenty-four year old school marm, brunette with brown eyes. She stood five-foot five with a pleasant personality. She had also heard about the gunfight in town from a passerby who wanted to assure her that her brother hadn't been hurt. Brenda watched as her last pupil scurried out of her one-room schoolhouse before she sat down. Even though Steve played on her mind, for the next hour, she continued reading and preparing her lesson for the next day. She didn't believe in taking her work home and, knowing that Steve was all right, she stayed at her desk. She enjoyed her solitude at home with her brother in a small unpretentious farmhouse. They each had a horse, a buggy they shared, a few pigs, chickens, corn in the yard, assorted staples, and a smoke house. Their parents had died of cholera three years earlier while Brenda was away at college. She had no inkling of an idea about Steve bringing her a suitor home for supper, although she had heard about the fast gun.

"Matt," Steve said as they rode slowly, "this is one woman you'll never in a thousand years forget. No boyfriends. Nothin' but school work. Makes me dizzy."

"You married?" Matt asked.

"Nope. Oh, maybe one day. But when I do, she'll have to settle for me bein' a sheriff and not a farmer."

"You, a farmer?"

"Not enough going on for the town to afford two lawmen, full time, that is." Then he looked over at Matt's horse and added, "Got a real nice animal there."

"Skeeter? I like him. My pa gave him to me on my fourteenth, along with a saddle."

"Sounds like a real nice man. Rancher?" Steve asked, presumptuously.

"Nope," Matt answered. "I wouldn't call him nice. And, yeah, he's a rancher." He pushed his hat back on his head and gave Steve's horse the look over. "Let me ask you somethin', Steve. How is it a farm boy has such a marvelous lookin' stallion?"

"Oh, I worked on a ranch not far from here for coupla years. Busted broncs when I was fifteen 'til my butt and my back couldn't take it no more. They paid me off with my pick of horses one day. Then Sheriff Potter saw I was pretty good with my .36 and hired me on as his deputy. Said I could be a sheriff one day."

"Well, you're good. All's I can say about it. Real good."

"You saw me."

"Yep, Matt continued. "Had it not been for your fast draw, I'd probably be in that pine box instead of Sin. Yep."

"Nothin' compared to you, though. Right between the eyes. How'd you do it? Seems real natural for you though, like you did it before." He took out his chaw of tobacco and sliced off a piece and offered it to Steve. "Have you?"

Steve held up his hand, and Matt stuffed it in his mouth. "I'll tell you about it some day." Matt looked at the road and how straight it was and asked, "Think your horse can outrun Skeeter?"

Looking at Matt putting the chaw in his mouth and pulling down the brim of his hat, Steve didn't have to be asked twice. "To the big oak at the bend." He spurred his horse without saying another word. The pair of quarter horses kicked up dirt and sprayed the country side with their dust. Skeeter passed the big oak, beating out Steve's horse.

"Next time," Matt said, catching his wind, "let's count to three." He spit to the ground.

"Skeeter's quite a horse. How'd you beat me?"

"You made the mistake of lookin' back to see where I was. Gave me the edge."

They continued to ride their horses slowly at a walk, until they reached the barn beside Steve's house and dismounted.

"Brenda'll change your mind about goin' back to Tennessee." Steve took Skeeter's reins and led both horses into the barn. "Skeeter's hungry. Ain't cha, fella? Let's give our horses a good rub down."

Matt followed Steve to a stall in the barn and Matt picked up a currycomb on the way. Once Skeeter was in and settled down, Matt began combing his mane while Steve got the water and feed ready.

"Don't over do it, Matt yelled. "Like to let him cool down a bit."

Steve noticed the buggy was in and Brenda's horse was in its stall, which told him she was home. "Brenda'll grow on ya."

"Got serious plans back in Tennessee."

"With that gal you sent the post to?"

Matt nodded.

"Damnation! And me wantin' to interduce you to Brenda. Suppose you gotta do whatcha gotta," Steve countered, coming around Skeeter to face Matt squarely. "But we'll have a good time at the dance tonight," Steve shouted out excitedly. He twirled around and crushed his hat in his hand. "It'll do Brenda a lot of good to go dancin'." He waltzed around his horse and continued, looking straight into Matt's eyes. "She ain't gone to a dance with a fella on her arm since she took up teachin'."

"Whoa, friend," Matt replied almost overzealously.

"Well, since you're goin', you can at least escort her. 'Sides, you owe me one, sorta."

Looking over Skeeter's haunches at Steve's smiling face, Matt broke down and said, "Didn't mean to sound ungrateful. Hell, you helped me get the man I was after. Since you put it that way, why not?"

"You and me and Jesse," Steve said, strutting out of the barn with Matt. "We're the town heroes. Shucks, every gal in town will want to dance with us."

When they reached the porch, Brenda opened the door and greeted them. Matt saw what the young deputy had been bragging about. She stood in the lantern-lit kitchen at dusk time, and her body was illuminated from behind.

She appeared angelic in the crimson glow. She was dressed in a full blue cotton dress with an apron in front, not at all like the schoolteacher she was an hour ago. It was evident to Steve that she had heard about the dance that evening, and that was why she was wearing her best dress.

"Brenda," Steve said with hat in hand, "this is Matt Jorgensen from Tennessee."

"Mr. Jorgensen," she replied with a smile, her hand held out for Matt to take. "Right pleased to meet you."

"Yes, ma'am," Matt mumbled and shook her hand.

"I presume my brother brought you home for supper. Am I right?"

"You sure are," Steve answered, shoving Matt into the house. "Go on in."

Brenda caught Steve and shoved him back off the porch. Steve stumbled and fell down the stairs, bringing Matt with him as he tried to hold on to him for support.

"Oh! I'm sorry, Mr. Jorgensen."

"Quite all right, ma'am." Picking himself up, Matt helped Steve to his feet.

"I'm really pleased that you've come for supper, but my brother is showing no manners. He should have stopped by and told me so." Brenda looked at Matt regaining his composure and continued. "I saw you putting your horses up. And, no matter how pretty you smell, our wash basin is to the side. You'll find some soap there, too."

"Some woman," Steve said, picking up his hat and putting it on his head. "Didn't I tell ya?" He stood up, dusted the seat of his pants and walked to the back.

Matt looked up at Brenda, simply smiled and followed Steve.

"Supper will be ready in a half hour," she said with a slight lilt in her voice. "You best lite somewhere. I'll call you when it's ready."

Steve made certain that Matt was dressed a little fancier than usual that evening by loaning him a set of his own clothes. And seeing Matt in clean clothes, only made Brenda's heart beat a little faster.

A lot was said over supper of corn bread, okra, ham, black-eyed peas and buttermilk; plain ordinary southern-fried cooking.

"Can you believe it?" Steve started in. "A bum comes into town, and I set him up with a job. Then, he accuses Matt of ambushin' him, and I arrest Matt for stealin' his rifle from him. And then, Matt gets me into believin' his story's true, so we goes after the other guy." He continues at a clipped pace while buttering his bread, almost demolishing it. "He tries to get away on his horse, which was a tellin' me that he was a bad-un, but it had a loose shoe, see. Well, if you could'ave seen it. His horse fell and he tumbled off."

"Oh, my," Brenda said, rather startled. "Is this true?" She looked at Matt.

"Yes, ma'am," Matt answered.

"Then what happened to this poor man?" she asked. She already knew more than Steve was telling, but wanted to hear the story from his lips, without spoiling it for him.

"Poor? He weren't poor," Steve rebounded. "He was a ruthless killer. A good thing the smitty was watchin' the whole thing. He shot the guy's leg with a rifle. I 'spect it was more'n a hundred yards. Wouldn't you say, Matt?"

"At least. Maybe more."

"And, he went down," Steve continued. "Then he got back up and started to shoot at Matt. But I drew and shot him in the chest. Knocked him down."

"You killed him, then?" Brenda asked, her eyes wide open, staring at Matt.

"Not really," Steve answered. "He got up and shot at Matt again, and that's when Matt shot him, right between the eyes. That killed him."

"Both shots did," Matt jested.

Brenda looked startled, first at Steve and then at Matt, and, stumbling for words, blurted out, "And, neither of you got hurt?" Her face froze as if to apologize for asking such a question, seeing both men standing before her.

"Nope," Steve answered.

"Then, that's that," she said, wiping her hands on her apron. She looked back and forth at the two men with much curiosity.

"He was a mad killer. Killed a coupla people at least. Right, Matt?"

"Yep. Two. A house nigger and a marshal."

"Oh, my," Brenda reflected. Then, trying to change the subject, she asked, "Do you have house Negroes in Tennessee?"

"Yes, ma'am," Matt replied, shrugging his shoulders. "Quite a lot."

"Then the Sheriff rode back into town from fishin' somewhere out at his favorite spot," Steve continued, excitedly.

"Oh! What'd the Sheriff say when you told him?" Brenda asked nonchalantly, staring at Matt.

"He called Matt and me big heroes." Steve replied proudly, strumming his gallowses. "Oh! Speakin' of which, the town folks are throwin' a dance for us in town, and this bein' only Tuesday."

Brenda turned back to Steve and then toward Matt again in a frivolous state. "I heard."

"You did, huh?" Steve asked. "Well, figured since you don't have a date, Matt could take you."

"Well, that's nice. Is he going to ask me?" she asked, a softer tone in her voice.

"Ask her, Matt."

"Well, I don't know, but . . ."

"Yes, I'd love to go."

"I didn't ask you."

"You most certainly did. You mumbled it, and I accept."

"I'll hitch up the buggy while you do the dishes," Steve said, taking off for the barn and leaving Matt alone with Brenda.

"You don't have to help me wash the dishes, Matt," Brenda said as she handed him a towel.

"A gentleman always pays his respects to the cook, ma'am. My ma would've tanned my hide if'n I was to have walked away without helpin' with the dishes."

"You got a room in town?" Brenda asked Matt as she placed the dishes in a pan of water.

"Nope. Figured it wouldn't be much trouble gettin' one later on, me bein' a hero and all."

"That mean you might be staying for awhile?"

"Maybe. Jest 'til Skeeter gets rested up a bit."

"Skeeter's a funny name for a horse,"

"Smart horse, though," Matt replied, drying the dishes as fast as she cleaned them.

Steve brought the buggy to the side of the house as the two finished up.

"That didn't take long," she sighed, untying her apron. Seeing Matt's stack of dishes on the table, she added, "We'll leave them there for now. I'd best be getting a wrap."

"Eleven years with me," Matt continued as he followed her. "Got him when he was ready to be busted, saddle and all. He don't cotton to skeeters, so I ups and calls him Skeeter."

They both laughed. She picked up a white shawl and a string-tie purse for her wrist. She wasn't one to pull punches when it came to getting her man, and she certainly had that feeling about Matt.

She turned gently and walked back towards the door. Then a magical moment seemed to fill the air as she stopped in front of Matt and their eyes locked on to each other.

"So, you teach school?" Matt whispered as he pulled the wrap close around Brenda's shoulders.

"Yes. And what do you do, Mr. Jorgensen?"

"I was foreman of a large plantation in Tennessee," he answered, looking down at the back of her neck. "I took the job away from the guy who had it. Guess that's why he got crazy like he did and done those killings."

"I see." She walked away and turned the lantern down on the table by the window. "But you're not a lawman."

"Nope. But he almost killed me, and that house nigger he killed were my boss's property. When my head got well where he clobbered me, I set out after him. But a marshal had already started the chase ahead of me. That was his mistake, 'cause he got ambushed. Sin killed him, too. That's his name. And, that's when I followed him here. But then your brother let him go and arrested me instead."

"Why did he arrest you?"

"'Cause I had this man's rifle, see, and he had told Steve that I stole it from him and to watch out for me when I came into town. It had his initials on it. That's why."

Brenda turned down a second lantern on the table and Matt enjoyed watching her move. "How did you get his rifle?"

"He ambushed me. But I was quick with my pistol, and when I shot at him, he dropped the rifle down a cliff. I got it, and he hightailed it out."

She looked at his brawny physique, and feeling good about him, she changed the subject rather subtly, "What's it like being a foreman of a plantation?"

"Nothin' much," he replied, turning the wick down on a third lantern by the door, causing the whole house to go dim. "Jest seein' that cotton and corn are planted, corn plucked and cotton baled at the right time. Things like that."

"That's all?" Brenda walked ever so slowly outside and waited for Matt on the porch.

"Yep. I reckon." Matt followed her and closed the door. "Takin' care of horses and such was my main thing, besides bein' foreman."

"Have you always been a foreman?"

"Nope."

"No?" she repeated. "What then?"

"Cowboy." He wanted to hold her hand, but held himself back.

"We've got cowboys here in Texas. Plenty of cowboys," she quipped. "How are cowboys in Tennessee?"

"Don't rightly know." He looked at her, then asked, "You got somethin' agin' cowboys?"

"Nothing at all," she said with a cute lilt to her voice, "cowboy."

"Yeah. Well, ya see, I come from Montana, originally."

"Oh?" she replied coyly, trying to look into his eyes, from which he had shied away. "Then why did Steve say you were from Tennessee?"

His shyness was unusual, for he was never one for loss of words around a woman. He knew she was playing with him. "Yep. But I was born and raised in Montana. Good country."

Steve watched the couple from the buggy and shouted, "You two ready?"

"Why'd you ever leave it?" Brenda asked, carefully, taking Matt's hand as they walked down the steps.

"Oh, no mind I s'pose." He took her hand in a strong clasp and helped her up into the back seat of the buggy. "Gee. You're light as a feather."

"Thanks."

"Jest wanted to see the rest of the country for myself before settlin' down." Then he looked at her staring intently at him. "And you?"

"What about me?" she asked.

"Where've you been?"

"Nowhere," she responded with a smile, watching him appear to act clumsily. He walked around the horse slowly and was aware of her gazing at him. He settled down in the front seat next to Steve and pulled his hat over his eyes, coyly like.

Steve made a motion with his hand for Matt to get into the back seat with Brenda, but Matt shrugged off his suggestion with a wink and a dry grin and sat down beside Steve.

"Never been out of Texas?" he asked.

"Nope. I received my teaching credentials here in Texas. You know, cowboy, Texas is big enough for just about any thing without having to leave it. I suppose you've been all over the country."

Snapping the lines over the mare's back, Steve yelled out, "Get up there, Sally," and drove the buggy out onto the main road to town and a dance being held for some heroes. "Matt's gonna stay on an extra day or two and teach me some fancy gun tricks."

"Now, I said a while, not a few days."

Steve parked the buggy in a small grove of trees, and the three of them walked up to the town hall, a small rectangular building set just off the main street and behind the general store, where many of the gathering greeted them warmly. Matt and Steve doffed their hats, shook hands and exchanged smiles. Brenda stood alone until Sheriff Potter walked up to her and offered his arm. "Ma'am. May I have the honor of the first dance with you?"

"Why, yes, Sheriff. Thank you."

"Jesse's already inside at the punchbowl, boys," the Sheriff threw back to Matt and Steve as he escorted Brenda to the dance floor.

The two heroes smiled and continued shaking hands with everyone.

"Great job you men did for our town," the town mayor complimented them.

Once inside, Matt fixed his eyes on the Sheriff and Brenda dancing until some of the available ladies made their gestures towards him and Steve. The two heroes were immediately lost in their charms.

Brenda patiently waited her turn to dance with Matt, but it seemed to her that he was fully occupied with the other ladies. She knew it wasn't that he didn't want to dance with her; more that the others were a little more aggressive in their efforts to impress themselves upon him. They weren't a bit awkward in their conversations as they waited for him to ask one of them to dance. In the meantime, she also wanted to be asked, but she refused to use her flirtatious whims on him. Then, when he got around to asking her, he caught Sheriff Potter whisking her off to the dance floor one more time.

Matt didn't want to do wrong to his Ginny, and felt he had a good reason for not dancing with Brenda, but he still kept his envious and longing eye on her as she danced the night away with some of the locals. Every time she glanced his way, he'd shy off in the other direction or find his way to the convenience of the punchbowl. The punch got stronger each time, for it seemed that Steve, Jesse and a few others had been spiking it with good ol' Texas red eye corn liquor made strictly for Texians. They made sure Matt's glass was always full.

Midway through the evening, Brenda asked her brother, "Is he going to ask me to dance with him or not?"

"Little sister," Steve replied, "he's a mind of his own. But I kinda guess he's thinkin' of his girl back in Tennessee."

"Oh, balderdash," Brenda blurted out and walked away to sit by herself. "He's danced with every girl in town."

"Well, well, Brenda," Steve said, laughing, "I didn't think schoolmarms were allowed to swear."

As the band played an easy Texas waltz, Steve twirled his lady friend around to Matt and his partner and said, "Brenda wants to know if you're goin' to ask her to dance."

"She's doin' pretty good on her own, from what I can see," Matt returned. "Is that Sheriff friend of yours crazy on her?"

"Him?" Steve asked, closing in on Matt. "See that woman over there carryin' on with the other biddies?" The woman he singled out was a mildly attractive woman in smart attire with her long hair wrapped tightly in a bun.

"Her?"

"Yep. A preacher's daughter. Real religious. They have two kids."

"Then what's he doin' dancin' with your sister?"

The lady Matt was dancing with giggled, "He never got religion."

"And," Steve added, "she's agin' dancin'."

The night wore away, and still Matt had not danced with Brenda. Steve walked over to him with a couple of drinks in his hand through the maze of congratulatory people and asked him, "You gonna ask her to dance or not, chum?" He watched Matt teeter on unsteady legs, and said, "No, I guess you're not." Then he took one of the drinks himself and toasted to Matt. "Might as well join ya."

Watching her brother and Matt appear in their inebriated state, Brenda rose, and snatching up her shawl as the last dance was being played, walked to the door. She waited for Steve to catch up and accompany her. She didn't look at Matt. She feared she would embarrass herself at wanting to give him an unlady-like piece of her mind. She pshawed a little like a jealous mare, turned, and with Steve by her side, walked outside. Seeing Matt follow them, she waited for him to help her up into the buggy.

Matt walked around to her side and offered his hand to her as he drunkenly gazed into her eyes.

Brenda refused to look at the cowboy, and once in the buggy, kept her eyes straight-away down the darkened road that was barely lit by the moonlight, filtering through the trees.

Matt somehow managed to climb in front with Steve. He sank back and pulled his hat over his face as the three rode lazily back to the farm house. Nothing much was said on the ride back, but much was thought by Brenda as she sat in a bad mood all the way home.

Wednesday 10 April 1861

In Charleston, South Carolina, a young, forty-three year old, medium stature gaunt Brigadier General Pierre Gustave Toutant Beauregard, a graduate of West Point, and now Commander of the provisional Confederate forces at Charleston, South Carolina, demanded Major Robert Anderson's surrender of Fort Sumter.

Major Anderson, Commander of Union forces in Charleston, had relocated his troops from Fort Moultrie on Sullivan's Island across the channel to Fort Sumter, having considered it to be a more defensible position, as it was strategically located on an island at the entrance to Charleston Harbor. He refused General Beauregard's demand, and the two men with their garrisons, one defending a fort, and the other demanding a surrender of it, began a standoff that would change the course of history for America.

That same morning in Texas, Brenda opened the kitchen door and slung the dishwater out into the yard, sloshing some on a surprised cowboy, standing just outside.

"Mornin', Brenda," Matt said, knocking the dishwater from his wide-brim hat and vest. "I see you're still mad."

Brenda's eyes widened as she dropped the pan and wiped her hands on her apron. The sudden noise caused Steve to run out of the house with a Navy Colt .36 in his hand.

"What happened?" he asked, looking dumbfounded at the couple sharing a moment with each other. He saw Matt wiping his face and saw the dishpan on the ground.

"I dropped the pan," Brenda said, looking first at Matt and then at Steve as he knelt down to pick it up. "Sorry. I don't know what came over me," she said, blushing. "Come on in."

"Mornin', Chum," Steve said. He watched Brenda as she straightened up her hair and smiled like she just had a birthday surprise, and he knew she had a feeling for Matt. He continued his conversation with Matt as he grabbed the coffeepot from the stove. "Didn't want to wake ya. Sleep good? Hungry?"

"A mite," Matt answered, following Steve's welcome into the house. "Smelled the coffee from the barn."

Steve poured Matt a cup, then picked up a chair and joined him at the table. "We jest ate," he said, pointing to the dishes that had been cleaned. "Got some biscuits left, though."

"What time is it gettin' to be?" Matt asked, grabbing his cup and a biscuit.

"I have to be at the schoolhouse to welcome the kids, so we get an early start. And no, I'm not mad any more." Brenda rushed out in one breath. "I trust you had a good time last night, Mr. Jorgensen."

Matt nodded and grinned at her.

"I'm going to be late if I don't go right now." She headed out the door to her buggy tied up by the side of the house. "See you boys when I get back?"

"I'm always here, Sis," Steve said.

"And, you?" Brenda shouted back, climbing into her buggy and waiting for Matt to answer.

"Maybe," Matt said, walking out on the porch. He took a swill of coffee and grinned again.

She took that for a yes, then whipped the lines over the mare's back.

Matt and Steve watched her head down the road.

"Brenda's the soft-spoken type," Steve said. Then he realized Matt was still wearing his suit, now soaked with dirty dishwater. "Hey. Look what you done to my suit."

"Yeah," Matt returned, "it's a mess. Guess I owe ya."

"You know, for a drunken cowboy, you sure sobered up fast."

Matt continued to watch Brenda as she and her buggy disappeared around the bend. "I might not have been that drunk, friend," he said with a smile as he took another swig of coffee. "Jest cautious."

Unbeknownst to the three, an evil wind blew across the country that day.

CHAPTER 1

TEACHING A FARM BOY NEW TRICKS

12 April 1861, 4:30 a.m.

From Fort Johnson, located on James Island in Charleston, South Carolina, a mortar shell broke through the cool morning air under the orders of General Beauregard and opened the momentous bombardment of Fort Sumter. On the following day, Major Anderson knew his men could not withstand the surrounding forces of the Confederate troops, and without the necessary provisions to help them hold out, he honored the General's demand to surrender the Fort. At 2:30 p.m., Saturday, 13 April, Anderson surrendered his forces without any casualties and on the next day, he evacuated the garrison at Fort Sumter. The Civil War had officially begun.

Matt stayed on the farm a few days longer as he had promised Steve to show him how to better handle a Colt .36. He also wanted to mend fences with Brenda because of the way he treated her at the dance. Friendship was hard to find and even harder to forget, and besides, he needed the rest before trekking the long way back to Tennessee.

Those days were like an Indian summer. Both men took time off from their chores to practice their shooting. It had already become second nature with Matt for he had kept up his practice since the days he had spent with his friend, Rod Best in Kansas the year prior.

"Yours isn't tied down," Steve noted. "Mine is. So I should be faster. Right?"

"It would seem like." Matt took his holster off and handed it to Steve.

Steve examined Matt's holster more carefully. "It's tied down in the back with leather latchets."

"Yep. Your holster slides on your belt. That slows you down. I found, by latching my holster, there's no slack. And notice my pistol rides at a slant. That way, it comes out easier."

"Seems awkward."

"Not necessarily. It shaves at least another second or two off my draw. You're drawing with a tied down holster and your pistol's pointed straight down. Mine's pointed a little upward because my gun grip faces away. Your grips have to be pointed more downward if you're gonna use your holster like that."

Steve removed his gun belt, handed it over to Matt and watched him carefully. "Work on tying it here and you'll improve your draw maybe one half to a second, but it could make all the difference between who hits the dirt first.

"Try my gear. See how it fits you."

Steve exchanged gun belts and strapped Matt's to his hips.

"Damn," he thought as he eyed the slickness of Matt's Navy Colt .36.

"My gun should be evenly balanced in your hand," Matt instructed Steve. "You'll find that the pearl handle is not only for looks but it should feel smooth, light and natural, not like yours which is a swollen wood stock and heavy."

At first, it felt awkward to Steve to draw with the holster slanted, but after several tries, it started to become natural for him.

"Now, draw and shoot." Matt pointed to a nearby tree.

Steve drew and fired several times while Matt watched.

"Real nice draw, but you missed the tree." Matt laughed. He drew the Navy fast and fanned it at the tree, splitting a branch.

Steve turned and fired at a branch on a nearby tree knocking it down with one shot.

Matt drew Steve's pistol and fanned off three rounds, clipping the branch as it fell.

"Damn!" Steve said, as he stood there with his mouth agape. "And, with my gun, yet. I've gotta learn that."

"A mite sticky on the hammer, Steve. Keep your sweetheart clean, and she'll never fail you. If your tie is loose anywhere, you lose. With my holster, again one doesn't need it tied down."

The men returned each other's gun belts and strapped them back on. They eyed each other as if they sensed that each of them had to play out the hand that was being dealt him and each felt a need to help the other.

"The reason I got Sin was because he hesitated. That's the only difference between us. Oh, he killed a marshal, but that was in the back. Facin' a man is another situation. Sin didn't know how to handle me."

"Did you kill a man before Sin?"

"Yep."

"Where? How?'

"Kansas. Too long a story to go into now, but take my word for it, I had to learn fast. Don't worry, it was legal."

For the next hour, Steve learned with the Colt Navy .36 all that Matt could teach him.

"The only way to improve," Matt continued, "is to practice 'til your hand is raw. Now, try a fan."

Steve drew and fanned his Colt three times, then twirled it and holstered it.

"Notice anythin'?"

"An easiness about it," Steve answered, putting his hands on his hips.

"Look at your hand."

Steve looked down and saw blood. "Damn. I cut it."

"Your hammer is razor sharp. I felt it when I fired yours. File it down smooth. Else you're gonna bleed to death every time. Notice my hammer is larger. That's for fannin'."

Steve wrapped his hand with his bandanna, and the two men called it a day.

On the morrow, they saddled up and went riding.

"You've got an excellent quarter horse,' Matt said as they rode out. "Nothing wrong with it if you're lookin' for quick speed."

"Yours is a quarter, too," Steve remarked, looking at Matt's horse carefully.

"A gelding. Yep. One of these days I'd like to trade him in on a thoroughbred. Kinda like to have speed for more than part of a mile."

"Where're we headed?" Steve asked as they kicked their horses into a gentle lope.

"Out in that clearing. I want to see what our fast horses can do."

They rode out to the center of a cleared field where the mud had dried from the rain a few days back. The ground was hard and the grass was soft.

Matt dismounted and tightened his girth.

"I suppose what got Sin killed was his negligence to his horse. Seemed he let his horse lose a shoe. If you're gonna be a sheriff, I'd look after my horse. Jest like I done said about a gun being your sweetheart, so's your horse. A man's only as good as his best horse," he smiled at Steve, and finished, " and at his worse time."

"Where'd you learn all this?" Steve asked, dismounting and tightening his girth.

"The guns or the horse?"

"Both."

"I learned the guns from an old friend of mine up in Kansas. Rod Best. Met him and his brother in Kansas. He was the fastest gun I'd ever seen. The only one I'd ever seen, sides me. What I learned you?"

"Yeah?"

"He learned me. 'Ceptin', he wore two guns to my one. He could draw and shoot them both faster than I could draw my one."

"What happened to him?"

"Got hooked up with some gal. Beautiful lady. Rode off to places unknown, I suppose. Wanted to be a marshal, some day. Like you. Probably is one by now."

Matt mounted up and said, "Let's ride."

"What cha gonna learn me today?"

"How to ride, mister. How to ride. Follow me."

The men started out in a walk across the field, then urged their horses into a trot. Without warning, Matt spurred Skeeter into a fast gait, and Steve's horse followed.

"Whoa, boy," he commanded Skeeter.

"What's the matter?" Steve asked.

"Two things, Steve," Matt said propping his leg upon his saddle. "First, let's have a chew."

"You noticed that when my horse went faster, yours did, too." He sliced a bit off his chaw of tobacco and gave a piece to Steve.

"Because I made it?"

"Nope. Some horses like to follow other horses. They don't take time to think for themselves. Yours is a follower."

"That bad?"

"A sheriff can't afford to have a horse that follows another one. He's got to have a horse that can outthink the other one. Kick your horse into a run."

Steve put his chaw between his teeth and spurred his horse into a lope. After a few moments, he looked back and saw Matt still sitting his horse.

"I see what you mean," he yelled and rode back.

"Take complete control of your horse."

"You learn this from Rod Best, too?"

"Nope. Jest from ridin' day and night for months on end. You probably rode a mile or two to town and back."

"No need otherwise."

"I've chased and been chased. Had my horse shot out from under me. You learn to respect your horse after a few encounters. Different than bustin' broncs. Trust me. He's your best friend out there alone." He spat out his wad while watching Steve wallow his around in his mouth. "Now, let's ride."

Steve bit down on his chaw and leaned into his saddle, kicking his horse into a trot.

"Control, Steve," Matt said, looking back. "All we'll be doin' now is controllin' him."

For the rest of the morning, Matt rode Steve into the ground with more instructions on riding a horse. Towards evening, when his buttocks sprouted blisters, Steve was ready for a good rest.

Sleep came short for Steve as Matt slipped through his bedroom window and roused him out of his bunk with the slap of a horse blanket.

"Your sister has some flapjacks on the skillet. I smelled 'em. Figure we could chug a few down and then do some more ridin' this mornin'."

Steve looked up at Matt and wrinkled up his face. "Oh, no."

"I'll be leavin' in a few days, and if you want to learn how to become a sheriff real bad, you best be takin' advantage of daylight."

Sure enough, after breakfast, Matt and Steve waved to Brenda and tore off towards the clearing again while she rode her buggy to school.

"Good lookin' woman, Matt," Steve said with a mouthful of the flapjack he carried with him.

"Matchmakin' again, Mister Andrews?"

"Ever' time I get a chance."

And, so it went for the next several days. Steve enjoyed Matt's companionship more than anything he had known as a kid, and he found in him something of a father image to replace the one he had lost. He also found a sincere friend, one who cared enough about him to help him towards his goal of becoming a sheriff.

"Sheriffs get shot at a lot," Matt warned him again as they rode and shot their way across the prairies of Nacogdoches.

"Hate work, Matt," Steve said. "Love to hunt and fish, though, and it seems to be a daily routine with Sheriff Potter. Yep. I guess I can handle a shoot out now and then. And huntin' and a fishin'".

Matt dismounted Skeeter, took out some tin cans from his saddle bag and placed them on a stack of rocks in the clearing.

"When I count three, draw as fast as you can and see how many you can hit."

Steve dismounted and tied his horse to a nearby tree. He took a position to draw.

"Naw. Not like that. Don't expect to draw. Act casual like nothin' was goin' to happen." He waited for Steve's relaxed moment, then yelled, "One-two-three."

Steve drew and hit all five cans. While one was spinning in the air, he shot it with his last bullet.

Matt drew and kept it in the air with six more shots. "Reload and keep it up there," he yelled out.

Steve reloaded quickly and got off three more shots, hitting it as it came down. Then he was startled by a rifle shot from Matt's side, and the can spun into oblivion. Turning, Steve saw Matt standing with a smoking rifle.

"Got to be a quick thinker," Matt said, placing his rifle back into its boot. "A man standing in the street with an empty pistol is likely to get hisself kilt. Know what I mean."

The pair continued throughout the day and the next, shooting at cans, bottles, tree limbs and flower buds, trying to outdo the other. Steve improved with each day of practice. Matt lost his sense of hurry to get back to Tennessee; he was having a good time with a new-found friend.

At the same time, Matt's days around the farm, learning feats such as slopping the hogs, making soap out of lye and castrating pigs and eventually smoking them proved to be quite an experience for him. It brought back remembrances of the days he journeyed through Kansas with his sidekick, Toothless. He had seen Toothless do the same chores as a farmhand. Now it was his turn. He didn't mind being a farmhand after having been plantation foreman just short months before. And do it he did, to Brenda's consternation. She laughed at him as he wrestled the pigs while Steve did the nipping.

Then one day, three riders spurred their horses onto the Andrews' property, passing Brenda's buggy headed in the opposite direction. Reining up at the house, a tall, gaunt man took off his hat and waved it, yelling, "We're at war! We're at war! Jest got the news!"

Steve ran out of the house almost knocking Matt down. "What's this you're yellin', Zeke?"

The riders were neighbors who had just heard the news in town. War between the States had finally come about, and they were zealously spreading it through the community of farms.

"Fort Sumter. It all started at Fort Sumter. The South broke away from the North. We're at war, people."

"You sure, Zeke?" Steve asked.

"Yep," replied a second rider who was shorter and a little older than the rest. "Jest heard about it. Ain't that sumpin'?"

"Yeah!" Steve threw his hat up in the air, caught it and screamed out, "Yahoo!" Then, as quickly as he began celebrating, he stopped when he saw Matt hadn't joined in.

"Hey, Matt, boy," he yelled out. "We're at war. Ain't that somethin'?"

Matt's face showed the other gentlemen he wasn't excited. If anything, he was confused and concerned.

"What's the matter, boy?" Zeke asked, walking over to him. "This is good news, son."

"Yeah," Matt replied. "I'm just not sure what your good news is. I'm from Tennessee."

"He's a Yankee," another rider remarked threateningly, dismounting and walking over to him.

"Hold on, Jerry!" Steve yelled out as he caught his arm. Jerry was a skinny redheaded teenager who had no other up-bringing than that in his strong redneck environment.

"Bein' a Tennessean don't make him a Yankee, necessarily" Steve continued. Then he turned to Matt and said rather dumbfounded, "Tell 'em, Matt."

Matt stood silent for a moment, not knowing exactly how to answer. He felt like he was back in Virginia City again fighting his pa about having to leave Montana or get hung as a robber and killer. Now he had to make a fast decision about on which side of the war he was going to fight. It wouldn't be an easy one.

"Come on, Matt," Steve said, giving Matt a clip on the chin. "You're a rebel, same as us. Tell 'em."

Steve saw he was going to have trouble with his neighbors, and laughed to lighten the mounting tension.

If Matt admitted he was a Yankee from Montana, he would be a dead Yankee. Rightly so, now that war had been officially declared. If he said he was a rebel, then he'd be asking himself, "What the hell does a rebel do?"

He plumped for the lesser of the two evils and sounded off. "There are southern sympathizers in Tennessee. And, then there are those who favor the North. . . . I'm a foreman on a Tennessee plantation with over fifty slaves." Then he asked rhetorically, "Do a Yankee have slaves?"

His answer brought a big sunshine grin to Steve's face and he let out a rebel yell that echoed throughout Texas. "There! Ya see, boys. We've got ourselves a war."

"But I thought you wanted to become a sheriff like Potter," Matt replied.

"Not when there's a war, chum. A war. Don't cha see. We'll be out there in the woods, a huntin' and a shootin' at no-good uns. Jest like they were all the bad guys. Shucks, Matt, what am I sayin'? They are the bad guys." He twirled around and laughed with the other men. "Yeah. We're the good guys."

Matt saw he was going to be caught up in a war whether or not he had any part in starting it and no obvious reason he could find to take either side. He had fought in Bloody Kansas helping to keep it a free state, free of slave owners. That seemed like a hundred years ago to him, now. He thought over and over again as to how his convictions were changing from one way of living to another ever since he had met Ginny McBride, a southern belle and plantation owner with slaves.

He was a Yankee from the territory of Montana-- much like Tennessee with both Northern and Southern sympathizers. He was caught deep in rebel territory, and he ached to go back to Tennessee and his Ginny.

Right now, Tennessee seemed a far ways off to Matt. It wasn't as distant as Virginia City, Montana, his hometown, but somehow Tennessee now felt like his real home because Ginny was there. He had made his decision right then and there; he had sided with Ginny's convictions and became a rebel. How he was going to personally make the transaction from Yankee to Rebel was the biggest problem he had to wrestle well at that moment.

CHAPTER 2

NO RUSH TO GET INTO ACTION

It still took several weeks for the news of Fort Sumter to spread through the region before many men joined up to fight. Their spirits had been lifted to great heights, but to keep themselves together at that point, they went out on a binge that lasted many, many days. Their objective, naturally, was victory for the South, fast. However, their other thoughts were for staying alive, and they figured it might be the last time they would taste whiskey as civilians.

They reasoned among themselves that the war might be over before they got involved, or at the latest that this might somehow be over by Christmas. They wanted to get into it and get it over with, yet at the same time, go slow and not do things too quickly.

"Hell," a young man said, taking a chaw as he stood under an oak tree set by a brook, "I ain't a hurryin' none to become a hero. Least wise a dead hero."

The men talked among themselves at every creek and bend in the road, trying to muster up enough courage to enlist. For days they argued as to how they would fight in this war.

"You suppose we should join the infantry or the cavalry?" Steve asked.

"Don't know," Matt answered. "How 'bout if we simply be guerrillas?"

One of the boys, tall and gaunt and mean looking, gave Matt a vicious stare of distrust. "You still talk like a damn spy."

"He makes good sense," Steve came back in Matt's defense. "We don't need uniforms to fight. Think about it."

They did, for about ten seconds, and then set back to talking about how they would join up, hoping something would eventually come along to change their minds.

"I think we need to join a real rank and file regiment," Steve settled on.

Some boys already did. Others went on home, hoping no one would come after them.

"How do you see it, Matt?" Steve asked, sipping the last drop of his Texas red eye at the Calico Saloon. "We're tighter than a whore's corset and we still haven't made up our minds what to do."

Steve had convinced Matt he would be killed if he went back to Tennessee, if not by Union soldiers, then probably by their own. Matt figured he was a dead man, coming or going. He reticently chose to stay with Steve.

Matt's face was buried in his hat as he sat slumped over a table.

All that Steve heard was mumbling out of Matt. "As I see it, friend," Steve swirled his empty glass in his hand with his thumb and two fingers as if saving a sip for later, "my drink is gone, and I'm drunk." He took the glass and threw it up against a far wall and watched it bounce and land on the floor, spinning. "Didn't break. And I threw it hard, too. Know what?" he asked drunkenly. "That's the world, spinning around and around. Columbus said so."

"What?" came a question from the man with his face in a hat.

"Columbus," Steve answered. "He said the earth was round, and that's what that little bitty glass is over there on the floor. Round and spinnin'."

"Ginny?" Matt mumbled.

"No, chum, not Ginny," Steve replied. "Spinnin'. Like my head."

The two men had been in the saloon for hours, and only a handful of people remained to keep them company. All were strangers.

The bartender, a robust man in his mid-fifties wearing an apron and carrying a cleaning rag, stepped over and retrieved the glass. A little disturbed by the incident, he walked over to their table and said, "We're closing, gents. Any more drinks, or have you had enough?"

Steve looked up at the bartender and vainly attempted to parlay his drunken stupor into sobriety. "Enough, my friend? There never is enough." Then looking at Matt, he added, "Right, chum?"

Matt couldn't respond but fell asleep in his hat and began to slide off the table. Steve caught him by his collar, stood up and brought Matt with him. "Enough, my friend," he said again. Picking up Matt's hat from the table and placing it on his head, he placed a silver dollar on the table and hauled Matt's body out of the saloon.

Leaving the saloon and panting for air, Steve pushed Matt's body up onto Skeeter. He wearily climbed into his saddle and exhaustively added, "Enough, and good night, good ol' red eye," and the two rode towards home.

Brenda was still up when they dismounted their horses and put them in the barn. Matt sauntered over to some hay on the ground, fell on it and passed out.

Steve had finished removing the saddles to put the horses away when Brenda stepped inside the barn.

"Drunk again?" she asked, wiping her hands on her apron. It was a habit she had of keeping them busy.

"Not me, Sis," he replied, winking and pointing to Matt

"What's to become of us, Steve?" she asked, walking slowly to his side as he placed the horse blankets over the rail. "I mean the war and all, now. When are you both leaving?"

"I suppose this was our last night out around here, Sis." Steve grabbed her gently by her shoulders and looked deeply into her saddened eyes. "Didn't see anyone we knew, except the bartender. But, we're way out here in Texas country and it'll be a while before we'll know where to enlist. We'll have to ride towards Houston I recken

Standing beside Matt, Brenda knelt down and bunched some hay around his head as a pillow. "Tomorrow?"

"Give or take a few days," Steve replied, watching her take care of Matt. He knew she was falling in love with him and he also knew that Matt still only had eyes for Ginny.

"Maybe get into a cavalry unit," Steve said. "They gotta need good riders and good marksmen, I reckon. Should check 'em out before signin' on with anyone else."

Most of the able-bodied men in Nacogdoches chose the infantry. Steve and Matt had good mounts and so they leaned towards the cavalry. Matt's ulterior motive was to pick a place far enough away to delay signing on with any company or regiment. Houston was a larger city, far enough away to travel, and yet close enough to be in their backyard, so to speak.

"You two are better than most with your pistol shooting and riding horses," Brenda said, rising to her feet, still looking down at Matt's drunken body.

"Shot that thar killer feller right between the eyes at fifty paces," Steve reminded her. "I'd say he's the best."

"And, you figure you're just as good now as he is?"

"Are you kiddin'? Close, maybe, but no one's as good as Matt."

"Well, if he's going to join up with you, I guess you'd better be watching out for each other," Brenda said, still looking at Matt.

"We'll do jest that, Sis," Steve answered, putting his arm around her as he walked her out of the barn.

CHAPTER 3

THE LONE STAR TEXIAN FROM MONTANA

The night dreamed itself slowly into dawn, as Brenda stayed awake, looking out her bedroom window towards the barn where Matt slept. When morning came, Steve found her still sitting by the window in deep slumber with her chin between her knees. She had finally given in to sleep. She awoke into a positive state of awareness the moment she felt Steve's gentle touch when he attempted to carry her to bed.

"You oughta get some sleep, Sis," he said softly
. "It's been a long night."

"I did sleep," she yawned. "You woke me up, stupid. I'm all right now."

He let her down easy and watched her as she flew down the stairs and outside. On her way, she looked towards the barn, but no sign of life stirred and so she lazily began her morning chores.

The waft of coffee floated inside the barn, waking Matt to a bright new morning. Stretching his arms ever upward and opening his eyes as if to ask where he was sleeping, he had gained his momentum for the day, appearing wide awake and bushy tailed as if he had never been drunk the night before. That lasted a few moments until he stood up and found himself still wobbly. As his eyes looked through the barn doors towards daylight, he squinted and then made his way to the nearest stall where he found relief. He found that Skeeter had preceded him earlier in the same place.

"Mornin', Skeeter," he said as he stood there, finding himself coming alive. "What time d'ya get in?"

"About ten, but I wasn't drunk like you," Steve answered, coming through the door and flinging it wide open. "How'd ya feel, chum?"

"Better now, thanks," Matt replied, pulling himself together. "For a moment there, I thought Skeeter got the gift of talkin'." Fastening his britches, he asked, "Hey, I smell coffee?"

"Yep. Brenda got bacon and eggs fryin'. Hungry?"

"Ugh!" Matt complained with an aggravated tongue hanging out of his mouth. "Jest coffee. Got any tobacco?"

"Sure," Steve replied, taking his tobacco from his shirt pocket and giving it to Matt. "Want me to slice it for ya?"

"Yep. Then just stick it between my lips, friend," Matt said, running his fingers through his thick hair.

Taking the wad between his lips, Matt said, "Let me ask you a question."

"Fire away."

"What do winners get and what do losers lose?" He started chewing down hard on the wad.

"How d'ya mean?"

"We're gonna enlist in a war we didn't start. Fight people we don't know, who we might have known sometime back or in the future, I don't know. For what? I mean, if we win, what do we win?"

"Freedom?"

"The hell you say. Freedom from what? Hell, we're as free now as we ever want to be. I've been thinkin', friend. You have a nice home, a sister who is a school teacher, a job where you'll some day be a sheriff of a town that's really just startin' to grow. What more freedom do you want?"

"I don't know," Steve returned, taking his hat off and tossing it on a pile of hay. "You say you've got slaves. If the North wins, say, then they'll take the slaves away from us. Then what?"

"Maybe it's a good thing, the way I see it," Matt answered. He thought about the McBride Plantation and the slaves he had, such as Hezekiah and Nancy with their three kids, and Naomi the house nigger, and the rest working hard in the heavy sun. He saw them living in their slave quarters, tending a garden in front and behind. He remembered their singing and shouting. He especially remembered when they buried big Bertha, and they sang all night and all day long over her body before they buried her, "She's Gonna Rise Up and Git Down Her Ol' False Teeth".

He remembered the Christmas where several of them were baptized together in a nearby creek that was too cold for swimming but just right some how for being dunked. He remembered all the good times and the bad. And he remembered Ginny, his girl he left behind to chase across country to capture the man who killed big Bertha and a kindly marshal just doing his job.

"How can you say it's a good thing?" Steve asked, sitting himself on a rail. "It's a good thing for them to destroy your girl's plantation?"

"Would they?"

"As sure as you're chawin' that wad, they would. They say those niggers have the same rights as you and me. If thet be true, one day we'll be workin' for them. Hell, Nacogdoches would have a black sheriff. Can you jest see that?"

"And if we win, say?" Matt began uncoiling a rope. "What do we win?"

"You serious?" Steve looked down at Matt quizzically and drew a conclusion. "You ain't one of us, are you?"

Matt spat on the floor of the barn. He had waited for someone to recognize him for who he was. Now it came time to admit it, to his friend, Steve.

"I'm from Montana," he answered. "I told Brenda. Didn't seem to bother her."

"A Yankee?" Steve jumped off the rail and picked up his hat.

"Born and bred, friend."

"I'll be damned." He dusted his trousers with his hat and plopped it on his head.

"Not like you think, though."

"How do you know how I think?"

"Been around you long enough the past few weeks. Don't that mean nothin'?"

"But, a Yankee! Damnation! How did you happen to settle on a plantation?"

"Jest happen to. Hell, Steve, I never set eyes on a black person in my life until I came across the McBride Plantation. I saw a white man whipping a black man. Didn't make sense. I shot the whip out of his hand and then she came after me with a whip. Ginny. The next thing I knew, I was in love with the most beautiful gal I ever laid eyes on."

"Thet don't change you from bein' a Yankee, none."

"Yankee! Hell, I didn't rightly know what a Yankee was until Ginny and her pa talked about them quite a bit. And we discussed it, recken because they owned slaves and didn't want the *Yankees* to take them away from them."

Steve stood still and stared at Matt as if searching for an answer, but said nothing. Just kept listening to Matt's tirade.

"I come from the North, Montana. We didn't talk any about them. Not to my recollection. I don't know what to tell you, Steve," Matt spat his wad on the floor . "It's gonna be hard as hell for me to want to kill a human bein' jest because some side says we want to free the slaves and the other side says no."

"In Kansas?" Steve asked with his hand on his gun grip. "What side were you on?"

Matt tightened his insides as he watched Steve's muscles twitch in his hand. He had seen that look before and it wasn't something he thought he'd see in Steve, standing against him.

"I stood on the first side that would have me. Plain and simple. I was there to break up the two gangs."

He eyed Steve's hand, twitching at his gun butt.

"You're standin' all wrong, Steve," Matt said, pointing to his gun hand quivering above his grip. "You'd be dead before you touched it, and you know it."

Steve bit his lower lip and stood firm facing Matt, waiting for Matt to make a play.

"I'm removing my gun belt, friend," Matt said as he unbuckled it and let it fall to the ground. "That's somethin' I've never done before."

Steve stood strong and silent, trying to find words to say.

"You see?" Matt turned his back on Steve. "You and I. We're in a grudge fight right now jest talkin' about sides." He turned with his hands in the air and continued, "And we're friends. You gonna shoot me jest because I helped to free Kansas of slave owners. Hell, Steve, they were shippin' 'em across the Kansas border from Missouri faster than you can imagine. And for money. For money, Steve. And power. They'd kill to get slaves into Kansas so they'd control the state and become rich. We're not like that. You and me."

"What d'ya do to make you choose one side agin' the other?" Steve asked, looking at Matt's gun belt lying on the floor.

"I was a government agent, given the choice of joinin' either side jest so's we'd bust 'em up. There were two men who had gangs in the area."

Matt saw Steve eyeing his gunbelt.

"To make a long story short, a U. S. Marshal got word of a gunfight I was in and liked how I handled myself. He came down and told me what was goin' on and asked for my help. I didn't do it for any patriotic reasons. I simply did what I did for the sake of humanity. There was too much killin' goin' on.

"I got in with the anti-slavers. We didn't call ourselves Yankees or Northerners or anythin'. The gang jest wanted to keep the pro-slavers out of Kansas and got to me first."

"Where was this?"

"Fort Scott, Kansas. I made a lot of good friends, and we had ourselves one hell of a war. But, to this date, I can't talk about it to either side for fear of someone wantin' to get revenge on me. So, I took up plantin' cotton for a pretty little lady."

"Wow!" Steve exclaimed. He picked up Matt's gun and holster and gave it back to him. "I've heard about that fracas. Hell, you done made history. You've already been in a war."

"Don't know about history, but, yep. I've been in a war. And it ain't pretty, friend."

"Then, what're we gonna do, now?"

"If word got out down here in Texas about what I did in Kansas, I'd be tarred and feathered. Guess I have only one choice. Tag along with you and make sure you don't get shot up, Friend."

"I'll keep my mouth shut about it." Then he thought. "You told Brenda?"

"Only that I'm from Montana."

"Good. Let the rest be our secret."

"Still the question."

"What's that?"

"What do we get if we win?"

"By 'we', you mean the South, I take it. Damned if I know. The right to own slaves, I suppose."

"And . . ." Matt continued, "you don't own any."

Steve stopped in his tracks, looked up at Matt and said, "Yeah."

"How about a light, friend?"

They walked over to the house and entered the kitchen where Brenda took the broom from the corner of the kitchen and shooed them back outside. "Not on me life, young Matthew," she said. "And you, too, big brother. Wash your face and your hands. I know where you've been, and it ain't over by the wash basin."

The men turned, jumped down the steps and headed for the washbasin where they found cold water and a bar of lye soap.

"She'd make a hell of a wife," Steve said, drying his hands.

"Yeah," Matt agreed, "someone else's, I reckon."

It was Saturday and there was no school, so Brenda took her time with the breakfast and cleaned up afterwards. She also took her time in primping herself up for the likes of Matt, thinking it could be their last day together and she wanted to look especially pleasing to him. Yet, her premonition, like that of many wives and sweethearts during a war, kept rolling through her mind. "He's leaving me and may never be returning. And I should be getting on with my life and preparing for his funeral."

"Oh, blast!" she shouted aloud and flung her hairbrush out her bedroom window. "Oh, my! I did not mean that," she said, and went quickly down the stairs and outside to retrieve it.

Matt held it up to her as she got to the door. "It's not every day a fella gets to see a flying hair brush," he said and then grinned from ear to ear. He brushed his hair and took his time about it. "Beats a comb any day."

"I . . . I lost my temper," she said, accepting it from him. "Give it here."

"Steve and I are goin' into town for a newspaper. See what news there is. We should be leavin' now."

Her face turned from anger to sadness as she watched her brother and Matt ride away.

Steve picked a paper up in town and read through it. "Here. It says they're recruitin' horsemen for a cavalry unit, chum."

"Where?"

"Houston."

"Far piece?"

"Yep."

"Take maybe several days to get there?"

"Yep." Matt took the newspaper and read the ad.

Mounted Rangers!
Terry and Lubbock Regiment!
For Virginia During the War

He read on further down,

Transportation from Alleyton to Virginia free.

"Do thet mean what it says, I'm supposin'?" Matt asked Steve.

"Only one way to find out."

"Sounds okay to me," Matt hesitatingly agreed. "I suppose first thing in the mornin'?"

"Yeah. Wait 'til Brenda hears this," Steve said, mounting his horse. With Matt in his saddle, they rode back to the farmhouse.

They were up early the next day, and after a good breakfast, a swim in the river, and a few shots at wild fowl, they prepared themselves to leave for Houston.

Handing Brenda the pheasants, Steve excused himself and went to saddle the horses. Now was the time to be readying for the ride. They were not infantrymen, not by a long shot. They enjoyed horses too much. The news that a strong unit of horsemen was forming somewhere around Houston appealed to them, and knowing that they had put off their joining much too long, they opted for meeting the challenge.

"I suppose you won't be coming back, young Matt," she opined, putting her hands into her apron pocket. "I mean until after the war, that is."

"Brenda," Matt said, taking her hands into his to offer her some assurance. "I'll be comin' back. Me and Steve together. Soon. But, I won't stay. I've been here much too long as it is. I should have gone back to Tennessee like I had planned."

"Ginny?" she remarked, turning her back on Matt. "You told me about her many times, and I believe you."

"I've got word from her that the war is thick in her parts. I wrote back that we were joinin' a cavalry unit. Now, with this unit goin' to Virginia, it will give me the chance I've been lookin' for. I told her, if I get into this unit, we'd meet in Richmond."

Turning back to him, she looked fondly into his eyes. "Just promise me one thing, young Matt. Promise me that if it doesn't turn out all right with . . . her," she said with tears welling up in her eyes, "then will you be reconsidering coming back this way for good?"

"But it'll turn out all right, Brenda," Matt replied, taking her hands again into his. "I know Ginny, and I know she wants me. And, just as important, I want her."

She placed her arms around his waist and brought him into her as she let the tears flow onto his shirt.

"I realized my love for her when I tried kissin' you, Brenda," he whispered in her ear. "I tried to make myself love you, and forget Ginny. I really tried. Maybe that's why I got drunk all the time. I jest couldn't face the truth and hurtin' you. Everythin' you did for me brought back memories of her, and I found myself wantin' her all the more. Does that make sense?"

Still holding onto him, she answered, "She's a dang lucky woman, Matt darling. A dang fine lucky woman and what I wouldn't do to be in her shoes right now."

"You are one hell of a lady, Miss Andrews," Matt said, holding her tighter. "And it's a good thing I'm sober, else I'd probably take advantage of this moment and make love to you."

"In front of Steve?" She giggled like a little schoolgirl. "I love you, Matt Jorgensen. And I mean it."

Breaking away, she saw her tears on his shirt, and said, "Oh, my. I am sorry for getting your shirt all wet." Taking a kitchen rag from her apron pocket, she tried to wipe the tear stain away.

"Let it stay," Matt said, taking her arm and putting it down by her side. "I'll keep the tears on my shirt for later, when I'll be thinkin' of you." He brought his lips to hers and gave her one last kiss, long and tenderly. Then they turned and walked towards Steve who had brought up the horses.

"I've got some things for your saddlebags," she said, turning to go into the house. "I'll be but a minute." She picked up the hem of her dress and quickly ran into the house.

"Well, chum," Steve said, turning Skeeter's reins over to Matt, "looks to me like you've made a young spinster happy."

"No, friend," Matt replied, taking the reins, "you're wrong there. Not a spinster. Not by any stretch of the imagination. Young, but not a spinster." Climbing up on Skeeter he added, "Happy? I hope she'll be happy the rest of her life. She'll find a good man somewhere, some day. Better'n me by a long shot. That's for damn sure."

The men waited for what seemed to be an eternity for Brenda to return. They enjoyed a smoke together, and did less talking. It was more a moment for silence than joking, like they had become accustomed to doing.

Brenda returned and stuffed their saddlebags with cooked chicken, biscuits, coffee, and a few other sundry items for the road.

"Well, little sister," Steve said dismounting, "take care of the farm, hear?" Then taking her into his big arms, he said, "We'll be back. Both of us."

Brenda gave him a kiss on the cheek, and smiled without any tears showing in her eyes. They were red from crying inside the house, but were dry now. She turned to Matt, reached up and gave him a kiss on his cheek as he leaned towards her from his saddle.

Matt slid out of his saddle, dropped his reins, turned into her, and kissed her hard on the lips. The kiss was long and sweet and unexpected by Brenda.

Steve sauntered away with both horses.

Matt wiped the new tears from her eyes. "What happens when we return?" he asked. "We'll jest have to wait and see."

Watching her face turn into a huge smile, wrinkled up by teary eyes, he walked over to Skeeter, climbed up and started him into a walk. Steve climbed up on Buddy and the two men rode down the road, south, towards Houston. They shifted in the saddle and continued to look back until they could see Brenda waving no more. They were going to war.

Brenda and Matt had said their good-byes and sealed them with a kiss. Still, Brenda felt then and there that she would never see Matt again, and so resigned herself that it would be that way. She had put a note inside the sack lunch she fixed for the two of them.

For Steve, her note read, *Be home for Christmas, big brother. That's your promise to me, and you're going to keep it.*

For Matt, she wrote, *When you come back, Matt, I'll have an apple pie in the window for you with your initials on it. If you decide to keep riding, give my love to Ginny. Love, Brenda.*

She stood in the road and waved her arms high until the two cowboys had been out of sight for several minutes. No one but God saw her sit on the lawn and cry herself to sleep that hour.

CHAPTER 4

TERRY'S TEXAS RANGERS

T he trail to Houston was slow as the men weren't anxious to get there in any hurry. In fact, they purposely stopped at many places to hunt, fish, and eat or just to have a cup of coffee since they figured they had plenty of time to arrive in Houston to enlist. *Maybe,* they each thought to themselves, *jest maybe, the war will be over by the time we get to Houston, or maybe it will never really have gotten under way."*

Every time a clearing popped up, just like a fish splashing in water bringing attention to a good fisherman, the two men would take off and do some trick riding. Matt dropped his hat, rode off, turned, and rode back at a fast clip where he bent low to retrieve it.

Steve followed up and did the same from the other end. Each time it seemed to get easier. Then, to ease the monotony of picking up a hat, they'd drop a neckerchief to retrieve.

Finally, Matt sat his mount in the middle of the clearing, looked over at Steve and flipped a silver dollar in the air. He nudged Skeeter to the other side of the field, turned and rode towards the dollar.

Steve looked for it but couldn't find it.

"A dollar says you miss," Steve yelled out.

Matt bent real low. His eye caught the shimmer of the metallic object and his fingers fetched it. Bringing himself back into his saddle, he reined up and raised the dollar in his hand for Steve to see.

Steve rode over to the site and carefully surveyed the area for a lost dollar he was sure was still in the grass. Not finding it, he took his own silver dollar and placed it in the grass where he knew it would be.

"Want to try again?" he asked Matt, as if not believing him.

"For not trusting me, I get to keep it?"

Steve looked at Matt for a moment and then said, "Why not?"

Matt pulled the brim of his hat down and nudged Skeeter again to the edge of the clearing. He gave a touch of the spur and rode him fast and low towards the dollar. He once again caught the shimmer, picked up the shining object with his nimble fingers and pulled himself upright in the saddle. He held up the dollar for Steve to see, and when he sided Steve, he pocketed it.

"Thanks."

Steve sat and eyed Matt for a while until finally he asked, "Think I can do it?"

"Up to you, friend."

"Can I have it back?"

"I'll loan it to you." Matt dropped the silver dollar in front of Steve's mount and rode away to the opposite side of the field.

Steve stared at the silver dollar carefully, looked at the sun, then at the other end of the field. He looked once more at the silver dollar and rode to the edge. He turned his horse, pulled the brim of his hat down tight and looked for the shimmer. Once he found it, he spurred his horse slightly into an easy gait, bent low and rode towards his target, the silver dollar. His eyes lost sight of it and he fell from his horse.

Matt laughed and rode over to help him. "You okay?"

"Just my pride. Get my stupid horse for me."

Matt brought the horse back and handed the reins to Steve. "You get to keep it if you pick it up, friend."

Steve remounted, looked at the silver dollar in the grass and rode back to the edge. He turned, eyed the shimmering piece, rode out easy again and bent low to pick it up. Again, he lost sight of it but stayed on his horse.

The sun was quick to set that day, but Steve was determined to pick up the silver dollar.

"If you can, I can," he yelled out from the edge of the field.

"This is the last time, friend," Matt yelled back. We've got to catch a rabbit or somethin' if we're gonna eat."

Steve turned his mount, eyed the shimmering dollar, and kicked his horse into an easy gait once more. He bent real low, his eyes glued to the slightly shimmering object, and his fingers touched the dollar. He stayed on his horse and rode past it.

"I can do it, Matt. I touched it."

"Okay, Friend. Remember how you did it. One more time."

Steve turned his mount again, caught sight of the object and rode easy towards it. His eyes stayed glued to the target even though the sun hid its face. He bent low, his fingers touched and retrieved the silver dollar. He sat back up in his saddle, reined up and held the dollar up high.

"I did it, Matt!" he yelled. "I did it!"

"Fine. Tomorrow we'll do something smaller."

On the next day and the day after, dimes became the object of retrieval. But the news they received at stops in saloons and general stores along the way let them realize that the war was any thing but far from being over. There was fierce fighting throughout the states and the toll of death kept mounting. They knew it was only a matter of time when their wearied and tired bodies would catch up to Houston.

At the last stop before Houston, the men had caught themselves a rabbit and cooked it. As they were skewering it over the fire, they began their last conversation for the evening. Matt was still thinking and talking about Ginny, and Steve was still playing the matchmaker for his sister, Brenda. It was something to do to keep their minds off the war, and it happened every night about the same time.

"If I were to head north, Steve," Matt asked, "figure it would take me a month or so to get to Nashville?"

"Perhaps," Steve replied, stoking the fire to cook the rabbit better and quicker. "Why d'ya want to go to Nashville?"

"Ginny," Matt replied.

"Still Ginny, huh?" Steve inquired.

"Yep. Always has been," Matt answered, taking the pot from the stand over the fire and pouring himself a cup of coffee.

"Brenda not good enough for ya?"

Jerking his hand from the heat of the coffee pot, Matt said, "Brenda's beautiful. She's good. Sweet. Educated, too. Everything a man would ever want in a gal."

"She can cook, too, ya know," Steve added. "Sew, darn, knit, paint, milk the cow, and ride a horse better'n any other gal I know of."

"Yeah," Matt answered, carefully sipping the hot coffee. "Yeah, she can, I suppose. And she could possibly make love, too. You forgot to mention thet."

"Well, then," Steve said, shrugging his shoulders. "Too good for ya, ya figure, huh?"

"Well," Matt went on, "when you put it that way, yeah. Yeah, she's too damn good for me. Look at me, Steve. I'm in my early twenties, and I drink too much, smoke too much, and cuss too much." I'm jest not any good for a gal like that, Steve."

Steve took the rabbit from the fire, sliced a piece of meat with his Bowie, and tasted it. Then he said, "Done!"

"Well damnation, then, give me a piece," Matt said, handing Steve his plate.

"What kind of a gal is Ginny?" Steve asked, portioning out the meat with Matt.

Taking a leg of the rabbit to chew on, Matt drew from a picture in his mind how he remembered Ginny to be. Then he said, "She's, well, she's . . . she's . . . ."

As he stuttered, Steve broke in, "She's what, Matt? Can't you describe her?"

"Sure I can. Jest don't rightly know how. That's all."

"Try," Steve said, setting his plate down and using his hands. "Is she tall and skinny? Short and fat? Old, young, snappy, or sassy?"

"Now, don't go puttin' any words like thet on her." Matt placed his plate on a nearby log and stood up to describe her. His mind went back to his last recollection of her as he said, "She's beautiful."

"So is Brenda," Steve added, carving another piece of meat with his Bowie.

"No. No. I mean, ravishingly. She's jest right. About this tall," Matt described with his hand so far from his shoulder. "And, she has blue eyes, and long, long auburn hair, like woven wheat. She's skinny, but not too skinny. Jest right. She wears pants like a man."

"Well," Steve interrupted, "you've got my attention. But can she cook? Sew? Darn?

Matt lifted up his hat, scratched his head and said, "Dunno. But . . ."

"I know," Steve interrupted again. "She can make love."

"Yeah!" Matt answered with a big grin, and then added, "And she can use a bull whip like no man."

"Now thet," Steve replied, "thet jest makes my mouth water for a chunk of apple pie."

"You read my note," Matt said, picking Steve up by his collar.

"The one you put inside your saddle bag for safe keepin'?" Steve asked, grinning him down. "Yep. Jest wanted to see what little sis had to say to ya."

"Well," Matt said, releasing Steve and returning to pick up his plate of rabbit and cup of coffee, "I 'spect Ginny can bake an apple pie, if she had a mind ta."

"Jest one thing bothers me, Matt," Steve said, as he resumed eating his rabbit. "What'd she use the whip fer?"

Matt looked at Steve, and then at the rabbit he was eating. To change the subject, he said, "This thing's too chewy. Don't taste like rabbit."

Steve looked at his piece of meet, and answered Matt. "Not good this time of year, but," he took another bite, "it's meat. Supposed to taste like chicken."

"Well, it don't." Matt took another bite and said while chewing, "Next time, we get chicken."

It was past noon when Matt and Steve rode into Houston. A group of men had gathered in front of the city hall, which acted as a recruiting station. Some tables decorated the lawn, and men were sitting behind them writing on pads of paper. Matt and Steve rode over to a tree in the park, dismounted and tied their steeds to a branch. Cautiously, they sauntered over to the tables to inquire about enlisting.

"Excuse me," Steve asked, looking at a man at the closest table who seemed to be taking a break from writing. "Is this where we sign up for the cavalry?"

The man looked to be in his forties with two chevrons on his sleeve and a corncob pipe in his mouth. "This here's the infantry," he answered about as gruff as he could. "Only men need apply." He looked both men over from top to bottom, and asked, "Why ain't you men in uniform?"

"We've been lookin' for a place to sign up," Matt answered with his hat in hand. "Cavalry. You know."

"It's our understanding that a cavalry regiment was forming here in Houston," Steve continued, "and we rode as fast as we could to join up with them," He strayed a little from the truth, for they had stopped and puttered along the way to Houston.

"Where you from?" the Corporal asked, standing up to inspect them. He walked around Matt first and then Steve, attempting to wear them into confessing their sins.

"Tennessee," Matt quickly answered.

"Nacogdoches," Steve added.

"Which is it?" the Corporal asked, looking confused.

"He's from Tennessee, and I'm from Nacogdoches," Steve answered, standing more erect than before as he eyed the Corporal walking around him. "My cousin from Nashville. Came all the way down to get me, and then we come to Houston. We're ready to fight."

"Cavalry," Matt repeated.

The Corporal cringed when he heard the word cavalry, then sat back down.

"Don't know, son," the Corporal said, spitting out a wad of well-chewed tobacco onto the lawn. "Check in town. Unless you want to join up with us *men*, best you be gettin'."

Matt grabbed the reins of both horses, untied them and handed Steve his reins while he mounted Skeeter. Hardly a man was in sight at the Red Garter Saloon except for two black boys pitching pennies with each other against the side wall, leading to the alleyway.

"Boy!" Steve yelled out to them as he stayed mounted, "You see a group of horsemen around here anywhere?"

"No, sah," said one of the boys, a young lad of about ten or eleven.

"How 'bout you, boy?" Matt asked the other lad.

"Outside ob town, ober by the groves," the older lad of about twelve answered. "Youse goes behind the warehouse. They's be a few horses."

"A few?" Steve stammered. "That can't be a regiment. Let's go check it out though, Matt." He turned his mount and rode towards the church at the other end of town and Matt followed.

On the lawn behind the warehouse, a man with sergeant major's chevrons on the sleeves of a coat was addressing ten men. He appeared to be a Confederate soldier, although the uniform was a hodgepodge. He was a horse soldier, about six feet tall, muscular, and sported a handlebar mustache. By his accent, Matt and Steve could tell he had Irish blood in him.

As they rode up, the Sergeant looked their way and stopped talking. Waiting for the men to dismount, he kept his eyes on them before saying anything else.

Dismounting, Steve asked, "Is this the cavalry?"

The Sergeant pushed back his hat and looked intently at the two saddle tramps that had invaded his terrain. "And what, may I ask, are you children?"

"You mean, 'who', don't cha, Sergeant?" Matt asked as he dismounted.

"Sergeant Major, Son," the Sergeant replied. "And I say what I mean, and I mean what I say. Now, I said 'what are you', and I meant *what are you.* And I'll ask jest one more time, what are you? You look tender and I worry about young-uns like you."

"We're cowboys," Matt answered, smilingly.

"The hell you say," the Sergeant hit back, walking over to Matt and standing in front of him. "Well, we ain't got no cows around here."

"We're lookin' for a place to sign up," Steve added.

"Sign up for what?" the Sergeant badgered back at the men.

"Is this the place?" Matt asked.

"This be a muster center for recruitin' men. I don't see none."

"We're men," Steve countered. "I was a deputy sheriff back in Nacogdoches."

"Can you shoot?"

"Yes, sir," Steve answered.

"I'm talkin' to your sister here, son," the Sergeant continued. "When I get through with him, I'll start on you. I said, can you shoot?"

"Yes, sir," Matt answered, pulling his .36 from his holster. He aimed from the hip and shot two twigs from a branch fifty feet behind the Sergeant who ducked for safety. Matt showed that he was both swift and accurate.

Steve radiated with pride just knowing Matt, the man who drew faster than any man he had ever seen. He awaited his turn with great anticipation for he, too, was ready to show off his expertise with a pistol for which he and Matt had practiced so long.

"You just made a believer out of me, son," the Sergeant replied, wiping his brow while lifting up his hat. Then he started on Steve. "And you, son. Can you shoot?"

Steve turned, crouched, drew his .36 and shot two more twigs off the same branch.

Matt drew again and fired at the two nubs Steve left on the twig.

With his pistol still out of its holster, Steve fired his four remaining bullets and blasted the branch apart from the tree. Matt followed with his last two bullets and made the branch dance before it hit the ground.

The rest of the men, standing around with their jaws opened, joined the Sergeant with a sigh of relief at the exhibition they had just witnessed.

"What side you on, boy?" the Sergeant cuttingly asked. "You'd better say the South, 'cause I'd hate to go up agin' either the two of ye."

Steve looked over at Matt with a smile and holstered his .36. Matt returned the smile and cradled his .36.

"So, where do we sign up?" Matt asked.

"Ye be a callin' me, Sarge. Sergeant Major John Foster O'Riley, that's who I am." Examining their horse's teeth, he said, "You got fine lookin' horses. Stout." Then with his hand wiping his mouth as if a bad habit, he said, "We ain't got any like these.

"Wanna see 'em in action?" Matt asked.

Whispering to himself, O'Riley answered, "Does I wanna see 'em in action, says he. Does I, indeed?" He felt the horse's shanks and ran his hand down its leg. "Fine animal. Go show me."

Matt grabbed mane, reins and saddle horn and threw himself into the saddle, pony express style as Skeeter took off. He galloped to the far end of the clearing, reined up and turned around. He took off his bandana and loped to the middle of the field, where he placed it on the ground. Turning, he cantered back to the edge of the field, turned and put Skeeter into a fast run. Bending down as far as he could without falling off, he reached for and picked up the bandana.

"Fine riding, son," O'Riley applauded, echoed by the men who were standing behind him. He looked at Steve, gave a broad grin and nodded in gesture for Steve to do the same.

Steve grabbed the saddle horn and flipped himself into his saddle on a running mount. After reining up at the far end, he turned and loped back to the middle and placed his makings on the ground. He cantered back to the edge of the field, turned and put Buddy into a running gait. Bending low, he retrieved the makings and sat back up into his saddle.

"Hmph. Your friend topped youse," he said to Matt.

Matt took out a double eagle from his vest pocket, flipped it into the air, caught it and put it back into his vest pocket. Steve mocked him with his double eagle.

The two men raced to the end of the clearing, dropping their double eagle in the center as they rode by. Skeeter out ran Buddy by a nose. They reined up, turned and at a faster pace, rode towards the middle. Simultaneously, they both bent low and retrieved their coins to O'Riley's applause, which was echoed by the other men looking on.

"That was great riding," O'Riley shouted. "Great!" You men ride a horse like, like you were part of the animal. I've never seen such ridin', 'cept for our Commander, Benjamin Franklin Terry that is."

Matt looked at O'Riley and asked, "Where do we sign up, Sarge?"

O'Riley took off his hat and squashed it in his hands. "You read the papers, son?" he asked, handing him a copy of the Houston Gazette he had in his back pocket.

"We did." Matt took the paper and read aloud for Steve also to hear.

Mounted Rangers!
Terry and Lubbock Regiment!
For Virginia During the War

He scanned the paper, mumbling in short fashion then read slowly,

... with a short rifle a double barrel shotgun and a pistol.
"I read all this. I like this part best,
Transportation from Alleyton to Virginia free.

"What's your point, Sarge?" Matt asked.

"Read on, son," O'Riley said while finishing his conversation with two other recruits.

Matt continued to read fast and then saw the date.

... will return to LaGrange on Saturday the 24th last.

"Well, Steve," Matt said, folding the paper, "looks like we found 'em."

O'Riley took the paper back and looked the two men over carefully, and read the paper further, *Louis M Strobel, Enrolling Officer.* That's what it says. He will be returnin'. What day is today, son?"

"Monday, the ninth, I do believe, Sergeant," Steve responded.

"And what month?" O'Riley asked Matt, breathing down his throat.

Matt conceded to O'Riley's request and responded weakly, "September?"

"That's right, *September*. The paper said, 'Last'. You, me fine friends, are one month late. Louis M. Strobel has come and gone." He removed his hat as if in mourning and then replaced it. "Son, we've had four times the men we need. We chose our men and sent the rest home to join up elsewheres."

"Wow! Who are these Terry and Lubbock fellas, anyway?"

A deep voice came from a man who had been standing a way off watching their feats, "I am Terry, son."

The men turned and saw a rather large, strapping man, seemingly past his thirties and a leader by all outward appearances. He was well dressed, wearing a cap decorated with a printed star on it. He sported a thick head of hair and a neatly trimmed goatee.

"Benjamin Franklin Terry," he said proudly with his hand on his saber. "Tom Lubbock is my second in command. I enjoy good horsemanship. And what I just witnessed, I admire most.

"I see you both have good taste for fine horses," Terry said without cracking as much as a smile. "I was watching you shoot from a distance. Together with your fine showmanship with the Navy, we can certainly use you. With shooting and riding like that, we'll shorten this damn war."

He looked at the other men around him and said nothing. Then he stopped and took O'Riley aside and talked briefly with him, "I need good horsemen who can shoot." Then he whispered, "You'll find another bottle in my tent. Don't' touch any of my good bourbon, though."

"Yes, Sir," O'Riley replied with a military chest. "I'll be a thankin' ye. Your bourbon is safe from me hands."

Terry returned to Matt and Steve and looked at the men's scabbards, "Rifles. Do either of you have a shotgun?"

"No, Sir," Matt returned.

"I presume you know how to use one."

"Oh, yes, Sir," Steve answered. "Raised on it in Tennessee."

"Both of you get one. I've a special spot for you two in my regiment. Sign them up as corporals with Company A. A few of our men got camp fever and had to be sent home. This will give Harrison his hundered men by my count."

The man he had referred to was Tom Harrison, an agriculturist and a graduate of the University of South Carolina. Like many of the volunteers in Terry's Rangers who were graduates of a college such as this one or Yale or Princeton, they considered it a privilege just to be in the company. He was also a strict disciplinarian and fighter who served with Lee's Rifles in the Mexican War and now was an officer in Terry and Lubbock's Regiment. Barely five foot seven tall and weighing one hundred and fifty pounds, he carried a Napoleonic attitude. He hailed from Waco, Texas, but encountered a relationship with Terry and Lubbock in Bratoria County south of Houston.

Terry turned and left.

Sign them up as corporals, the man says, says he. Me bein' in this man's army longer than any. O'Riley rubbed his chin and eyed the two men. Then he gave them their first order. "Now, go gets yourselfs acquainted with the other men 'til I be needin' ye."

Matt and Steve joined the other ten men. "When do we eat?" Steve asked, hoping to strike up a good conversation.

"You two were good," a young man replied. "Real good."

"Thanks. But when do we eat?"

"Time for that, lad," an older man answered, holding onto his rifle.

Steve noticed that he was dressed down with four pistols, a rifle and a Bowie. "Gettin' kinda serious there," he said to the recruit.

"Figured I had 'em, might as well keep 'em."

"Sounds like good advice."

Matt and Steve made the rounds with the recruits and introduced themselves as they went along. Steve kept eyeing the man with the artillery. He looked at his long rifle and Navy pistol and shook his head. "A lot of weapons. Matt. You figure we need to get more guns?"

Matt looked at Steve and simply answered, "Some men need to shoot more than others. Your one is equal to his ten."

"Yeah, but now we need to get ourselves a shotgun."

They found the chow and stood in line with their tins.

CHAPTER 5

MEN FROM THE BRAZOS

Matt and Steve took their coffee tins and sauntered over to O'Riley, who was eating alone.

"Who is this Benjamin Franklin Terry, Sarge?" Steve asked.

O'Riley wrinkled up his face, "Him? Ye be a askin' me who be this fine sport of a man? Well, me lads, I'll be a tellin' ye. He's Benjamin Franklin Terry, about the finest leader in the Confederacy. Now ye be a thinkin' you're a good rider. Well, me fine friend, let me be tellin' ya that there goes a better horseman you'll not be findin'. And he can shoot straighter and faster than either of you two with his hands tied behind his back. Yeah, he can do thet."

"I believe you," Matt replied, watching Terry walk straight down the road in strong military style. "Where's he from?"

"Where he be from? Well, now. Ye might be thinkin' he graduated from West Point, but ye'd be wrong. Ye might think he grew up in the military, but him being young like he is, ye know that'd be a lie."

"He's all military, I know that much," Steve chimed in.

"Before this here war, Mister Terry was one of the wealthiest sugar and cotton planters in all of Texas." He strummed on his gallowses. "Rich man, he is, I be tellin' ye. I understand he was born in Kentucky. That be where he learned about horses. Best in the land. He'd be a wantin' some of them here, if he could. He was raised a Texian right here in Brazoria County."

"A plantation owner," Matt shouted, smacking his hat on his leg. "Damn! I knew there was somethin' about him I liked." He looked down the road with a smile at Terry as he disappeared over the hill.

"If he's a plantation owner, how'd he get his own company of soldiers?" Steve asked.

"It's like this. He volunteered right away when that first shot was fired, and him not a military man. I be with him one day when he stood on the banks of the Brazos. Thet's the river here in Texas and runs past his ranch. I heard him pray thet day, I did.

"He told me, O'Riley, says he. 'The Brazos River is 870 miles of twists and turns. One would suspect nothing unusual about a river, but a sense of awe seems to be trying to tell me somethin'. The name is Spanish, *Brazos del Dios*'

"I asked him what it meant. He said, 'translated, it means *the Arms of God*. Legend has it that great warriors would some day rise out of her waters.'

"I heard him pray, like I says, and I heard him sorta answerin' the callin' of the River." He looked at the two young men and wiped his mouth with his handkerchief as if he were trying to hide back a tear. "You may not believe this, lads, but I know thet River has called him. Yes, sir. She came to his back door and placed her hand upon his shoulder. Thet's why he volunteered and started this here cavalry."

Matt leaned in closer to O'Riley, then looked far off as if to look upon the Brazos. "So, you're sayin' the Brazos River called Terry to be a warrior?"

"Take it as you like, me lad. I only know what I heerd from the ol' man's lips hisself."

"And then what?" Matt asked.

O'Riley continued his story of how Terry's Rangers got started:

Thomas S. Lubbock, Terry's second in command, rode to Montgomery, Alabama where he discussed the situation of wanting to form a cavalry unit with the War Department there, but he never received any satisfaction. And he was denied his request for getting any horses. When he returned to Houston, he met with Terry at the headquarters' tent.

"How'd it go, Tom?" Terry asked, offering him a cigar.

"They refused our request on the grounds that Texas was too distant from the real action." He took the cigar and accepted a light from Terry's match.

"Too distant?" Terry barked back.

"Frank, they're thinking a short war and short boundaries. They don't expect the war to reach Texas."

Terry preferred to be called by his middle name, Frank for Franklin rather than his Christian name Benjamin.

"We need horses Tom, if we're going to fight in this war. How persuasive were you?"

"They said it would be less expensive to use men on horses who needed them where the action was."

"Damnation! I figured as much," Terry answered, looking outside his tent at a few scroungy looking animals many of his men had been using as horses.

"They're thinking right, Frank," Lubbock added. "We're a long way from the fighting. It'll take us months to get into the war. And that's if we had good horses. We haven't got months." He watched Terry pacing the floor and knew he was not a man to let this stop him.

"Tom. We're going to Virginia. You, me and Wharton. Right now. Right away. Tell John to pick out fifteen of his best men to go with us."

Since Lubbock's ride, the Capitol was moved from Montgomery to Richmond, Virginia.

"What about horses?"

"We'll buy them once we get to Richmond."

"What I couldn't do, you figure eighteen of us will."

"What have we got to lose?" Terry asked, slapping his glove against the palm of his hand. "Nothing but time."

"Now you're talking," Lubbock said. "If we had done this the first time, we'd have our cavalry already."

Terry and Lubbock were much more aggressive by taking fifteen Texians, including Sergeant O'Riley to Richmond. John A. Wharton, a tall man with a strong will and determination, joined them He took a short cut which landed him in jail for a spell, long enough to make him late for the meeting with President Davis.

"It's a damn large mansion," Lubbock observed as he and Terry walked down the hallway of the Capitol. "Bigger than the one they had in Montgomery."

"Wharton make it, yet?" Terry asked.

"No. He should have met us already. Said he was going to take a short cut."

"He'll be here," Terry assured Lubbock.

"I know. He's never disappointed us, yet. Still, sometimes his shortcuts get him into unnecessary trouble."

"None that he can't handle."

"You men look lost," a tall good looking man with a full-length black beard and wearing a Confederate General's uniform approached them.

"Yes, Sir," Terry answered. "We're looking for President Jefferson Davis."

"Kinda figured that, gentlemen. What would you want with him? Excuse me. Please allow me to introduce myself. I'm General James Longstreet."

The men from Texas removed their hats as courtesy to the General as Terry spoke. "I'm Benjamin Franklin Terry and this is Tom Lubbock. We're Texians and we have a cavalry unit that we want to bring into the war."

"Texas? What for?"

"What d'ya mean, what for?" Terry asked. "As we see it, the South is going to need every able bodied man it can get if we're going to win this war."

"You don't really think it's going to get all the way down to Texas, now do you?"

"Sir," Lubbock spoke up. "I visited the War Department in April when it was still in Montgomery and they said the same thing. When I returned to Texas, Frank here ate into me fiercer than any Federal could."

"We don't expect the war to last long, either," Terry said. "That's why we're here. We want to fight. We've organized a cavalry force of a thousand good fighting Texians and we'd like to get them into the war before it's over."

"I admire your tenacity, gentlemen. It's splendid. But I don't think seeing President Davis is going to do you any good. You'll need help more like from a couple of senators."

"Please let us be the judge of that, General," Terry returned almost bitterly, biting his tongue so as not to get mad. "Tom here came alone last time. This time, we've brought fifteen of our best men with us to help prove our cause. One other was supposed to have met us here. Seems he's a mite late. But he'll show up, I'm certain." He looked at Lubbock and gave him a nod of assurance about Wharton. Both men knew Wharton had other plans along the route, perhaps amorous plans mixed in with his gun running, but come hell or high water, they were certain he would not miss this meeting. He looked back at the General. "Now, just how do we get to see the President?"

"Fifteen men?" Longstreet thought deeply. "Good men?"

"Yes, General. The best."

"You figure you have a good enough cause to argue your case?" Longstreet asked, sticking two long fingers inside his vest pocket.

"Beg your pardon, Sir," Lubbock interrupted. "Now if we didn't, we wouldn't have ridden all this way, and me twice."

"No. I suppose not. Now, I think I might be able to do you some good."

"Anything you can do for us would be greatly appreciated, General," Terry answered with a feeling of relief.

"Would you be willing to, say, prove your ability as leaders by joining my brigade as volunteers? Just for awhile?"

"What would we need to do to prove ourselves?" Lubbock asked.

"My brigade is in training. I have very few men, if any, who could do what I think you might be capable of doing."

"We're listening," Terry returned.

"I need to know where the Federals are. Right now."

"You want us to scout for you?" Terry asked.

"I need to know everything I can learn about them. I'm concerned about the safety of my men going up against the strength of the Federals. If I knew something about them, I'd be in your debt."

"Would that help us get authority to form a cavalry?"

"I would be able to speak up for you to Jeff Davis."

"I'd like to see the President, now, General," Terry reminded him. "Let's see what he has to say."

Longstreet thought for a moment, put his hands behind his back and then turned to look out the window. He saw the fifteen men Terry and Lubbock brought with them. "All right," he said and turned to face the two men directly.

He took Terry by his arm and led him down the hallway where he stopped a couple of well-dressed men. "Senators," Longstreet spoke up. "These are two men who have a cavalry regiment of over a thousand men and they need our help."

One of the senators spoke up and asked, "How can we be of service?"

After the formalities of introducing one to the other and dispensing with superfluous remarks, Longstreet explained the situation to them. "What these gentlemen need is our help in their petition to our President. If you would, I'd like you to accommodate them."

"Certainly," one of the senators agreed. "We'll help in whatever way we can to petition their request to the President."

Terry addressed Longstreet. "We'd like to meet with the President first before we make any agreement."

"I fully understand, and I concur. He's coming down the hall, now." Longstreet stepped up to another six-footer, gaunt in face with wavy black hair, handsomely dressed, and with a seemingly good demeanor about him. It was President Jefferson Davis, himself.

"President Davis, Sir." Longstreet greeted him at attention along with the two senators.

"General," Davis returned. Then he looked at Terry and Lubbock. "I don't believe I've met these young men."

"Mr. President," Lubbock addressed him. "My name is, Tom Lubbock. This is Frank Terry and we're from Texas."

"Ah, yes. I remember you, Tom. You met with my war department in Montgomery a while back. Mr. Terry. My pleasure in meeting you." The three gentlemen shook hands. "You have some men you want us to authorize as a guerilla unit."

"They told me they've been here before." Longstreet added.

"We have another gentleman meeting us from Texas soon. John Wharton." Terry stuttered a little and looked over at Lubbock. "He said he was taking a short cut. Rest assured, Sir, he'll be here."

"We have come to listen to them," one of the senators said. "With your permission, Mr. President."

"By all means. Come on into my office, gentlemen.

23 June 1861

It was late evening in President Davis' office where he, a General and two Senators listened to the men from Texas petitioning for authority to establish a regiment of guerrillas in Texas. What impressed President Davis the most was their status as rich men with a commitment to fight, and their traveling the distance to make him aware that they meant business.

"I must say, I admire your tenacity," Davis replied. "Your second attempt to get your way. Why? Why would you want to leave your families and fight a war that will probably be over with by the time you get yourselves back to Texas?"

"We're both seasoned veterans of war, Mr. President," Terry answered. "We know what war is like. We'd like to offer our services to help end the war that much quicker for the sake and the cause of the Confederacy."

Terry went to the window and pointed out to some men resting on the lawn. "We've brought fifteen other Texians with us. If you please, Sir, to show you our allegiance and our ability to command an army, General Longstreet offered us to fight as volunteers. If the war ends before we get back, we've done nothing more than helped win it."

Davis looked at the men below, turned and faced the General and two Senators. "They talked you into this?"

"I can use them as scouts," Longstreet offered.

"Does that set with you gentlemen?" Davis asked, lighting up a cigar.

"Only to show you that we are as good as we say we are," Lubbock returned. "We're anxious to get back to our men."

"And you have a thousand men ready to ride with you?"

Terry nodded his head, and with Lubbock, waited for Davis' next move.

"Very well. Be that as it may." Davis went to his desk, sat down and took pen to hand. "You'll be assigned to General Longstreet's command. He's the Commander of the Fourth Brigade. Fine man. Don't get him mad at you. His report to me will help enforce any further decision I may make concerning your request."

Lubbock and Terry took their fifteen Texians who had ventured with them and organized themselves into an independent band of guerillas and joined up with Longstreet.

"Gentlemen," Longstreet addressed them, "the Federals are north of us. At least I hope they are. I suggest you lead your men on a scouting expedition in that direction."

Terry and Lubbock's men quickly scouted north of camp and shortly came across a Federal camp of a few troops.

"By gawd," Terry said, "our first battle. Men, ride quickly before they awake."

With his command, the newly formed guerillas captured two of the enemy, wounded a third, and confiscated a horse and an unerring rifle without firing a shot.

Terry and Lubbock reported back to Longstreet with their find and captured prisoners.

"Scouting," Longstreet started in on Terry and Lubbock, "is scouting. Not taking prisoners. You took two prisoners and a horse."

"And a rifle," Terry added with a smile.

"You may keep the rifle, and the horse, and go out again. Find me something to shoot at."

"If I may, Sir," Terry returned. "These men are on a reconnaissance mission, and they know where their main body is. That's why we brought them back to you, Sir."

"They are?" Longstreet asked, turning swiftly to look at the men.

"They've already led us to the main body," Terry returned.

"Where?" Longstreet asked while looking at the prisoners.

"If I may use your map, General," Terry continued. "I'll show you." Terry went to the map and pointed to the spot designated by one of his captives, and said, "Bull Run."

21 July 1861

The General showed that he was well pleased with the Texians' report and continued letting them scout for him. Taking the information given to him from the Texians, he marched his brigade out, and as expected, encountered firing power on his men across Bull Run.

In the next hour, Terry and Lubbock's men discovered that Federal troops were moving in heavy columns against Longstreet's left. Upon hearing the news, Longstreet showed his trust in them by expediently ordering a retreat.

"Fall back!" Longstreet ordered from his command post. "Fall back!

"By thunder!" he exclaimed. "I thought we had them on the left flank."

"What's the situation with their batteries?" Longstreet asked after his brigade came to a halt.

"We know where they are, General," Terry answered. "It'll take us time to get there and back with the information you'll need."

"Go man! Go!" Longstreet ordered, pulling another cigar out of his vest pocket.

In the ensuing hours, Terry and Lubbock's men snuck back across the scrimmage line and found the batteries they were looking for.

"Sketch it out, Tom," Terry said, keeping his eyes glued on the Federals' camp.

Lubbock got a pad out and began sketching what they saw. He finished it just before being spotted by a sentry. "Let's get the hell out of here."

They turned and crawled back through the Virginia thickets.

At command headquarters, Longstreet reviewed the findings. He didn't waste time, and instantly met with his Field Commanders. "Once the batteries are ready, order your troops to lie down and cover themselves from the artillery fire as much as possible. It's going to be one hell of a battle."

And it was. Terry and Lubbock's men found cover behind trees and laid low.

"Fire!" Longstreet commanded and all hell broke loose. Immediately, they commenced firing upon the enemy's position with the Eleventh Virginia and the Fifth North Carolina posted in front of the battery on his right.

He broke through the enemy's lines and eventually marched towards Centerville where he halted his attack. After an hour of staying in position, Longstreet directed his troops to return to Manassas for water.

At dawn the next day, Longstreet met with Terry and Lubbock.

"I want to compliment your men for an excellent job," Longstreet said while inside his tent. "Thank you."

"Yes, Sir," Terry returned.

"I don't know how many prisoners we have," Longstreet observed. I had them sent on to headquarters."

"More than you probably realize, Sir," Terry said, sipping coffee out of a tin.

"Now for the dirty work," Longstreet said as he sat down.

"What's that," Terry asked.

"I want you to pick up the stragglers and any property that the Federals may have abandoned. Guns, bayonets, anything. Ordinance, if you find some. I've got Captain Whitehead's troops to give you protection."

When they rode through Fairfax County in Manassas, Terry saw the Federal flag waving over the Courthouse.

"Hold up, Captain," he said as he took the rifle they had confiscated in their first raid. It had the appearance of a six-shooter with a rifle barrel attached to it along with a rifle stock. He aimed it and hit the lanyard that held the flag and broke it.

"There. Now, with your kind permission, Captain, I'd like to have one of my men shimmy up the building, take our flag and place it up there where it belongs."

Captain Whitehead looked with his jaw dropped and eyes widened. "That was one hell of a shot. You've my kind permission, Frank," Whitehead returned, and ordered the flag to be given to Terry.

"Got a volunteer?" Lubbock yelled out.

"I'll do 'er," a young lanky boy said as he took the flag and scaled the courthouse.

The men waited until the flag was securely in place and flying, then, with the young man standing below it, the rest of the company came to attention and saluted the Confederate Stars and Bars; the flag bore seven stars and three bars of red, white and red respectively, and a blue union.

When Terry and Lubbock returned to General Longstreet at his command post later that day, they were met with cheers and hoorahs from the men in his brigade and a strong sturdy handshake from the General.

"My report will go to Davis by courier with you gentlemen in the morning, Terry. Lubbock." Longstreet instructed them. "President Davis is already quite pleased."

Then he sat down at his desk, opened a drawer and took something out. "Our first job is to make you each a colonel," he said, handing both men a set of epaulettes. President Davis had already ordered these for you gentlemen on my last meeting with him."

He looked at the men and waited for them to say something. It was long in coming, as both men felt uncomfortable about receiving their ranks.

Terry gazed up at Longstreet and haltingly said, "Sir. We appreciate the honor, and we'll accept these epaulettes as an honor, but until President Davis himself recognizes us as Commanders of our *own* cavalry, we will not wear them, nor shall we have our men address us as such. That day will come, I promise you, when we will ride as a cavalry unit on this lawn and in front of this Capitol."

The walk back to their tents was slow and deliberate as Terry and Lubbock's men could hardly restrain themselves. Once in their tents and lights were out, the fifteen men gave out a horrendous rebel yell.

"I've been reading General Longstreet's report," President Davis said to Terry and Lubbock as they sat in his office the next day. "It is one of the best I've received. Let me read you a portion of it."
Taking it from off his desk, he stood up to read.

HEADQUARTERS FOURTH BRIGADE,

28 July 1861.

"Down here at the bottom." President Davis continued reading:

Volunteer Staff. - Colonel Riddick, Assistant Adjutant-General, North Carolina, was of great assistance in conveying orders, assisting in the distribution of troops, and infusing proper spirit among them. Cols. B. F. Terry and T. Lubbock were very active and energetic. When unoccupied, they repeatedly volunteered their services to make reconnaissance. They were very gallantly seconded by Capts. T. Goree and Chichester, and so forth.

I remain, sir, very respectfully, your most obedient servant,

JAMES LONGSTREET
Brigadier-General.

"Splendid, indeed. For your information, your Captain Goree has elected to stay with the brigade and has been appointed to serve with Longstreet." He paused for a moment, looked out the window and at the rest of the Texians resting under the tree.
Then he said, matter-of-factly, "It is my understanding that you refused your ranks as colonels."
Terry's opened his eyes wide as he answered, "Yes, Sir."
"And your reasons?"

"Sir," Terry stood straight and caught President Davis' immediate attention. "We need for you to authorize us to organize a cavalry unit to serve in the Confederate Army. When you do, and we hope you will, Sir . . . and when we parade as a regiment upon these grounds, then we would be honored to have you hand these to us. Duly respective of the honor for which they were presented to us by General Longstreet, we would wear them at that time, Sir."

Davis looked at the two men with consternation and quivered his lips. He reached down and took three cigars from his case, offered one to each of the men and took the third one for himself.

"Thank you, Sir." Lubbock took a match from his vest, struck it and lit the President's cigar along with Terry's and then his own.

Watching the two Texians enjoy their cigars with him, Davis said, "We need you men here."

"Mr. President," Terry started in again. "With all due respect, we can do this until the war is over. It will prove absolutely futile. We have an army ready to fight for you in Texas."

"Texas," Davis fumed. "Texas. Good gawd man, do you honestly realize how far away Texas is?"

"Sir. We came from Texas."

"Yes. Yes, you did. How many men have you in Texas?"

"Over a thousand men fully equipped with their own guns. All we need is your authorization . . . and horses."

"Horses?" Davis asked. "Now you add horses? You are trying my patience, Colonel Terry. We do not have horses in Virginia to give to you in Texas. You are much too far away to be of any good to us at this juncture. The war is in our backyard. Not yours. If it ever crawls over into yours, God forbid, then we can and shall give you horses. Why not join up with Alabama and fight in the infantry, for crissake?"

Terry tightened his fists and grit his teeth. "We'll get the horses, Mr. President. All we ask now is your authority for us to organize an army."

"You will consider my suggestion then, I'm to take it?"

"Sir? Alabama?

"I only said Alabama. Maybe the New Orleans 1st. They're closer to you, and they need good men like you and your brave men outside."

"Yes, Sir. We'll take it into consideration."

"Then, under your word, I'll authorize you gentlemen to organize a cavalry, but only on that condition. Right now, however, as good as you are, we can't support a cavalry in Texas. Like I said, if it ever happens and we are drawn into Texas, then we'll use your services to the hilt. Agreed?"

Terry drew in a deep drag from his cigar and exhaled it before he answered. "Yes, Sir. We'll bring our men to New Orleans. By that time, we should be ready to serve with a brigade there."

"Good. I'll draft up the documents immediately and you may return to Texas." He sat down at his desk, looked up at Terry and Lubbock and added, "Unless you want to stay and fight with me."

"No, Sir." Terry replied.

"Doesn't hurt to ask one more time."

"We'll remember that, Mr. President."

The President looked up and handed the documents to Terry. These will help you get started, Colonel Terry. Colonel Lubbock."

Terry took the documents and gazed eye to eye at the President. Davis got the message. "Frank. John.

"Yes, Sir? Thank you, Sir."

With their small detachment, Terry and Lubbock started their trek back to Texas, whereby on the road out of Richmond, they met up with their colleague, John Wharton, sitting on a tree stump with the reins of his horse in his hands.

"Are my eyes deceiving me, Frank, or is that a mirage?" Lubbock jestured, seeing Wharton smiling up at them.

"Just where in the hell have you been, John?" Terry laid into Wharton. "You've been missed over a month. Some short-cut."

"Gentlemen," Wharton began, "I got waylaid on the road. Seems someone with authority wanted to talk to me about something or other, didn't make sense to me, so I refused to stay and talk."

"What about, John?" Terry asked.

"Now, Frank, does I have to tell ya? Can't you just trust me?"

"It's a woman," Lubbock smiled at Terry. Then he looked down at Wharton and asked, "You couldn't have just ridden with us and stayed out of trouble?"

"Now, Tom," Wharton smiled his pleasant smile," it wouldn't be sportin' for a gentleman to reveal his secrets of amour with the likes of his brethren, now would it? Take it from me, I could have outridden the sheriff, but I just didn't feel right about it, so I surrendered to his jail."

"You what?" Terry asked, laughing loudly.

"Well, you see, Frank, it was either that or getting shot right then and there by someone akin to the fair damsel."

"How did you argue your way out of that one, you being a magnificent lawyer and all?" Lubbock asked, joining in the laughter with Terry.

"Well, now, Tom, it was taking days for me to get a fair trial, the circuit riding judge being busy and all, so I did the next best thing, habeas corpus like. After I saw the futility of it, I broke out and ran like hell."

"You what?" Terry shouted out with more laughter. "You escaped jail?"

Wharton mounted his steed and sided the two gentlemen. "Truth of the matter?"

"If you have it in you," Terry returned. "As long as you don't break out in poetry, like usual."

"Like always," Lubbock chimed in.

"Fellas, give me a break. This was for real. A couple of Yankee patrol boats ran me aground. I was running guns between New Orleans and Galveston when they caught me and jailed me."

"Now that makes more sense." Terry spurred on. "But, you knew this mission was more important."

"Yes. Sorry for that, I thought I could do my job and still meet you on time. Well. So be it. I realized I had to get here on time, didn't I, Frank? So, here I am. As they say, *Better late than never.*"

"More like five weeks later, may I add," Terry continued.

"Any one after you?" Lubbock asked.

"Not likely. One has a headache right now and can't ride. The other I lost in the woods. I told you I could out run them." Wharton looked at the men traveling south and asked, "I'm really late, aren't I? Did we meet President Davis?"

"We?" Terry smiled and motioned for Wharton to ride. "We've had one hell-of-a time, John. One hell-of-a time. We'll explain on the way back to Texas."

"Us eighteen men returned to Texas and Terry was authorized to raise a regiment of cavalry to serve in the Confederate States Army," O'Riley continued as the three men kept walking. "And that's how it all happened."

Then he stopped and looked at Matt and Steve, and with a bit of pride about his face, he repeated, "But at Manassas, he and Colonel Lubbock and me fought together. It was there that Terry shot and broke the pole that held the Union flag over the courthouse, and he did it on horseback. And then they wents and replaced it with the Confederate colors and seven stars. With me eyes, I witnessed it. Them men proved they had savvy for fightin'."

"Some shootin'," Matt said. "Wish I had seen it."

"You mentioned Lubbock?" Steve asked, siding O'Riley opposite of Matt.

"Lieutenant Colonel Thomas S. Lubbock. Ah, a grand and glorious man he be"

"What's he like?" Steve continued.

"Short on temper, long on courage. Much like Terry. He's a strong man and cusses a lot. He be a wee bit shorter and older than Terry by a few years. He's a rich man, too." He stopped and laid an arm across the men's shoulders and confided, "You never heered that from me. Common scuttlebutt, though. But not from me."

"Neither of them knew soldierin'?" Matt asked, slicking off a chaw of tobacco he took from his shirt pocket.

"I said Mister Terry was a dirt farmer. Mister Lubbock was the military man. He was with the Nawleans Gray when he came to Texas. He saw battles, and became a peddler somewhere in Texas. That's when he became rich." Again, he turned and hushed his lips. "Ya never heered that from me."

"Well, Sarge," Matt said, sticking the wad in his mouth, "you've convinced me they know what they're doin'. Question is, where're they goin' once we've won the war?"

"They'll own all of Texas, I'm countin'," O'Riley said with pride. "Mister Lubbock's brother is already runnin' for governor."

"Lubbock?" A light went off in Steve's head and he stopped short in his tracks. "I heard of Lubbock in Nacogdoches when he brought a company of Greys in when the Texas Revolution started."

"That he did."

"But, he's the same man? I remember hearin' about him."

"It be him," O'Riley confirmed. "A finer soldier you'll not be findin', either. And don't be thinkin' his size stopped him none. He drove the Mexicans across the Rio Grande, he did."

The main of it was that Terry, Lubbock and Wharton, all three were neighbors in Brazoria County. Like Terry, Lubbock worked with cotton in New Orleans until he got caught up in the Texas Revolution.

Steve was interested in the romantic one of the trio, John Wharton. "What's Wharton like?" he asked O'Riley, spitting his juice to the side. "Can hardly wait to meet the gentleman."

"Yeah," Matt chimed in, "me, too."

O'Riley rubbed his face with his dirty handkerchief, looked pie-eyed at the two men and answered, saying, "Well, Mr. Wharton, first of all, he is the clean shaven of the lot, good looking man, I'd say in his early thirties. At one time he owned a sizeable amount of property in Brazoria County called *Eagle Island* I unnerstand he has a sizable amount of slaves, over a hundred. You can readily see why he don't want no Yankee govement."

O'Riley pointed to Terry galloping smooth across the meadow like he and the horse were one. "Have you ever seen anythin' prettier that that, now I ask ye?"

"Sure seems to love to ride," Matt said, watching Terry ride like the soaring of an eagle.

O'Riley took a pad and pencil from his vest pocket and began writing. "Now, me lads. You provide your weapons," he said, looking at his note pad and writing, "one Colt, one carbine."

"We each got a good horse, Sarge," Matt said, grinning as if he were Davy Crockett killing his first bear. "Both of us."

"And we ride like the wind, too" Steve answered, smacking the dust off his hat against his pant legs. "Put that in your notes."

"I seen ye," O'Riley continued. "'Now we furnish one saddle and blanket. You furnish the rest." He resumed writing.

He looked back up from his pad at the two men and repeated, "Like the wind, you say? Good. Good. More like a cyclone. I see ye wit me own eyes.

"Now, you saved us from havin' to get you a horse," O'Riley continued. "Both of you. Now, right here, son." He handed the two men some papers to fill out. "Sign your names and you'll belong to the finest cavalry unit in all of Texas."

Matt took the wad from his mouth and cast it aside. Taking the pen, he signed the document and gave the pen to Steve.

"I heard about Manassas," Steve said, sticking his hands in his pockets as if he had nothing more to say.

"Yeah, and I was there, too, let me remind ye, me young buckaroos, along with many others here."

He had told the story a hundred times, but to him, each one was a fresh experience of which he was proud. "And before long, you'll be in the thick of it, me lads." O'Riley turned and walked briskly towards a group of men grooming their horses.

Matt took the pen and hung onto the papers as they walked.

"Ever kill anybody?" O'Riley asked the two men as they followed him.

"Yep," Matt answered.

"You?" O'Riley asked Steve.

"Yep"

"Who'd you kill, Mr. Jorgensen?"

"A man up Kansas way," Matt continued.

O'Riley stopped, turned and looked at Matt. "Kansas, you say? Where 'bouts?"

"Mudd Creek. A bad one took my earnings."

"That it?"

Matt became apprehensive about wanting to talk any further as he realized he was on the other side of the fence in Kansas. He remained silent, but O'Riley sensed something in his behavior.

"There's more?"

Matt said nothing.

"Wanna tell us over a beer?"

"Sounds good to me," Steve answered.

The three men waltzed into the saloon close by and sat down. Matt decided that he was not going to talk any further about Kansas.

"Beer," O'Riley yelled out. Me friend's buyin'." He smiled and looked over at Matt. "Now, tell us all about yourself. You wanted for somethin'?"

A few of the locals in the saloon stopped their conversing and turned towards their table to listen.

"Aw, goes back to your jabberin'," O'Riley told them. "We're talkin' soldier talk."

The bartender brought them each a beer and collected from Matt.

"Wull?" O'Riley asked. "You're not wanted for anythin', are ye?"

"Nope."

"Then out with it, me lad."

Matt fidgeted with his fingers, then wrapped one hand around a glass of beer the bartender sat in front of him.

"Know of Nacogdoches?" Matt asked, swallowing his first drink.

"Naga - whatches? That be in Texas?"

"Yep."

"I heard some about it," O'Riley said. "What happened there?"

"Had a shoot out."

"Who got it?" O'Riley asked.

"Well, I'm here, ain't I? The other guy bought it, but we both had to bring him down."

"You bose? How cha do it?"

Steve broke in, adding, "Well, I was a deputy and this guy was a wanted killer. He drew down on me, but I outdrew him and hit him in the chest. He went down firing at Matt, and Matt drew and fired. Hit 'im right between the eyes."

O'Riley sat there, drinking his beer, meditating on what they just told him. He listened to Matt's accent and decided it wasn't southern enough. He hated what he was thinking and tried to put it out of his mind, but the thought etched itself deeply into his subconscious, *Matt's a Yankee.* He bit his lip and drank his beer down without stopping. "Where'd you say you're from?" he asked Matt, again looking intently into his eyes.

"Tennessee."

O'Riley wiped his lips with his gloved hand and looked at Matt and Steve, and then glanced around at the rest of the people in the saloon. He felt in a sense that they all knew what he was thinking and he had to be quick to counter it. *Tennessee?* he thought. *Could be either way.* He grinned and showed his teeth with two missing in front. "Thet's me boy," he said for the whole saloon to hear.

"Yeah." Matt smiled and drank his beer.

"It took ye bose to bring him down, huh?" O'Riley quipped. Bose of ya. But ya got 'im. Thet's what counts."

Matt let O'Riley believe what he wanted to believe, and hoped he believed that he was for the South, and that it would be the end of the matter. He said nothing more about Kansas, and O'Riley asked him nothing more about it. When they finished, they went back outside and continued walking.

"So how many are there of us?" Matt asked, stepping in line with O'Riley.

"In our cavalry unit? Like I told you. There'd be a tousand expert horsemen who could shoot as well as they could ride. And twelve more now that we have you and the others."

"Sarge!" Matt said matter-of-factly.

"Sergeant John Foster O'Riley, son," he quickly reminded him. "You be rememberin' that now 'cause you'll be ridin' under me whip."

"Is this all there is?" Matt asked, looking at the enlistment paper he held onto all this time, to which he had not yet signed.

"You be lookin' at that paper and you still be askin' 'Is this all there is?' Well, me fine gallopin' cowboy, what day it be again today?"

"Tenth of September," Matt answered O'Riley, taking off his hat and dusting it on his pants.

"Well," O'Riley reminded him, "for your information, we began signing up on the eighth of August. The newspaper's a month old and so are you."

"And we jest made it!" Matt exclaimed, signing the papers with Steve, and looking at the other ten men.

Addressing the ten men who had come together with Matt and Steve, O'Riley said, "We have a tousand men in training right now, and you will make it a tousand and twelve when I gets you there."

By actual count that day, there were actually eleven hundred and ninety-three armed and equipped men who were signed up and sworn in. Sergeant O'Riley was not far off on his count. Terry was privileged to select one thousand and four men to be sworn in for duty as his cavalry unit. However, he added more as others kept coming, and replaced those who were killed. The unit eventually totaled thirteen hundred and five men. Matt and Steve were two of the last men to be sworn in as horsemen in Company A. There were eleven companies all told with over one hundred men in each, counting the officers. Tom Harrison was Major of Company A.

Sitting around the campfire one evening, Matt asked O'Riley a curious question. "You told us that Major Wharton went to Richmond."

"Thet's what I told you, and that's a fact, son." O'Riley answered.

"Well, if Harrison is the major of this here A Company, why didn't he go with them? Looks to me that they passed him up for Wharton."

O'Riley stood up and walked away, motioning for Matt to walk with him. Steve joined them. "Aye, thet they did, son," O'Riley told them as they walked into the darkness. "You'll learn this sooner or later, so you might jest as well hear it from me. But remember, you didn't hear nothin' from me, unnerstand?" He looked at the two men and wiped his mouth with his bandana. "This here Harrison is a sly one. He has pull because he knows many people in high places, but lots don't like 'im. No sir. You see, he fought in this here Mexican War, like me, with Jeff Davis."

He stopped, looked around. "He says he fought with us. He served with us. Wharton is a better man all the way around. And, Harrison, he has bitter feelings for him from the first. He knows our commanders like Major Wharton all too well, and he knows thet they trust him. Thet's why he's always with them. Major Harrison, well, I know he's here for only one reason, and our commanders know thet, too."

"What's thet?" Matt asked, lighting his makings.

"He wants to be governor of Texas, and so's he's pretendin' to be a horse soldier to get his wishes. Thet's what me thinks. And so does a lot of others. He figures this war will be over real soon and he'll be out shaking hands." He continued leading them back to their tents and left them in the field, as he went to his own. "But mind you, he is the Major and you better be a doin' what he says, if'n you know what I means. See you children early in the mornin'."

CHAPTER 6

FIRST NIGHT – LONELY NIGHT

The camp for Terry and Lubbock's guerillas was set up twenty miles north of Houston in a clearing. Because the terrain was mostly prairie and the existing bramble was cut and thrown away, it made for good training for horsemanship. Terry was obsessed with making his regiment the best cavalry unit in the war, even though he lacked the horses to do so at the time. He was confident horses would be provided him. After all, he had the finances and contacts for which to acquire them. He was playing out the hand dealt him and waiting for the proper time and place.

Sergeant O'Riley led the twelve men to the camp where other soldiers were already in training. Most were privates, many with little skill in horsemanship or firearms.

"Those men you see on the green are cavalrymen. Some have seen battle in another war. They're good. These men you see ridin' in close formation have been doin' so for a month now. You have one week to catch up to 'em, and I'll be ridin' ya every minute of the day.

Matt and Steve stood with their reins in their hands, holding their horses while surveying the campsite. The men, whom O'Riley called "good", rode like they owned the grounds and no one was going to show them any new tricks, while the ones in close formation bounced on their nags.

When O'Riley left them, Matt and Steve walked over to some horses that were tied together to a rope hitch.

"Those look like they're fifteen high and fifteen year old, Matt," Steve said as the two men examined the lot. *A tousand expert riders, now he says, says he,* Steve mocked O'Riley. "Look at 'em, Matt. No horses. No uniforms. This is the cavalry?"

"Yeah," Matt said with disgust, taking his hat off and dusting it on his pants. "And we're goin' to Virginia?"

Towards evening, the men chowed down around a campfire with their new-found, so-called friends.

"When do we get our uniforms?" Matt asked the group. "I don't see any one here wearin' any except O'Riley , and his sister must'ave made it for him."

"And you won't," replied an older soldier, cleaning his rifle. "We wear what we want to wear in this here outfit until they decide to issue us uniforms, which is doubtful."

"That's it?"

"Yep," replied an older man who appeared to be in his thirties named, Gus. He lit his corncob pipe and continued, "We're supposed to be guerillas. And some of us don't have horses. Most of us who do, don't brag about 'em."

"I wouldn't either," Steve chimed in, sinking his teeth into a chicken leg.

"They're supposed to get horses for us," another man added. "That's what they said. We supply our carbine and pistol and horse gear. They supply the horses. Glad I kept mine."

"Why guerillas?" Matt asked. "I'm all for it, mind you."

"We're volunteers, son," Gus spoke out. "Far from the front, and never been trained. We'll fight like the minute men of old, exceptin' our leaders kinda think we'll become a cavalry unit attached somewhere in this damned war."

For the rest of the evening, the subject was mostly about women; women they left behind or women they were hoping to meet. It seemed that most of the men didn't want to talk about the war, as if it were a thing of one's imagination.

Gus stoked the fire a bit with a twig and asked, "So, you joined because we're goin' to Virginia and you wanted to go, too?"

"Seemed good at the time," Matt answered. "Why?"

A young man sat away from the fire and played "Dixie" on his harmonica low and quiet like. Some of the men who knew the words to the song sang along .

"Nothin'," Gus replied. "I have some kin in Virginia."

"Terry won't let us call him colonel 'til he gets his commission from President Jeff Davis, hisself on the lawn of the capitol," O'Riley interrupted, walking into the circle of men. "That's pretty much why we're goin' to Virginia. And he'll get thet, and we'll parade in on horses, alls at the same time."

"How're we gonna get to Virginia without horses?" Matt asked.

"We'll get there," O'Riley answered, rubbing his face in his right hand. "Don't you no never mind."

Then the subject of the evening changed as abruptly as it started.

"Ever kill anyone, Gus?" another young man asked. "I don't much like killin' any one. Not right away, anyways."

"Nope," Gus replied, putting a branch of wood on the fire. "I don't relish the thought either. But I'll do it when I have to, I reckon. Jest like all of us."

"Supposin' we're gonna see action any time between here and there, Sarge?" another asked, sewing buttons on his shirt.

"Hope not," an older man answered. "I'm a farmer, down by the Brazos, outside a'Waco. I know about plowin' and ridin' a mule bareback. That's about all I know how to do."

"Terry wants us to use shotguns," another old codger joined in. "I'd rather use my long rifle."

We ain't gonna do no damage with shotguns if'n those Yankees come at us with carbines and such."

"The hell we can't," another Ranger joined in. "You seen what a shotgun can do? Hell, it could tear the guts out of a man."

"If'n we get close enough afore they bring us down," another voice from a younger man close to the fire added.

"I still carry my carbine," another joined in, lying against a tree trunk with his hat over his eyes as if feigning sleep. "And I got four sets of pistols I carries with me at all times."

"We can use our shotguns, if'n we get in close enough," O'Riley offered. "That way we can do more damage among the Yankees." He rubbed his face and said, "Now, get some sleep, all a youse."

A heavy-set man seemed to have nothing better to do that night, so he picked an argument with Matt.

"You don't speak like none of us, mister. Where'd you say you're from?"

"Didn't."

"Well, where're ya from?" the man asked indignantly, trying to rile Matt.

"Tennessee."

"Why didn't ya enlist with those fellas up there, then?"

"Thought I'd come down here and ride with you fellas."

"Think you're good enough?"

"Don't ride him, Troy," Gus cautioned him. "Leave him be."

"Jest talkin' with him, Gus," Troy returned. "Ain't I, Tennessee?" He referred to Matt.

Matt kept silent and poked at the fire with a stick he found lying on the ground.

"I asked you a question, Tennessee. You better be answerin' me. I said, you think you're good enough to ride with us?"

"Name's, Matt, and I'm better," Matt answered without looking up.

"Oh! The hell ya say. Think you can teach me?"

Steve stood up, took his tin cup and swished the cold coffee into the fire. "Gonna get me some shut eye." He walked into the night on the far side of camp, picked a tree, sat down and pulled his hat over his eyes, hoping what was about to take place wouldn't. He listened to the argument going on but soon, his tired body found sleep.

"Can't," Matt answered Troy.

"Ha! 'Can't', he says," Troy retorted. "Can't cause ya can't."

"Nope. Can't cause jackasses can't be trained."

"You're askin' for it," Troy came back, kneeling down and grabbing Matt by the front of his shirt. "We don't like men who come from the North."

"That's a good shirt, mister," Matt replied, tightening his fist. "Unless you got a better'n, I suggest you let go of it."

The heavy-set man rose to his feet, bringing Matt with him by his shirt. "You call this thin' a shirt? I call it a piece a rag."

Matt's fist came fast and hard and made its impact into Troy's face, causing blood to spill from his cheek bone.

Troy stumbled backwards and fell. He got up quickly and caught Matt around the neck, falling into the fire with him. The two quickly rolled out of the fire with smoldering clothes. Matt sprung up and squared himself off with Troy who got to his feet, rubbing his bloody face with his dirty hand.

"I suggest you've had enough, mister," Matt warned from a crouched position.

"I'm jest warmin' up," Troy snarled, and threw his body into Matt's.

The two men rolled again over the fire spreading embers around the lined pit. This time their clothes caught fire. Some of the men standing around took a bucket of water and doused the fire out on both of them. They continued to fight. Troy's fist found Matt's chin a convenient spot to plow into and sent Matt reeling backwards. Without losing his balance, Matt turned back into Troy with his fist to his midsection. Troy doubled over and gasped for air. His fat didn't protect him. Matt followed through with an uppercut and sent Troy flat on his back into the fire pit again where he laid. Matt reached down and rescued him from the fire by pulling him up. Again, the bucket of water found its mark and doused the flames from Troy's back.

"Had enough?" Matt asked, reaching out to shake hands with him.

Troy straightened up in pain, looked at Matt, turned and walked away.

"You beat him fair and square, lad," O'Riley said, putting his heavy arm around Matt's shoulders. "Now, why don't cha go dry off and have yourself some whiskey on me. I'll join ya."

O'Riley was proud of Matt that night and shared his pride by drinking with him the rest of the evening until Matt passed out.

"Well, me lad," O'Riley whispered in the ears of a drunken soldier sound asleep at his feet, "I hopes you is as good a horse soldier for the South as you are a liar." He was sure that Matt still had Northern blood in his veins. "You be gettin' your sleep, now"

Looking at the rest of the men, he continued. "'Cause y'alls gonna be needin' it come sun up. Lights out, girlies."

Matt wasn't as drunk as O'Riley thought. Once O'Riley left the tent, Matt rose and staked his place of solitude by a lantern and prepared a post to Ginny and Jim telling them the good news. In his letter, he told them that if there were any way Ginny could meet him in Virginia, she would have to look for him as a guerilla as they had not yet received any uniforms.

You can't miss us because I'll be riding Skeeter. If that don't beat all. Matt.

Seeing Matt, Steve got up and sauntered over to him, stretching out from a good nap. "You writin' Brenda?" Steve's voice broke Matt's power of concentration.

Matt stood up, folded his letter and stuck it and his pencil into his shirt pocket. "Hello, Steve."

Steve looked at Matt's beaten-up face and asked, "What the hell happened to you, chum?"

"Made some friends," Matt answered. "Where the hell was you when I needed ya?"

"Oh, me? Fell asleep.?

"That O'Riley's not such a bad guy after you get to know him."

"You beat up on O'Riley?"

"Nope. Another fat-ol' geaser."

"What's this about O'Riley?"

"He didn't stop the fight, like I thought he woulda. Instead, we spilled a bottle together over at his tent."

"Well, I'll be. Where's he at now?"

"Restin', I suppose. He had already been nippin' before the fight."

Steve put his hands on his hips, looked round the camp site, and seeing only a handful of men milling around, sat down next to Matt.

"Writin' Brenda?" he asked again.

"No. Ginny."

"Oh. Well, it'll be some time 'afore you'll send it. We won't be in town for a while. Got a lot of trainin' to do."

O'Riley was right. Before the sun rose the next morning, with the waking call of the bugle, he banged the pan and went around the site, waking everyone.

"Youse heard the bugler. Gets your asses off the ground and chow down. We've got trainin' to do."

Training. Matt and Steve were reminded that they were a month behind and had to catch up. Riding a horse was second nature with Matt and Steve, more so than many of the others. But to learn it the military way was a disciplinary lesson for both men to learn, and learn they did.

O'Riley sat his mount in the middle of the field as his two aids rounded up Company A and placed them on the edge of the field facing him. They stood by their horses with reins in hand.

"Youse men who are experts now," O'Riley bellowed out, "mount up and show these girlies what to expect."

Eighty-nine men mounted their steeds, and in single file, trotted to the end of the field. Once there, O'Riley gave them the order, "Right-dress!" The men lined up shoulder to shoulder and readied their mounts.

O'Riley rode his horse to the edge and joined his aids. The newly enlisted men watched. Then he yelled out, "Trot!"

The men started out in unison at a good gait, nose level with each other.

"Gallop!"

The Rangers leaned into their saddles and rode fast.

"Charge!"

The horsemen spurred their mounts and gave a loud and thunderous rebel yell in unison. When they reached the end of the field, they pulled back hard on their reins, stopping their horses, then turned and lined up for O'Riley's further command.

O'Riley rode out into the center of the field again, grunted and said, "Now, girlies, you will do the same thing in short order fashion."

He gave the command to his aids, "Keep working with these children, men. I wanna see what my new girls can do."

"Follow me, girlies," O'Riley commanded the new men. O'Riley's eyes focused in on Matt and Steve. He led them to another field on the other side of camp. When he had them in the center of the field, he reined up and yelled, "Whoa!" He rode around the men and continued addressing them. "That means for youse to stop. Now, I'll ask ye. Can any of you ride?"

The men took note of one another without answering him.

"Well," O'Riley answered, sitting tall in his saddle, "we've got 'em."

Major Thomas Harrison, Commander of A Company watched from his tent, and then out of curiosity, walked down to the arena for a better look where O'Riley was working his men.

"Tighten your girth, girlies," O'Riley ordered his men with a swat of his quirt against the palm of his hand. "Or you'll be suckin' up dirt for your dinners. Get out there and show 'em how it's done, Corporal Jorgensen."

Then Harrison heard O'Riley add something in a mumble while wiping his nose. "You Yankee."

"Sergeant!" Harrison called out.

O'Riley turned and saw Harrison standing behind him and realized that he probably heard what he had said.

"Line up your horse with the rest of the girls, Private," he yelled at a recruit falling behind.

"Yes, Sir," he snapped to at Harrison's voice.

"What did you just call that corporal?"

"Oh, eh, nothin', Sir. I assure you."

"I heard you say 'Yankee'. Did you or did you not?"

"Oh, no, Sir," O'Riley stuttered. "I said, my 'hankie'. I blew my nose." He straightened up, and then continued, "Now why would I be callin' me beloved Corporal a Yankee? Oh, no, Sir." He laughed a bit and repeated himself with his handkerchief in hand, "hankie, Sir."

"Very well."

Harrison noticed that O'Riley never gave a reprimand to either Matt or Steve. He stood there and watched them as they rode head-and-shoulders over the rest. He now began to feel doubt about Matt's allegiance to the South, but kept his feelings to himself.

"Trot! Gallop! Charge!" O'Riley kept repeating over and over. He wiped the sweat from his brow with his bandana as if in disgust as he watched a soldier fall from his horse and another as his horse tripped and fell.

"Youse gotta learn to sit in a saddle before you can trot, girlies," he reprimanded the recruits.

Several times he watched Matt and Steve finish a ride and wait at the end of the field for the rest to catch up. They rode figure eights until the men caught up.

"Youse men got plugs for horses. Look at dose men there." He pointed to Matt and Steve. "They ride well because they got good horses."

"When are we going to get ours, Sarge?" one of men shouted out.

"Make yours do for now, girly. We'll get youse some good horses when you show me you can ride."

"Keep up the work, O'Riley," Harrison said. "And just to let you know, I don't believe your story."

He turned and walked away.

O'Riley rubbed his mouth with his gloved hand and spat on the ground.

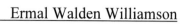

CHAPTER 7

ON TO RICHMOND

Terry met with Lubbock to map out a strategy to get their cavalry unit into the war.

"If somehow we could rapidly train some of these men to ride like cavalry." Terry hit his gauntlet against his leg. "By picking the best riders we have, we could ride to Richmond, I'm thinking, and get right smack into the war. It's a challenge, and by gawd, we're up to it."

Lubbock's face lit up. "Why not, Frank?"

"Yes, by damnation, we'll show President Jefferson Davis that we're cavalry, or my name isn't Benjamin Franklin Terry. And we'll show him that we're the best damn fighting cavalry he's ever seen."

"How are we going to do that, Frank?" Lubbock asked. "You see the animals we have to use. They're slower than molasses in January."

"We'll get some champions on the way, some how."

"Like last time, and use up our money to finance this war?" Lubbock returned. "That's ridiculous."

"No, Tom. It's idiotic. I'm thinking we'll boat it to New Orleans, hook up with a brigade like President Davis wants us to do, and they'll supply us with horses."

"What if we don't find a brigade that'll have us? A thousand men on foot."

"Then we'll take the train to Richmond. Somewhere along the way, the Confederacy will get us our horses."

"You're going to take our entire regiment to Richmond by train, Frank? That's doing exactly what President Davis wants us to do," Lubbock came in. "I thought we were going to ride on his lawn as a well, disciplined cavalry unit."

"And we will, Tom. We will. We've got some good horses, Right?"

"Some is the word," Lubock answered. "Some are pretty good. Good enough if we had the right men to train the right riders."

"I'm looking at two animals right now tied up just outside. Fine looking animals."

Lubbock looked out and saw the two horses in front of an adjacent tent. "Who do they belong to?"

Terry smiled and answered, "Two of the finest horsemen in our regiment. Jorgensen and Andrews. I like your idea, Tom. By damnation, I like your idea. We're not licked, yet. Not by a damn sight. Tom. Let's get our men ready. We're going to Richmond."

"When?"

"At daylight."

"Just like before," Lubbock came back. "They're going to get tired of seeing our faces."

Terry laughed. "This time we're going in as a regiment." He turned and walked back to his desk. Removing a bottle of bourbon, he uncorked it, poured two glasses, and when finished, he raised his in a toast. "To Lubbock and Terry's Regiment."

The two men gulped their drink down in one swallow and returned the glasses upside down on the desk.

Terry stepped outside the tent and caught O'Riley's ear. "Sergeant!"

"Yes, Sir!" O'Riley straightened up and came to attention.

"We're going to Richmond."

"Again, Sir?"

"All of us this time, O'Riley."

"All of us?"

"The whole damn regiment. Tell Majors Harrison and Wharton to step this way."

With a salute, O'Riley double-timed over to the tent where Harrison and Wharton were standing outside. After informing them of Terry's order, he saluted, turned and quick-marched back.

Horsemen are as quick on their feet as they are in their saddles. Wharton and Harrison made fast time to Colonel Terry's tent, catching sight of Matt and Steve mounting their steeds. They entered the tent and removed their hats, as was protocol.

"Sit down, Tom. John." Terry ordered, rolling his cigar between his lips.

Lubbock spoke up. "We have news for you, gentlemen."

"Have the Company Commanders ready their men to move out at dawn," Terry ordered with his strong determinant voice.

"Move out?" Harrison asked. "Where?"

"We're going to Richmond." Lubbock lit his cigar and gleamed at Harrison.

"Yes, Colonel," Harrison returned. "It's about time." He was excited because he knew this time he was included.

"That's not all, Tom. I want two of your men to pick the best riders we have and train them to ride and shoot like the devil. Think you can get them to do it?"

"Two of my men? How do you mean, Frank?" Harrison asked. "Who?"

"I've watched your two new recruits ride. I like their style. Almost as good as me." Terry rose and walked over to Harrison's side and pulled back the tent flap for a better look at Matt and Steve.

"Andrews and Jorgensen?" Harrison showed a lot of dismay in his voice as he stood next to Terry. He still had suspicions about Matt not being totally truthful about being on the side of the South. He hadn't told Terry for fear that Terry would think he was saying it for spite, if not for vindictiveness. His allegiance was truly for the South. If he could prove that Matt was what he suspected, he'd have him before a firing squad. At the present, Matt was Terry's fair-headed prodigy.

"I've paid particular attention to them," Harrison said matter-of-factly. "They're undisciplined and difficult to manage."

"You've come to that conclusion, have you?" Terry asked, rising from his chair. "Why do you say that?" He looked out again onto the training grounds.

"I can't talk with them."

"You've tried?"

"No. I just know their kind. Showoffs. Nothing but showoffs."

"I talked to them and I kinda like them."

"We'll see." Harrison said. "I'll work with them and give you my full report."

"I want those two men as lieutenants, Tom." Terry looked Harrison in the eyes to get his message across that he was serious. He turned and sat down.

"They're green, Terry. They haven't seen any battle, yet."

"I won't go against your wishes, Tom. But I will say this. I need officers. I do not have a captain for your company, and I only have one lieutenant who doesn't know his ass from a prairie dog's butt. Granted he's West Point, but he doesn't have what we need. Those two men do."

"I appreciate and understand your desire, but this is my company and I am and will run it the way I feel it should be run."

Terry stared at Harrison for a few seconds longer, and then walked over to his chair and sat down. "Tom. I'm going to remind you that I know what your stand is in this war. You're in it strictly for political reasons."

Harrison bowed his head for a moment, and then looking at Terry, he said, "Same as you."

"No. No, not the same as I."

"You're in it for what it will give you and your family, Frank, and all of your brothers and their families. We're no different. That's why you're in this war."

Terry stood back up, put his fists on the table in front of him and looked Harrison in the eyes once more. "I'm in this for all that, yes. But, I am not going to run for governor of Texas."

"No. You're not," Harrison agreed. He reached into the cigar box and grabbed a cigar. "I am." He lit his cigar and waited for Terry's return.

"How important is it for you to become governor, Tom?"

"What are you getting at?"

100

"You know you have to win a battle to even put you in the running as a candidate against my brother?" Terry clinched his cigar tightly between his teeth. "And this war could be over any day without that win. Your envy of good men like those two out there on the grounds is overpowering your greed, Tom. Think about it. Those two men could lead you right into the governor's mansion. That's worth thinking about. Not that I could help you any. The incumbent being my brother."

Harrison took his cigar out of his mouth and, as if frozen for a moment, pondered on what Terry had just said. "You think they're that good?"

"I know they're that good. I've seen them fire their weapons like professionals. I've watched them pick up a silver dollar at full gallop."

"Pardon me, Colonel, but what the hell does picking up a silver dollar have to do with helping us become professionals?"

'Tom, you're missing it. The idea is make riders out of our men. The ultimate goal is to make them a unique cavalry unit that can win battles. I think these two men can help do just that. And, if they can train a few, they can train others to train others. And, more importantly, they can lead your men into many victories. And, again, all you need is, one!"

"And what if they don't? What if they get killed in their first skirmish?"

"You better damn well hope that never happens." Terry took a drag on his cigar, removed it and exhaled the smoke slowly. "Dammit, Tom. You'd be no worse off than you are right now."

Harrison walked to the entrance of the tent and looked out again. He wondered if he should reveal to Terry his suspicions concerning Matt. He turned and looked at Terry's big frame and cowered under his voice. He knew it was no more than a suspicion and he was afraid of how Terry would react if he spoke up. He kept silent.

"All right. I'll tend to it right away, Frank."

"I want them to select your best riders, and have O'Riley work with them first, teaching them the rudiments of a cavalry horseman. Train them. I'm going to have our Company Commanders involved, too. Everyone is going to be trained with skills they've never seen the like. I'll talk to them."

"That it?"

"No, Harrison. I need them trained as quickly as possible. When we reach Richmond, Terry's Rangers will ride in front of the Capitol like no cavalry unit has ever ridden before. I promise you that."

"Terry's Rangers? We're calling ourselves that, now?"

"I see no reason why we shouldn't. Do you?"

No, Sir."

"I want our riders to run their horses until they feel they can't ride them any more. They're going to stay behind while the rest of the regiment marches on foot, then join up with us in Beaumont. We'll get rid of the horses there."

Terry watched the look of doubt on Harrison's face, but he knew the potential that Harrison had for being a great leader, even if he didn't think so himself.

"Think they can do it?"

Harrison felt uncomfortable, sensing that Terry had treated Matt and Steve with favoritism since he first met them, almost to the point of disrespect for him. "They aren't regular, Frank. They haven't even had time to learn military discipline and rules and all that goes with it."

"Rules and protocol be damned, Harrison. They'll learn them in time. What I want now is a cavalry unit, and those two men out there can give it to me. Do I have your support or do I transfer them to John's company. I think John can hear me straight? Right, John?"

Wharton nodded and together the two officers waited for Harrison's answer.

Terry stared at the two men, chomped rigorously on his cigar and waited impatiently for Harrison to answer him.

"I just don't know, Frank" Harrison replied sheepishly.

"I know I'm pushing you. I'll respect your decision, Tom. You want some time to think on it. You've got one minute." He pulled out his pocket watch and opened it.

Wharton interrupted. "A week, Frank? You want those men to learn how to ride cavalry style within a week. On those horses? It can't be done. Not by my men."

"Give us some more time," Harrison said with his palms out.

"I want your best riders in shape as quickly as possible. They'll catch up to the rest of us."

Harrison watched out the tent door from the corner of his eye at Matt and Steve riding as professional horsemen. "Yes, Sir. Am I dismissed?"

"That's all, Tom. Do I have your agreement?"

"Yes, Sir."

"Get outa here. You've got two men waiting for their orders."

Harrison turned and walked out, pulling the flap down on the tent.

"What are you waiting for, John?" Terry asked Major Wharton as he stood as if he were still in shock. "Give Harrison a hand."

"Yes, Frank." Wharton saluted and joined Harrison back to their tent.

Terry turned to Lubbock and continued, "We've got a war to fight, and we're not in it. But, by thunder, we will be, and right soon. We have eleven hundred men. I'll settle for how ever many horses you can get me, Tom. Can I count on you to outfit half my men?"

"You want me to go back to the staff ahead of you?"

"Yes. Ahead of us. Get those damn horses for us. I plan to parade right in front of President Davis with a full cavalry unit."

"They said, *no* already, Frank. It'll be impossible. You'll be marching right into the thick of this war as infantry, if you don't watch out."

"Get us some horses!" Terry walked outside the tent, lit his cigar and looked at his regiment. "Good horses. Damn good horses."

He waited for Lubbock to say something, and then impatiently stormed at him. "Try, Tom! Dammit! Try!"

"All right, Frank. I'll try. I'll leave ahead of you in the morning."

"We'll be in New Orleans," Terry added. "I want to hear that you've got them. I'll wait there for your answer."

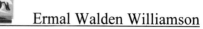

CHAPTER 8

TRAINING OF
TERRY AND LUBBOCK'S REGIMENT

T he officers realized Terry's zeal to have only the best horsemen and shooters in his outfit. When seemingly greenhorns from the outside like Steve and Matt who had these skills came on board and Terry showed favoritism towards them, it set their teeth on edge. They even felt worse when Terry made Steve a lieutenant without any combat experience. Harrison himself was commissioned a captain on the battlefield when he first served with Terry.

A week of training would tone up a cavalryman's body, more so, a major's mind. Harrison decided to march to a different drummer.

A young soldier rode across the grounds on his bay and reined up at a small group of men.

"Sergeant O'Riley, Major Harrison needs to speak to you."

"The Major?" O'Riley asked, looking up the road. "Well, let me have your horse. I'll not be a walkin' in this heat."

The young rider dismounted and turned the reins over to O'Riley. O'Riley climbed aboard the young man's horse and spurred him into an easy gait.

Harrison was waiting for O'Riley outside his tent. "Sergeant!" Major Harrison yelled out in a high pitch voice across the grounds as the sergeant alit from his horse in front of his tent. "Come on inside."

O'Riley followed Harrison inside his tent where he doffed his cap and waited for the Major to sit. He stood. Then, once Harrison did sit, O'Riley followed suit, and sat down.

"Yes, Sir," O'Riley replied, sitting tall in the straight back chair.

"These two new recruits, Jorgensen and Andrews. Either of them have college?"

"Don't know, Sir."

"Find out. Any college? Hell, any high school education will suit me. I want to make them officers. I want them to learn my ways and get into action with me right away. We'll give them special training. They've got what I'm looking for."

O'Riley sat up a little straighter and stared at Harrison as if confused.

"That's all, Sergeant."

"Yes, Sir," O'Riley responded. He left the tent, mounted and rode his horse back to the grounds. He found the young soldier who had loaned him his steed, and after turning his horse back over to him, ordered him to bring Steve and Matt over to the corral.

Matt and Steve walked over to O'Riley and planted themselves on the top rail of the corral.

Taking out a cigar without offering any to either of the two men, O'Riley lit it and exhaled the smoke into the gentle wind. "Either of you Texians have any college?"

"Nope," Steve replied. "Just high school." Then he smiled as proud as a peacock.

"Good. Good. You'll make fine officer material." He took his cigar out of his mouth and addressed Matt. "What about you, me lad?"

"Nope."

"Nope, what?"

"Nope, Sir?" Matt retorted, showing he didn't know how to address a sergeant.

"Ya don't address me as *sir*! I ain't no officer, son. Nope, you ain't got college or what? You don't sound Texian to me. You gotta be a Texian to join up with us."

"Hell, sarge, I ain't. I'm from Tennessee."

"Oh, devil be damned!" O'Riley threw his hat on the ground and then picked it up, dusted it off and put it back on his head. He thought, *The Major wants them both officers and this one ain't even a Texian. Hell!"*

He looked with disgust at Matt and asked, "Whatcha doin' in Texas if you ain't a true and bona fide Texian?"

"Came to ride horses like you."

But not a Texian! O'Riley reminded himself.

"Hell. Ain't my ridin' and shootin' good enough?"

"No, it ain't good enough. Those boys over there are all Texians. I'm a Texian. The Major wants officers and damn good officers but they gotta be Texians first and foremost.

"Come with me," O'Riley said, pointing to Steve. "You," he hit Matt's chest with two of his fingers, "stay here." He motioned to the young horse soldier again who brought his horse back. After the rider returned and alit, O'Riley mounted the horse and walked him towards Terry's tent with Steve walking behind him. He pointed to Matt and said, "You! Get better acquainted with your new sisters, if you can!"

Matt stayed behind, shrugged his shoulders to Steve, watched him trail alongside O'Riley and gave him a wave of his hand. Then he walked over to the ten others and began a conversation with them.

It wasn't long before O'Riley returned without Steve. O'Riley rode his horse to the corral, dismounted and returned the reins to the young horse soldier who had loaned him. "Two hours, lad. Walk him and then trot him for a few minutes." The soldier took him and walked him around the corral.

Matt noticed something different about Steve when he returned; a set of lieutenant epaulettes in his hands.

"What cha got there?"

"The Colonel made me a lieutenant, friend. Looks like you're gonna be salutin' me from now on."

"Congratulations, Sir," Matt said, coming to attention and saluting him. After receiving his salute, he grinned from ear to ear and gave Steve a big bear hug.

"He boosted you up to Sergeant 'cause he wants you to help me train this regiment how to ride horses." He took a pair of chevrons out of his pocket and tossed them to Matt. "Here. Sew 'em on."

"Train this regiment to ride horses? These animals? Who the hell is somebody kiddin'?"

He looked at his chevrons and tried them on his shoulder sleeve for size. "Well, damnation. How comes I don't get a set of them bars, like you?"

"You ain't a Texian, friend," Steve answered, hitting him in the shoulder. He lit a cigar, let out the smoke and added, "The word is that the regiment is leaving for Virginia in the morning."

"Virginia?" Matt's eyes opened wide with enthusiasm for he thought about Ginny in an instant. Ginny's hometown was Richmond and her wish was to some day go back with Matt.

As quickly as he was elated, Steve broke his dream. "You and I are staying behind to train some riders."

"What? The hell we are." Matt was quick to do an about face when Steve calmed him down.

"Easy, chum. Terry wants to groom an elite corps to show off in a parade. We're to take some of the best from each company, as well as their commanding officers, and join the rest of the regiment down the road later. They're marchin' out on foot. We'll ride out on horses once we're through training." He watched Matt's countenance change to a better mood. If a parade were in the offing, he would certainly agree to it as he felt it would be a good place to show off to Ginny and meet her again.

"Get a good night's rest, friend. We've got a lot of work to do."

The air was damp in Texas that morning in sixty-one. Steve rode Buddy into the arena under the watchful eyes of the other well-picked riders. He rode with such splendor that his precise movements demanded their attention. Starting from a walk he moved into a trot, and then a canter and kept their attention.

Matt rode out on Skeeter with the same precision, and met Steve in the middle of the field. They rode together the full length of the field, gently turned their mounts around with loose reins in hand and lightly spurred them forward. Both animals took off with lightning speed into a full gallop towards the men standing around. They never stopped, but rushed through the men, making them go for cover behind the trees. Clearing the fence ahead of them, Matt and Steve reined up, turned their steeds around, surveyed the situation and came back at full gallop. After jumping the fence once more, they brought their horses to a halt in the midst of the men and looked round and about at them.

"Men," Steve addressed Company A, "this is Sergeant Matt Jorgensen. An expert horseman who, with the help of our Sergeant O'Riley, will teach you how to expertly ride a horse."

Without any hesitation, laughter filtered through the air from the company.

"You're laughin' now," Steve said, "but you're goin' to be wishin' you hadn't heard of us by the end of the day."

An older rider, standing in back with a weed stuck between his teeth, sarcastically butted in. "What cha tryin' to prove to us?"

About that time, O'Riley walked fast into their midst with his quirt and gave the man who spoke up a whack across his arm with it. "Stand up, mister!" O'Riley ordered, sizing the heavy-set man up and down. "Your face looks to me like you lost a fight."

It was Troy from a couple of nights before and O'Riley grinned his devilish grin at him. "You'll be runnin' this course until I say otherwise. Now, mister! Now! Double time!" O'Riley ran the grounds with the heavy-set man to keep him going. O'Riley was truly a soldier and a good sergeant, fit and tough all the way. Having downed a bottle of scotch the night before, he was still in fit condition to run the course that morning.

The rest of the men sat and waited until the two men returned from their run. Troy, being heavy set and out of condition, fell down in just about the same place where he started from and laid there while O'Riley stood over him.

"The next one of youse who gripes will get twice what he got and I'll use me horse." He looked around at the men without showing too much strain at being exhausted from running. He smacked his quirt across the palm of his beefy hand.

"Beggin' your pardon, sergeant," a red-headed young lad spoke up, "but we already know how to ride."

"Well, mister," Steve interrupted, sitting tall in his saddle as the officer he had become. "You. The fella with the weed growin' out of his mouth. Get your horse and show me."

Troy looked astonished that Steve would ask him when he knew he was all in. But, realizing that Steve was meaning him, he rose up, walked to the rope line and picked out his horse. He saddled it and rode back to the grounds where the men were standing. Matt and Steve were still mounted.

After Steve motioned for him to go ahead and show them his expertise, the rider galloped out onto the grounds, reined up and looked back at Steve.

Steve rode out to the middle, took off his hat and placed it on the ground. "Ride at full gallop and pick it up, soldier."

Troy smiled and waited for Steve to move out of the way. He eyed the hat, spurred his horse into a slow gallop and bent low for the pickup. He tipped the hat with his fingertips and fell off to the laughter of the other soldiers.

"Any more takers?" Steve asked, spreading out his arms and turning on his heels.

A younger man galloped out to the middle, tipped the hat with his fingers but stayed on his horse.

"Any more?" Steve asked again. He looked at one soldier who raised his hand. "What's your name, soldier?" Steve yelled out.

"McTavvit, Sir," a tall, lanky, blond, blue-eyed horse soldier answered.

"Go for it, McTavvit."

McTavvit rode out faster, bent low and picked up the hat to the praise of the men. He raised it high in the air, smiled and returned it to Steve.

"Thanks for the hat," Steve said in gesture, "but I was referring to the silver dollar I placed under the hat."

McTavvit's face dropped as he looked back and saw a shining object on the ground.

"Wanna try?" Steve asked him, putting his hat back on his head.

"At a gallop, Sir?" he gulped.

"At a full gallop, mister," Steve added with a smile.

Matt had already accepted the challenge and spurred Skeeter into a full gallop. Bending real low with his eyes locked onto the shining object, he picked it up and rode back to Steve.

McTavvit and the others grew gravely silent as they witnessed what they thought to be one of the best riding tricks ever performed.

"You men liked thet, did cha?" Steve shouted at them. "Well, get used to it. Each and every one of you will be doin' the same thing before we get through with ya."

"Youse heard the Lieutenant, men," O'Riley said as he walked up to Steve. "Now, girlies, get to your horses." He watched as they walked towards the rope line. "Double time!"

"Well, Matt," Steve said, rolling his makings. "You and O'Riley have got your work cut out for yourselves. How d'ya feel?"

"Why are we here, Steve? These local jerks already know how to ride horses. What are we goin' to prove to them teachin' them to pick up a gold piece?"

"Colonel Terry wants this to be the best damned regiment in the Confederacy." Steve took off his hat and scratched his head. "Let's see if we can do thet. Go join 'em."

Matt looked at Steve and smiled. "Virginia, hey. We'll have the finest company ready for a parade inside of a week." He eased Skeeter into a walk, tilted back his hat. He counted on and got O'Riley's full cooperation in military discipline for horse soldiers.

Matt continued writing his letters to Ginny, but it was several days before he had a chance to give them to a rider. They were the last posts that Matt sent, for the balance of his stay in Houston was superimposed with such rigorous training that he had little time to write again, and when he did, he never mailed them.

It took a little more than a week, but Matt and Steve did get the men pretty well trained.

"You men were carefully chosen," Steve addressed them, "because Major Harrison said you are the best. Now thet don't mean nothin' to me. And it means even less to Matt. Now, he's got somethin' to say to ya'll."

Matt walked front and center with an empty tin can in his hand.

"You, with the red hair," he called out to a horse soldier, standing amidst the others. "Take this can and place it on the post yonder."

"You gonna show us some trick shootin'?" another horse soldier asked sarcastically with a laugh, while others joined in.

"Hold it soldier," Matt yelled out, stopping the red-haired man. "Give it to this dumb ass."

The man who spoke sarcastically walked over and received the tin can from the other man. He was taller than Matt and heavier built but his size didn't phase Matt any.

"Sure. I'll place your dumb can on a post for you to shoot at," he said and walked out to the post.

"No." Matt ordered him. "Stop where you are and hold it at arms length."

"What?"

"You heard him," Steve stepped in. "Arms length."

The man stopped, looked seriously at Matt and waited.

"Arms length," Matt repeated.

"I'm not gonna play this game."

Matt caught a bead on where the can was, turned around and faced the squad. "Well, if you don't . . . "

He turned quickly, drew his Navy and fired, hitting the can from the soldier's hand.

"I'll have to shoot it where it is."

Matt fired again as the can hit the ground, knocking it back into the air where he fired twice more, keeping it going.

Steve drew his .36 and fired at it, sending it home.

"You can return," Steve ordered, holstering his pistol.

The big man never moved, he just shook and quivered with his eyes opened wide as if in shock.

Matt walked over to the men and continued to address them. "We did thet to impress you. How many of you were impressed?"

All hands went up, including the big man's.

"Good. But thet's not the real reason we did it. I shot it out of your hand to scare the hell out of you. Thet's the secret, men. What's gonna make you better'n the rest in this cockeyed war is your understandin' of how to fight.

Looking at the big man frozen where he stood, Matt said, "You can return to the line, mister."

The man hobbled back as if he had his legs tied.

"First, you've got to get mad. Good'n mad," Matt instructed them. "But, you've got to control thet anger."

In the back of his mind, he wasn't buyin' any of what he was saying at all, because he knew he himself was not mad enough yet to kill his own kind from the north. So what he had to say was a sham for his own inadequacy.

"Second, you've got to scare the hell out of your enemy. Now I want you to pay attention to three things. Scare the hell out of your enemy. If you don't scare them, they'll sure as hell scare you. Your enemy. They are your enemy. No one else's. Hear me strong. They are your – enemy! You've got to hate them! It's hard to kill somethin' you like. Remember thet!

"Third, you've got to shoot to kill 'em! You don't, they will. Understand thet. You've got one chance and only one chance to kill them. So when you fire your weapon in their direction, you do it with the intent to kill 'em."

The message was pointing back at him. It's easy for one to say one thing and never practice it. Perhaps, just perhaps, Matt figured one day he'd escape this camp and ride over to the other side. He was a man with much conflict and confusion, and he was playing out this game of war within himself.

He knew his words were true; he just had a hard time swallowing the truth. He knew he was instructing men he might someday have to kill if he ever chose to go to the other side. He knew men from West Point had to commit to the same when fighting for their cause, for both sides had officers from West Point; some were buddies. It was no different for him, and he knew it.

"I've fought and killed before, like some of you. And, like some of you, I fired my gun for no other reason than to kill. You saw me hit thet can. Think of it as another person. There can be no difference."

He walked down in front of the men and looked at their faces. He stopped in front of the big man. "Sorry I scared you."

"Yeah," the big man answered. "So am I."

O'Riley had some of the men make up scarecrows which they placed against the back fence.

Seve walked to the perameter of the field, shaking his head. He watched as Matt prepared the men to attack the scarecrows, making certain he would not be in the way of the horsesoldiers.

"Now, we want you to do some target practice at those idiotic scarecrows Sergeant O'Riley so graciously had made up for you. Don't aim. You take time to aim, you lose. Shoot the hell out of 'em, then aim."

They did just that the rest of the morning, and to their self-realization, found that it was easier than they thought to hit what they shot at without aiming. All it took was confidence and practice. Practice and confidence. And, some help from Matt, Steve, and Sergeant O'Riley.

Next came horsemanship. The ground was hard but the leaves added padding for the horsemen when they took their spills, and took them they did. With Matt's expertise and O'Riley's enthusiasm, Company A spent each day going through its paces. The men were treated as if they never rode a horse before, and learned the right side and the left side of the horse, its mane, its tail and what the differences were. They learned to curry them and get the burrs out of their tails and manes. They learned when and how to pat them down when tired and hot, and when to let them water and when to let them eat. The men learned the life of a horse as they lived and slept with them. More importantly, they learned that they were dispensable and were to be ridden into the ground if the horse soldier's life depended upon it.

O'Riley would yell out, '"Dismount! Fix saddles and tighten' your damn girts!" The men would ride again until their rears were raw.

There was no want for sleep at camp those nights, for every man could hardly stay awake. Morning came and so did O'Riley. "Up and at 'em, girlies!" he yelled, clanging on a skillet with a ladle.

Matt got the men out into the field early after breakfast and showed them what he expected from them that day. Steve came around and encouraged them, performing his horsemanship again and again.

"Trot! Gallop! Charge!" These were Matt's commands for the next few days. The men heard Matt yell at them repeatedly while O'Riley walked his horse around the terra firma and watched the fun. "Trot that horse until I tell you otherwise!" Matt yelled. "Hold him back or you'll be no good to the company. Hold him, I said! When you go to battle, I want you to go as one body, in a line," he added. "Any one of you stray from your position and you'll weaken our body. We don't want thet. Right, men?" He waited for a response, but received none from the men.

"Well, so much for thet," Steve interrupted. "Let me tell you this, whoever breaks rank because they can't handle their horse will get extra horse duty while the rest of us eat. Is thet clear?"

"Now you heard it from our Lieutenant and I'll tell youse, too," O'Riley added, looking deep into the men's eyes. "Sergeant Jorgensen is in charge of training youse how to ride a horse the way he wants you to ride. Now who wants to show me how good he is? Private McTavvit. I saw you ride. Youse did a fine job at it, too. But not good enough. Mount Emma and let's see your style."

The men got their comeuppance from O'Riley and Matt without any further complaints that day. For that week, cavalrymen in each company heard commands such as, "Sit up straight, girly!" or "Tighten your girth!" Or "Who taught you to ride, your mama?" The men learned to hate Matt, Steve, and of course, O'Riley as they learned to ride as a well-disciplined unit. When each commanding officer rode through his company, he did so with a solid backbone of pride.

The morning came for them to rejoin Terry and the regiment in Beaumont. They were all proud of their new name, "Terry's Rangers".

When the Rangers reached Beaumont, Terry had the horses gathered and sent back to Houston. They acquired river transportation and traveled down the Neches River to the northern side of Sabine Lake and upriver to Niblett's Bluff.

"I'd like to know where we're headed now," Matt queried as they began disembarking their crowded vessels.

"O'Riley will tell us thet, Matt,' Steve answered.

"Alright, girlies,' O'Riley's voice yelled out that drizzling afternoon. "Get in formation."

"What for?" one of the Rangers asked, looking at the muddy ground around him.

"'Cause, me fine soldier of a boy," O'Riley bent into him, "we're gonna march. Now! Let's hurry it up."

And march they did. The rain subsided and the sun came out as they marched to New Iberia, Louisiana. As they arrived in different groups, they were piled into a boat with rickety old planks to sit on, and floated towards New Orleans.

"Where do you suppose we're at now?" Steve asked a tired Matt.

"Sign says 'Crescent City'," Matt noticed. "Must be Crescent City."

"Where's Crescent City?" another Ranger asked, walking by them.

"I heard tell we're in Louisiana, though no one tells us anythin'." Matt smiled at Steve.

"Can't be," another Ranger answered, catching up to the first man. "Thet'd mean we traveled over three hundred miles."

"I feel it," Steve said, rubbing his buttocks from sitting so long on dirty hard planks in the boat.

"Hey, soldier!" a local farmer yelled out as they marched by. "Where ya hail from?"

"Texas," a horse soldier answered.

"Texas? You them Ranger fellas we've been hearin' about? You them Texas Rangers?"

"Well," O'Riley yelled back, "You heard about us, hey?"

"Everybody up and down this here valley has heard about ya'll."

And the word spread far and fast. "The Texas Rangers were in town."

"And we're Texas Rangers?" O'Riley asked, walking up behind Matt and Steve. "I thought Texas Rangers were tough men."

"He called us 'Texas Rangers'," Steve said to Matt. He turned to O'Riley and asked, "We're *Terry's Rangers*. But, now they're callin' us *Texas Rangers*. Isn't thet what you heard, O'Riley?"

"Is thet because we're from Texas, Sarge?" A horse soldier asked, moving up.

"Yeah!" O'Riley proudly answered. Then he said to Steve, "You're from Texas. Your friend ain't."

He gave another innuendo that implied he was not altogether sure that Matt wasn't a Yankee. He yelled back into the ranks. "Yeah, we're callin' ourselves thet so thet these locals will know we're from Texas."

"But we ain't *the Texas Rangers,* Sarge," another horse soldier chimed in.

"They ain't no way no one is gonna know thet way out here," O'Riley said. "So, goes ahead and use it. Youse got me permission."

"Looks to me, Frank, that our men are kinda proud of our new name," Lubbock informed Terry. "Gotta admit, it's sounding better all the time."

"You see those Louisiana people yelling it. That's a battle call if ever I heard one," Terry added.

"Yeah. *Texas Rangers*."

Terry smiled and added, "*Terry's Texas Rangers*, Tom. *Terry's Texas Rangers*. You agree?"

Lubbock looked at Terry, furled his brow, smiled and looked out at the Louisiana people and the Rangers. "Damn right! *Terry's Texas Rangers.*"

Terry was ready to get his horses, but President Davis wasn't. Lubbock dispatched a wire to Terry and Wharton from Virginia with the discomforting news.

"Devil be damned!" Terry crumpled the wire in his hand and threw it to the ground. "I'll not let the tremendous amount of effort that went into training my men and getting them this far for this gawd-forsaken war go to waste."

"We're headed for Orleans," Major John Wharton reminded him.

"And President Davis suggests that we should come to Virginia if we want to receive our commissions," Terry added.

"Are we going?" Wharton asked.

"It's either east to Virginia for our commissions without horses, or Alabama as infantrymen, or back to Texas. I'll be damned if I'm going back to Texas with my tail between my legs."

"Then you're resigned that we're goin' to Alabama?"

"No. No, we're not," Terry said adamantly.

"On to Virginia, then," Wharton said with determination.

"No, John. Not without horses. I've got another plan. Some how we'll get our horses and then we'll show them we're a cavalry unit that those Federals had better not mess with. I've still got an ace up my sleeve, John. It's about time I used it."

"Al?" Wharton asked, rubbing his chin with his gloved hand.

"Damn right. Send out a wire, John."

"Now you're talking Texas style."

A disgruntled Terry asked another of his Brazoria County neighbors, General Albert Sidney Johnston for help. Wharton scribbled off the wire and got it sent immediately to Johnston's headquarters in Bowling Green, Kentucky.

The body of the wire simply read,

I've got eleven hundred rangers at your disposal and no horses. Where do you want us?

As the days drew closer for the Regiment to leave for Virginia, Matt's mind set himself into the arms of his Ginny. If any one could find Matt in Virginia, it would be her. He knew her family would put out the scouts to watch for him.

Ginny stood on a Tennessee hill overlooking her plantation. It was the same hill where she first met Matt. It was then that she had a whip in her hand, and he felt the brunt of it. He had saved the beating of one of her slaves from her foreman that day only to have her use it by whipping him. It was a whipping that made her recognize him for the man he was, and made him recognize the one woman who would share his dreams.

Today, she stood alone, waiting for his return from Texas. She clutched his letter of weeks before, which said he was coming home.

I sent Sin to his Maker,' he wrote. *'Not proud of it. Just grateful it was him and not me.*

'Got a friend. Name's Steve. This war broke out and we enlisted in Terry and Lubbock's Regiment. I'm what is called a 'guerilla'. But not for long. We already got word that we'll be parading in Virginia in full uniform. I'll be on my way by the time you read this. Watch for me, my darling.

She waited and watched, for she knew it would be soon.

CHAPTER 9

THE BONNIE BLUE FLAG

T erry's Texas Rangers landed in New Orleans. It was here that Terry gave the men some R & R to move about, But for his officers and non-coms, which included O'Riley, he had them attend a concert called, "Music in the Civil War" at the New Orleans Academy of Music which helped change their destiny considerable. It was put on by an English-born actor who billed himself as the "Arkansas Comedian", Harry Macarthy. A great many of the regular soldiers attended as well for the amusement.

With help from his wife, Lottie, Harry came on stage in a flamboyant outfit of various colors and feathers, dancing and singing across the proscenium to ethnic music. For each number, he also changed into a brighter array of wardrobe.

"He's funny," Lubbock commented to Terry as they watched him perform.

"What do we say when we talk about Jeff Davis, little one?" Harry asked his cockatoo.

The cockatoo squeaked out, "Three cheers for Jeff Davis" and the attending soldiers threw their hats high in the air and to mimic it, yelled, "Three cheers for Jeff Davis!" Matt and Steve sat behind their commanding officers and failed to keep from laughing loudly.

"Our men are getting out of hand, Frank," Lubbock commented.

"Let them," Terry replied. "This is pretty damn good. Good for the soul."

The show had lasted almost two hours when Macarthy stepped out of character, removed his hat and said, "Ladies and gentlemen. I have not been in America too long, but I realize that we are in a terrible time. Ah, Lottie and I should have stayed abroad where we performed at the Convent Gardens. But, alas, we are here.

"Having toured the south more than the north, we have come to pledge our loyalties to you. A few months back, we performed a special number to our soldiers in Jackson, Mississippi. They liked it so much that we want to present it to you tonight. So, if we may.

Lottie came out and carried a flag on a pole which she held beside Harry. It was a flag with a single white star on a blue field. A slight breeze blew from the flats along side them, causing the flag to wave ever so slightly. "Maestro." He motioned to the orchestra leader in the pit to begin.

His performance was inspiring throughout the evening. Then he sang his closing number, "The Bonnie Blue Flag".

Terry's eyes grew moist as did the rest, though no one noticed. Terry and Lubbock and the officers around him stood up and removed their hats. The rest of the Rangers also stood at attention with their hats in their hands.

After the show ended, Terry and Lubbock, along with Wharton and Harrison went backstage and met with Harry and his wife, Lottie.

"Mister Macarthy," Terry said as he reached out and shook Harry's hand. "I'm Frank Terry and this is Tom Lubbock. We're the commanding officers of the Texas Rangers. You may have heard of us."

"Throughout the people here shouting about your coming," Harry answered with a smile.

"May I tell you that your show was one of the best I have ever attended? It stirred my soul."

"Well, thank you, sir," Harry returned in his cordial English manner. "This is my wife, Lottie."

Terry bowed to her. She was a lovely young lady in her upper twenties with blonde hair and blue eyes. "Your being out there with the flag added just the right touch when he sang . . . what was the name of that song again? The Bonnie Blue?"

"The Bonnie Blue Flag", Harry answered with a smile that stretched from ear to ear.

"Why, thank you, General," Lottie answered. "I also had to open the outer doors to let the wind blow the flag. Sorry if it got a little chilly."

"I'm not quite a general," Terry said amusingly as he looked around backstage at the open door and knew what she meant. They all laughed and in the next few minutes got to know one another.

Then Terry looked around at his men, and back at Harry for a quiet moment, pondering carefully what he was going to say. Then he asked, "How's chances of getting this song for my troops?"

"What do you mean, Mister Terry? I feel awkward calling you a mister."

"It'll do. I mean, young Mr. Macarthy that your song was destined for me to use with my Rangers, and I'd like very much to carry it into battle with me. You have a price. I know we have to pay you. How much?"

Harry looked sternly at Terry for a moment, his countenance dropped and he turned back to Lottie. "Excuse us, please, gentlemen." They stole themselves from the presence of Terry and the other officers for a moment and walked back by the open doors where they talked.

Matt and Steve found their way backstage and stood by the back entrance, unknowing that Harry and Lottie were in a secret conference. They could see the actors huddled nearby and heard them talking about the flag.

"Good show, people," Matt yelled in.

Lottie looked up and walked over to Matt and Steve. "I'm Lottie Macarthy, Harry's wife. I saw you two gentlemen in the audience. You in particular." She pointed to Steve.

"Why me?"

"You were laughing the loudest."

"Do you always talk thet funny?" Steve asked. "The show's over now."

"You do not like the way I talk?"

Harry walked over to where they were talking and introduced himself. "You two intrigue me," Harry said, shaking hands with them. "Yes, this is the way we talk. But, we feel you have the accent. Not us."

"Man, your English is great," Steve said. "I love it. I could listen to it for hours."

"Didn't mean to interrupt what's goin' on." Matt apologized. "I mean your talking with our commanders."

"Oh, I see," Harry returned. "It is all right for me to call Mister Terry and Mister Lubbock, Commanders?"

"Yes, Harry," Matt agreed. "Their our Colonels, but they prefer to be called our Commanders for a special reason, which I can't go into right now."

Harry looked puzzled, then smiled and asked, "How did you like my final song?"

"You saw the audience. We all loved it."

"Your Commanders in there want to buy it."

"Well, this is where we should be leavin'," Matt continued. "My apologies. Comin', Steve?"

"No. No." Harry stopped Matt. "You represent the rest of the troops." Pointing to Terry and his officers, he continued, "I know the Commanders like it. But you're not an officer."

"I'm afraid you're askin' the wrong fella."

Steve looked at Matt and said, "It's the Bonnie Blue Flag, Matt. The flag for the Confederate States of America."

Matt was silent for a moment, and then realized that he might be telling on himself. "Well, if you want my opinion as a Sergeant, I would love for our regiment to have it. But it's not just for us, it would be for the whole South."

"That's what I wanted to hear." Harry shook hands with him and said, "Please excuse us," turned and walked away.

"Thet's what I wanted to hear, too, Matt," Steve said. "You sure do keep actin' strange. Can I ask you a question? Tell me to mind my own business, but I've got to ask it."

Matt stared at Steve, afraid of what he was about to be asked. "What?"

Steve looked around to make sure no one could hear him. "Ginny's a Southerner, right?"

"I said as much."

"Are you?"

Matt turned his head and looked out at the Mississippi, groping for an answer. "I told you, my heart is with her. Isn't thet enough?"

"It is with me, I suppose."

"Then what are you concerned about?"

"The men. Can they depend on you in a battle?"

Steve watched Matt stare out into emptiness. "Oh, I know. You fought a war in Kansas against the Pro-Slavers because you were given the job. Do you still feel thet way?"

"I don't know how I feel, Steve," Matt returned. "I'm from the North. I'm in the South and I'm told to fight agin' my own people. And, yet, it's like as if I had to fight my own brother. If he were livin'. It don't make sense."

"It does if you believe in it."

"I believe, Steve," Matt continued, "in doing the right thing. I believe in killing a person if he murders another. I believe in defending my best friend if he's being attacked. But for me to say right here and now thet I could rush up to and shoot another man because he was from the North, I can't say. I – I wish I could."

"Time will tell," Steve added.

"Yeah, friend. Time will tell. I hope you won't."

"Only if I see you turn agin' me," Steve said dead seriously. "I hope I don't have a gun in my hand if thet ever happens."

"Gentlemen," Harry continued when he reached Terry and the officers. "On January 9, of this year, I was asked to perform in Jackson at the convention of the People of Mississippi where they adopted an Ordinance of Secession. Afterwards, they raised the Bonnie Blue flag over the capitol building

"I had written my song for that occasion. What you gentlemen saw tonight was what I shared with the people that night. My song is to be shared with the Confederacy. Will you take my song with the rest of your, how would you say, your armies?"

"Mr. Macarthy," Terry answered, "we would be happy to share your song with the entire South."

"Then the song is yours."

"How much?"

"Victory!" Macarthy answered. "Give the South victory in what you are fighting for. The song is yours for that price, and nothing short of that."

Lubbock interrupted and said, "Thank you, Mr. Macarthy. The South will have her victory and your song will lead us to it."

Macarthy went inside his dressing room and returned with a set of papers upon which the song was written. "The song is yours. And I will sing it wherever I perform."

"Why not now?" Terry asked, taking Macarthy's arm to lead him back to the stage. "Let me announce it."

Terry stepped to center stage and waited for the men to quiet down. Once the place was absolutely quiet, he addressed them. "Gentlemen. The flag and song is ours. Mr. Macarthy will lead us and teach us the words."

Macarthy proudly took center stage and began leading the men in singing. Terry's cheeks looked like he was singing the loudest. The men yelled with joy as they sang, and a ruckus broke out that lasted a while before everyone could settle down. But, with the help of the mayor, they did settle down and returned to their camp.

Terry took the manuscript, thanked Macarthy and walked out proudly with Lubbock and the other officers, and the Rangers. Matt and Steve sided Terry and kept in step. Settled down they were, but ten mayors could not quell the singing once they got outside the building.

Terry could hardly restrain himself the next morning after breakfast as he shared the excitement with the rest of the troops. "The song is ours," he assured them again as he gave the manuscript to the regiment musicians.

"The song is good," one of the musicians said.

"Then," Terry commanded, "Take it with you and rehearse it with the rest."

The musician smiled, tucked it under his arm and took it with him as he walked proudly back into the group of horse soldiers who had already been singing the new song.

Afterwards, Terry held a meeting with his officers. "Now I'm not a good artist, so you fellas have to help me."

Lubbock advised the rest of the officers. "Terry is inspired that we should have our own flag,"

Terry added, "Yes. The flag as it is right now is dark blue with a white star in the center. I want to add something to it."

"What are you thinking?" Wharton asked, feeling and looking carefully at the one star flag.

"The Bonnie Blue has one star. Well, we're from Texas. Texas is one star. Why not?" He sketched the one star and then added *'Terry's Texas Rangers'* above it. "It fits."

Handing it back to Lubbock, he said, "Have someone sew the letters, using bright yellow thread."

And so Terry's Rangers' first flag was made. The musicians played the song at New Orleans while the men placed her on a pole and hoisted her high into the air. The Rangers sang the words with vigor and with hats in hand.

It took some time for General Johnston to answer Terry, but he did. The wire read,

As of this date, you and your regiment are independently assigned to my brigade in
Bowling Green, Kentucky.
I aim to go through Federal territory swiftly and need your strong cavalry regiment.
Signed: Albert Sidney Johnston, General
Commander of the Western Brigade.

Johnston was all army, being a graduate of West Point. He was a man looking for victories swift and sure and knew his friends from Brazoria County with eleven hundred drilled and disciplined men could help him accomplish that. He was not a man of any hesitation.

Terry read part of the wire again, emphasizing: *I need your strong cavalry regiment.* "That's it, gentlemen. We're going to be cavalry."

Terry gave the order for the men to head to the tented fields of Kentucky. The troops were sullen and saddened about being rerouted, but happy at the news of the possibility of getting horses. After another day and night at bivouac, they were ready to march first thing the next morning.

One of the musicians took pen in hand and wrote new lyrics and titled it *The Texas Ranger War Song.* They sang it to the tune of *The Bonnie Blue Flag.* It was an easy song to pick up on, and when they spread the word through camp, many of the Rangers picked up on the words quickly.

And they sang the *Bonnie Blue Flag* as they left New Orleans.

Terry regrouped his company and had the men saddle up in boxcars used for hauling cattle. They put in unshaved planks for seats without backs. That and the filth and smell kept the men awake and on their toes the whole twenty-hour trip as they headed to Bowling Green, Kentucky to join up with Johnston's regiment.

When they reached Nashville and settled in, Matt found himself a relaxing spot by a lazy stream of water and bit into a chaw of tobacco. The wind was quiet among the autumn leaves and the sound of the forest was absent as the birds and the animals sensed a frightening moment.

Upon hearing the news that the regiment would not be going to Virginia, but instead would assist Johnston's Brigade in fighting the Federals in Tennessee, Matt had good and bad feelings run through his body all at the same time. This would have appealed to Matt, also, had he known earlier, but now no posts were leaving the camp and there was no way to contact Ginny. He just knew there had to be some way to get a message to Ginny before she left for Virginia. His belief was short lived when it hit him that it was more probable that she was already on her way to

Virginia to see him in the parade. Knowing her as well as he did, he was surer of that than of her still being in Tennessee.

He looked out into the wilderness, spat his chaw into the stream and yelled out, "Ginny!" The forest got quiet.

A bullet shot out and reverberated through the distant forest deep in the Tennessee woods. A rider fell to the ground. Then all was still again.

CHAPTER 10

DEATH KNOWS NO GENDER

Ginny had received a post from Matt that his regiment would soon be parading in Richmond. She prepared herself to leave the McBride Plantation in Tennessee the next morning and ride towards Virginia to greet his entourage.

"I'll be perfectly all right, father," she said as she sat in her large comfortable bedroom brushing her hair and tying it back so she could push it under her wide-brimmed hat. "We're in Southern territory and no cowardly Yankee will even see me."

She dressed for the ride in her tight pants, shirt, and jacket. With her hair pushed under her hat, she appeared as a man on a horse. She always rode like a man, but now she was seemingly taking the unnecessary chance of riding through territories being fought over by soldiers on both sides.

Her father, Jim, walked her to her horse, which he had one of his slaves saddle up for her.

"I'd feel better if you took the buggy," Jim said with a concerned voice, "and drive only during the day time."

"And get there late, father? Really." She mounted her horse with her quirt in her right hand. "I'll take the road I'm familiar with and be there in no time. A buggy would slow me down. I don't want to waste words with you, father. If they can't tell I'm a woman," she said, sitting tall in her saddle, "then God placed the right things in the wrong places. Or they're blind."

Stretching towards her father, she leaned down and received a big hug and a kiss from him, which she reciprocated. With a smile on her face, knowing she would soon be seeing Matt again, she spurred Suzie into an easy lope and rode towards Virginia.

For the first few miles, the woods of Tennessee were familiar and the ride was easy, so her trip was pleasant. She camped out that night in a small clearing and built herself a fire to stay warm. She also built a lean-to out of some limbs and branches, and covered them with the loose leaves and dirt she found through the snow. She found herself warm and cozy by the fire. A cup of hot coffee, some bread and beans satisfied her stomach for the night.

She rose before dawn, got her belongings packed in her saddlebag, washed her face in the nearby creek, and rode off towards Virginia.

The fog was thick one morning along the river bed, so she rode easy, hoping to gain at least a little ground towards Virginia. She was careful with Suzie, stepping onto loose limbs along the way.

She could hear laughter and talking through the woods, and wondered if the voices were friendly. The laughter led her to believe they were friendly, and she kept riding towards their voices.

"We done shot her," a soldier said, telling a story to the others. "Norm and I were sittin' right here yesterday mornin', and she crept up on us, and we thought she was some Reb a-stalkin' us. We froze ourselves to our rifles with fear and trepidation until they came closer, and closer, and closer," he said ever so slowly to keep the other soldiers' attention.

It was a small camp of Union soldiers, mostly young fellows in their teens, having breakfast and telling some new recruits what went on the day before, when asked had they seen any war, yet.

"Well, sir," he went on, "when we were sure they were right on top of us, we let go of our repeaters and nailed those suckers like you never seen before."

"What?" one of the recruits asked, with his eyes wide open and his jaw just as wide. "What happened?"

"We didn't rightly know," the story-telling soldier went on. "We waited and never heard anythin' for quite a while. Then the fog lifted, and there she was."

"What?" another recruit asked impetuously.

"A stupid Bessie," he finished. "We shot ourselves a gawddam cow."

"Let me tell ya somethin'," another soldier chimed in. "It sounded like soldiers. She lifted up her left foot and put it down, and then her right, and she sounded just like soldiers walking through the woods."

About that time, a couple of the listening soldiers, young bucks that had never yet shaved, picked up their rifles to the tune of their ears and pointed out into the woods in Ginny's direction. "You hear that?" one of them asked the rest.

The noise they heard all right was that of Suzie stepping lightly through the snow, crunching twigs and branches. None of them could make anything out in the fog.

Then, she appeared to them out of the fog, and one of the soldiers, taking her for a Confederate soldier because of the color of her gray clothing, fired once and brought her down. He was a good shot for a soldier barely tall enough to fire a rifle. The bullet went through her right shoulder.

The soldiers ran quickly to her, ready to fire again, still thinking Ginny was the enemy and still alive. They had their first kill of the war, and they were excited over seeing their enemy lying face down in the snow, apparently dead.

"Hold on," a tall skinny soldier yelled out. He appeared to be barely eighteen by the looks of his smooth face. He turned her over, and seeing her gasp for air said, "He's still breathin'."

Another soldier brought his Remington into firing position at her chest.

"Hold it! He's as good as dead," the first soldier said who turned her over. "Let him be."

Ginny laid face up for the boys to see, until an older boy, short and skinny, recognized she was not wearing a uniform.

"It's jest a boy, fellas," he said. "Not a Johnny Reb at all."

"Well, hell," said the tall skinny soldier, "Let's get a medic over here real quick."

Two things were in Ginny's favor at that hour. The first was, the company doctor was on hand, so he answered the call instead of the medic. Secondly, he was a man in his thirties, and knew considerable about gunshots. It took him only seconds to find out Ginny's gender.

"It's a girl," the first soldier said, noticing her shape as the doctor opened her shirt.

"Get a litter ready, men," the doctor ordered as he applied a compressed bandage to her wound to stop the bleeding.

"Fortunate for you, young lady, it went clean through and missed the bone," the doctor said, finishing up the bandaging. He wrapped her coat around her and helped some of the men place her on a litter. "You should be fine." He hoped she heard his voice for she slept deeply from the wound and from exhaustion.

He followed the soldiers as they carried her to the field hospital tent.

Ginny awoke to find herself on a cot in a strange setting. Seeing only the white jackets of the medics and the doctor walking around, treating a few patients, she had no idea what side the soldiers belonged. Before long, she could make out the color of their uniforms in the camp's courtyard, and she knew then that they were the Union soldiers. They belonged to the 2nd East Tennessee Infantry Regiment.

"Where am I?" she asked, staring up into the face of a medic who appeared to be in his late twenties, thin with long hair and clean shaven.

"You're all right, Miss," he said as he looked around for the doctor.

The doctor heard her, and walked over to the cot. "How're you feeling, Miss?" he asked, taking a chair beside her. "You've been out for two days now."

She suspected that they did not know her patriotism was on the side of the South.

They must have assumed, she thought, *since I rode on the other side of the Tennessee River, that I would naturally be a Union sympathizer. But, why did they shoot me?*

"Why was I shot?" she inquired of the doctor again, looking quizzically into his face as she attempted to sit up on her elbows. She fell back upon her cot and stared up at the ceiling.

"The fog had hidden you, and the boys were pretty jittery."

"But I was on the other side of the river!" she clambered still looking up at the ceiling.

"We apologize for that, Miss, but unfortunately we are at war and we are next to enemy lines. They didn't want to take any chances."

"And they shot me, a helpless defenseless woman out for a ride."

"Beg your pardon, Miss," the doctor interrupted, "but, you were riding in the fog, and not just for a ride. They had every reason to believe you could have been the enemy. You were also packed for a trip. Mind telling me where you were going?"

"As if it were any of your business, but I'll tell you anyway," she said curtly and sarcastically, turning her head from one side to the other to avoid meeting his eyes. "I was on my way to Virginia to visit my folks."

"Alone? Why didn't you go by road and take a buggy?"

"Am I being held a prisoner, Doctor? If you are a doctor?"

"No, Miss. You are free to go as soon as you feel well enough to travel. And, yes, I'm a doctor. Captain Henry Paterson at your service."

"My, my. You are polite." She smiled and looked up into his warm and sensitive looking eyes. "I'm sorry. Bad manners of me. Not the way I was brought up."

"If I'm not mistaken, I hear a Southern accent in your voice."

"Well, Captain, I did say I was from Virginia, and I now live in Tennessee. So, I suppose I do have somewhat of a Southern accent."

"I hope that's all that you have, Miss."

"There you go again. Being suspicious. You have no right accusing me of being other than what I am."

"And, Miss, just what are you?" the Captain asked as he began buttoning her shirt.

"You may leave my shirt alone, Captain."

"The bleeding has stopped. I'll have someone bring you some food. Get some rest. I'll look in on you later."

"Is that all?"

He stood tall, and looked down upon her. "No. But we'll discuss your boyfriend later." He smiled and walked away.

He went through my mail, she said to herself as she watched him walk away. It was something in the way that he handled himself that gave her the confidence that he was on her side, and his light grin amused her.

On the third day, she sat in the sun in the camp's court yard and watched some soldiers drill, and others wrestle around among each other like cuddly bear cubs.

One of the soldiers eyed her and then asked, "Want to play around, little sister?"

Another soldier took a strong hold of the smart alec's tender area and threw him over his shoulder, then let him fall to the ground. The wounded soldier grabbed his groin with both hands and staggered away.

"I hope to God he's not an example of a good fightin' Union soldier," Ginny said, half laughing.

The soldiers saw she had made her point as they joined in laughter, and continued fighting each other. More soldiers practiced in the distant woods, using their Remington repeaters.

Sleeping in the opened tent for several days, she came down with a cold, and now she tried her best to shake it.

Captain Paterson, seeing her sitting outside her tent that morning, walked over to her. "If you're going to sit outside, then put these on." He had her get dressed in a Union soldier's outfit. "And blanket up, miss," he said, tossing a blanket to her. "I don't want to have to treat you for pneumonia."

She went back inside the tent and put her new clothes on. "How am I doing, doc?" she asked from inside the tent, buttoning up her britches.

"You'll live, young lady, as long as you rest and stay warm. This weather isn't doing any of us any good. We buried a young 'un yesterday. The cold took him."

"Oh?" was all she could say. She came out of the tent, looking like a young recruit, carrying her blanket. She sat back in her chair and wrapped herself in the blanket. "Better?" she asked Doc, with a smirk on her face.

"I'd feel better if you stayed in bed a while longer," he answered.

"I like it outside. The fresh air and all."

Ginny watched him as he turned and walked away. He was an attractive man, with a smooth face, salt-and-pepper hair and a matching moustache.

A few nights passed and the thought strongly haunted her that she was well enough to continue her journey. She got back into her own clothes, slipped out of the field hospital tent and saddled Suzie for her continued ride once more towards Virginia. Her mind was intent on seeing Matt, and if he were still in Virginia, she would find him.

The sentries posted at the opening of the camp that morning tried to stop her, but she spurred Suzie into a gallop and rode past them. A few miles outside of camp, she felt the chill hit her again, worsening her cold. However, she believed that by noon the sun would be up and would warm her body enough for her to continue. In less than an hour of easy riding, she stopped for rest. She found that her saddlebags were empty and she had no makings for coffee. In her hurried plan to flee the camp, she had forgotten to take along provisions. After awhile, she made her decision to return to the camp, even knowing how much she hated the Union soldiers. At least, there she had a chance with a doctor who seemed to be concerned with her health and not her patriotism.

The doctor was on hand when the sentries brought her to the hospital tent. "She don't look good, Doc," one of the sentries said, as he helped lift her out of her saddle and, with another soldier, carried her to an empty cot inside the tent. Another soldier tied Suzie up with the rest of the horses

Doc examined Ginny quickly and found her to be running a fever, and delirious as to where she was. He had seen it in other people in the north. He saw it in the soldier they buried two days earlier. Now he was witnessing a lovely young lady shivering from it. Pneumonia had settled into her body, and she was wet with perspiration.

"Get me some blankets, orderly," he yelled out as he began unbuttoning her shirt and pants so she could breathe easier. With the help of an orderly, he tucked the blankets around her body, and began wiping the perspiration from her brow. He knew from the color of her skin that she was in a second stage of pneumonia, and if he didn't bring her fever down quickly, he could lose her.

He stayed with her throughout the night and most of the next day, leaving other soldiers with lesser wounds for other medics to tend.

"Matt," she softly cried out, time and time again, turning her head from side to side, yet keeping her eyes closed. "Damn Yankees shot me, Matt, honey," she blurted out, shifting her head from side to side as having a nightmare.

When the doctor heard her, he muffled her sounds for no one else to hear. He looked around to assure himself that no one heard her. No one had.

The next morning found Doc weary and tired, but still making the rounds to attend to the soldiers. Captain John Rogers, his senior in the field, caught up to him, and, looking into his eyes, questioned him. "You're a little uneasy on your feet, Hank. You look like you stayed up all night."

"Mornin', John," Doc returned, throwing a blanket on a soldier he had summarily examined. "Yep. Could you spare me for a while?"

"How come? You're pet patient, what's her name?"

"Yeah. She's serious. Pneumonia."

"Let's take a look see, and then you get some rest. Hear?"

They walked over to Ginny's cot and looked down at the sleeping beauty. Hank felt her head and then took her pulse. At that moment, she began to show signs of awakening.

"Fever's broke, as I can tell." Hank watched her eyes begin to open and shut. "Our patient is waking up.

Doc knelt on the other side of the cot and placed his hands on both sides of her face, looking into her sleepy eyes. "Can you hear me, Miss?" he asked, hoping to keep her awake.

She made a few grunt sounds, opened her eyes and smiled at Doc, then went back to sleep.

John took his stethoscope and, opening her shirt, examined her breathing. "A little congestion, but, Hank, I do believe your worries are over."

Doc sighed, took his stethoscope and examined her for assurance. He stood up and smiled at John. "Thank you, Lord."

"Now, you can get some rest."

John threw his stethoscope back around his neck and walked away.

Doc walked over to a nearby cot, plopped down and went to sleep.

By noon, Doc was awake, shaven and had already checked on Ginny for signs of her awakening.

A nurse nearby caught Ginny's eyes opening and called out, "Doc. Miss Sleeping Beauty has entered our world again."

Doc smiled and quickly walked over to Ginny's side. He took his fingers and opened her eyes, and then took her pulse. When he placed the cold end of the stethoscope on her chest, she jerked.

"Cold," was all she could murmur. She looked up and smiled whimsically at Doc.

"You sure are handsome," she teased, looking into his eyes.

"Welcome back, kid," he replied with a big grin.

"Thirsty," she added, "and hungry." She licked her lips.

It was a good sign, a sure sign that she was getting better.

The day spun on and Doc made sure Ginny had full attention from the attending nurses, which were two females and three males on duty. In his mind, it was not enough for the wounded and sick coming in, mostly the sick from colds and scurvy. He had never seen so many men with diseased gums and losing their teeth. The disease didn't stop. Some died. Then many died.

He wanted to make sure that Ginny would recover by applying his experiences as a doctor and prayers as a Christian gentleman. Ginny saw him whispering to himself as he constantly examined her. She knew not that it was his way of praying, for she had not witnessed so good a man as Doc.

Her father had raised her after her mother passed on before she was yet a teenager. But he raised her in a home full of grace, but little prayer. He was a determined man who believed that his power was sufficient to get his work done without the Almighty's intervention. He used prayer only when it was deemed urgent, and that was seldom after the death of his wife.

Doc came to Ginny's side while she was sat up in bed, downing her chow for the evening. He pulled out a chair from nearby and sat down.

"How're you feeling, Miss?" he asked politely, hoping that he could spend some time in healthy conversation with her without letting his personal feelings get in the way.

"If you mean, am I ready to talk about myself, why don't you jest come right out and say it?"

"Is it that obvious? Okay. You have one over on me. Can we talk?"

"Sure." She smiled and continued eating without stopping.

"We were just getting around to finding out more about you when you rode away." He furrowed his brow and shyly looked into her eyes. "Can you tell me who you are, now?"

"Would if I could," she answered with a mouth full of food. "Thing is, can't."

"Can't?"

"Can't."

Doc looked perplexed, dipped his hand into his blouse and pulled out his well-worn pipe. Packing it with tobacco, he stared at Ginny and finally asked again, "Can't? You mean you won't tell me?"

"Don't know, Doc," Ginny replied, swigging down some milk. "Jest don't know."

Doc lit his pipe, inhaled and then blew out his fresh puff of smoke that wafted into the air above Ginny's bed. "Don't know?"

"Yep. Funny, ain't it?"

"No, it's not funny, young lady," Doc retorted. "You're playing with my mind." He leaned on his elbow and pointed his pipe at Ginny. "Now, what do I call you?"

"Call me?" Ginny stopped chewing and stared at Doc for a long minute. Then she answered him. "Bla-bla."

"Bla-bla?" Doc repeated.

"Bla-bla." Ginny mocked him. Then she giggled. "Stupid, ain't it. I just don't know my name, Doc, and thet's for sure. Bla-bla."

Doc sat for a moment and just stared at Ginny, not knowing whether to believe her or not. "You've got a name. Right?"

"If you say so, Doc."

"No. No. You have a name. What do people call you?"

"You've been calling me *Miss*. Seems to me you'd know what my name is, if anyone would."

"Miss, what I'm trying . . ."

"See? You did it again," she interrupted him. She put her spoon down on her plate, pushed the plate aside on her bed, and looked dumbfounded. "Doc. I don't know."

Doc rose, looked down at Ginny and excused himself. He came back to her bedside with Captain Rogers and found her sopping her plate with her last biscuit.

Rogers took a hold of Ginny's wrist and checked her pulse. He continued by examining her eyes. "Look to your right. Umm. Now look up at the Doc."

Ginny giggled again and said, "We playing games?"

"No, Miss, we are not playing games," Rogers answered, smilingly. "Captain Paterson here says you can't remember who you are. Is that correct?"

"Funny, isn't it?" She pondered. "No, it isn't funny, either." She looked up at Rogers then at Doc and asked, "What's wrong with me?"

"How old are you, Miss?"

"How old? Thet's simple, I'm . . ." She stopped, and stared out into space. "I'm . . . I don't know how old I am." Then, dropping her biscuit and plate onto the floor she asked, "What's happened to me?"

Both doctors looked at each other as if to say, *she's faking it. She's hiding herself from us, and maybe valuable information, too.* Neither man was sure of her condition at this point, for neither man had experienced a situation such as Ginny's.

The team of doctors left Ginny alone for that night, hoping the sleep would heal her into consciousness as to who she was. There was no improvement with her memory the next morning, either.

Later, on the same day, Doc ventured again with Ginny, sitting at her side, this time before she had her evening meal.

"Wanna talk, again, Doc?" she asked, watching him take his pipe out of his pocket as usual.

"Yes, Miss, I do. Can we?"

"By all means, Doc. I'm yours. I want to get well as much as you want me to, seems like."

"Good." He lit his pipe and stared at Ginny as she watched the smoke rise to the top of the tent. "Look at me, Miss."

Ginny brought her attention to focus on Doc, restraining herself from giggling. It was no game for her at this time, but it did appear to be comical to her that she could not remember anything about herself.

Doc stood around and summoned a nearby nurse. "When you've got a moment, bring her to my tent." Then he concentrated his attention to Ginny. "We'll be more private there."

"People will talk," Ginny teased.

Doc looked at the nurse, who was already preparing Ginny by putting a coat around her, and said, "Just bring her."

Ginny was at his tent with the nurse. They both picked out a cot and sat down while they waited for Doc to come. When he did, he excused the nurse and sat Ginny on the cot while he sat in his chair. He continued puffing on his pipe as he began questioning her.

"Who are you?" he asked determinately.

"We're going to play thet game again, are we?"

"Until we get some truthful answers from you, yes. Who are you?"

"For awhile back there I thought I was talking with a handsome man. Now, I'm not sure."

"No, no. We are not taking that route." Doc stood up and paced to the front of the tent, turned and looked back at Ginny.

"Miss. I admire you. You're too beautiful to be, well, cute. And right now, I think you're just being cute."

Ginny smiled and sat straight up. "You think I'm cute?"

"I think you're *being* cute. There's a difference. You're playing with my mind."

"You do have a mind to play with, Doc." She smiled and waited for him to answer. Instead, he humphed and chewed on the end of the pipe. "All right, I'll tell ya." She placed her hands on her knees and deepened her voice. "I'm the enemy, and I'm here to capture all you Yankees." She watched him loose grip of the pipe. He caught it before it hit the floor.

He got a grip on himself, relit the pipe and continued. "You mentioned the name, *Matt.*"

Ginny's eyes opened a little, then she looked intently into Doc's eyes as he bent low to her. "Nope."

"Nope, what?"

"Don't ring a bell."

"*Matt?*"

"Nope. Can't be. *Matt's* a man's name. Try again."

"Who is Matt?" Doc asked, standing straight and looking back down at Ginny.

"*Matt*, who?" Ginny returned.

"You're telling me that the name, *Matt* has no significant meaning to you?"

"Should it?"

Doc turned and paced back to the opening of the tent, stood there and watched outside as rain began to trickle down the slope of the tent. He patiently smoked his pipe and let the smoke exit through the front gap in the tent. He felt very amorous towards Ginny from the moment he had met her, when she was injured by one of the Yankee bullets. He grew more fond of her as the days grew on, a feeling of which he tried time and time again to get rid of and yet he could not even begin to hide. He did not know whether she knew of or felt any like feelings towards him. He certainly did not think she would feel the same towards him. But now, he was becoming infatuated with her beauty in front of him, alone with him inside his tent.

The moment broke when Captain Rogers opened the tent's flap and entered. He was suddenly face-to-face with Doc who was startled and lost his pipe to the floor.

"John, just what the hell are you doing?" Rogers stood erect and without waver as he addressed Doc.

Doc bent and picked up his pipe. "You believe in knocking before entering, John?"

"Where's your nurse?"

"I sent her away?"

"Why?"

Doc knew he had sent her away simply because he wanted to reveal to Ginny what he had heard her muttering in her sleep. *Matt. Matt, darling. They shot me.*

Doc led Rogers outside the tent and continued talking to him in a soft voice. "I need privacy, John. To question her."

"That's no problem, as I see it, but why didn't you tell me. It is not permissible for an officer, even a doctor, to see a female patient alone in his tent. You know that."

Doc lowered his voice to a whisper. "John. I know I should have told you. Sorry about that. But the moment came when I felt I had to prod immediately. I felt that she was going to tell me something, and I needed this moment."

"Good. Now you've got it. But with me here."

"Not good enough, John."

"That's how it has to be, Hank. You shouldn't have excused your nurse."

Ginny rose and walked to the front of the tent. "May I return to my bed, gentlemen? I feel rather weak."

The two doctors looked at one another while Ginny brushed by them and left the tent to meet the rain.

John rushed out, took his cape off and threw it over Ginny's head. Doc looked on, rushed to her side, took her by the arm and led her back to the hospital tent with John.

The days got warmer, and with the help of Captain Rogers, Doc began working with Ginny to help her regain her identity and anything of her past. Each time, the sessions got a little more personal, and less and less informative.

Rogers approached Doc as he neared the end of his session with Ginny and asked, "Any progress with our lovely and yet mysterious lady?"

"None, John", Doc replied, rising to meet him. He excused himself from Ginny's presence and led John outside the hospital tent. "I'm convinced she's telling the truth."

"How can you be so convinced? You see how she plays with our minds, giggling, smiling, smirking. She's a, a. I don't know what or who she is, but I'm just saying this one time. Watch out for her!" With that, Rogers left and Doc returned to Ginny's bedside.

"He still thinks I'm fooling?"

"Yes, I'm afraid he does. Some," Doc continued. "You've got to understand, Miss, we've never had a problem like this before. And to top it off, you are not our priority."

They both looked towards the door of the tent as more stretchers bearing wounded soldiers were brought in. Doc looked around at the five nurses in his tent, walked outside and watched the train of wounded being lifted and carried towards him.

It was then that he again realized more seriously the futility of an understaffed medical center with lack of medicine. With Captain Rogers, they had prided themselves with organized procedures and plenty of provisions. The procedures were now running short and the provisions, both food and medicine, were dwindling. They had sufficient for the time being, but both men could see the time approaching when they would need to send back to Richmond for supplies and medical attention for some of their more serious men.

The battle raged on, both on the field there in Tennessee, and in the mind of Captain Henry Paterson, the doctor in charge of helping heal a wounded beauty lost in a world of her own.

Ginny was on her feet and helping out with the nurses, caring for and attending to the medical as well as the personal needs of the sick and injured. Doc was not alone at admiring her prowess with the patients. It seemed the other nurses as well as Captain Rogers also recognized her talents. She was an amazing force to them, for she had recovered from a near-death situation, and was now helping others to get well. Some healed up and went back onto the battlefield to face the same evil that brought them here. Some succumbed.

Doc watched the wonderful improvement in Ginny's progress towards being healed, but he still had doubts about her amnesia. He had never heard of a case of amnesia lasting as long as Ginny's. Of course, he had never dealt with the subject before Ginny. He knew that if he were to help her get well, she would need more professional attention than he could offer her. She would need to go to Richmond, Virginia where he had colleagues that knew about amnesia. He sensed the need to send her back to Richmond with the wagon train heading back for supplies and medical provisions. Doc was seeing it as a way to get Ginny off the battlefield. He also knew that he might never see her again. Tension mounted up inside that tore him apart. He had some amorous feelings for her, feelings he was afraid and ashamed to reveal to her. But, somehow, he hoped she would learn of and maybe reflect her own feelings toward him, or maybe not. He knew deeply that he could not pursue his thoughts beyond this point because of his marital stature and his professional stature as a doctor. But as a man, his thoughts were, *How the hell is Emma going to take it when I send her home as a special patient?*

CHAPTER 11

THE FAIR AT NASHVILLE

"**H**orses," Steve said, sitting down on a felled tree.

"We're finally goin' to get horses?"

The word quickly spread through the camp and the men were no longer feeling sorry for themselves about not getting into the war. They knew that once they got horses, they'd show the rest of the regiments just what a cavalry unit was all about.

"It's about time," Matt agreed.

"Appears thet our Major Harrison is close friends with the Terrys and the Johnstons. They knew each other in Brazoria County. Gotta be good to the Major from now on, Matt. He's got clout."

"He's got nothin'. I don't give a damn for the Major, you know thet." Matt just knew he was close to Ginny. His craving to see her ate at his insides.

"Didn't you say your gal was in Tennessee?" Steve asked, rolling his makings. "Well, the way I see it, we're headed for Nashville. Close, friend."

Matt thought about Ginny again. *Yeah. Real close.*

And right he was about Nashville. When Terry's Rangers hit Nashville, they used the fairgrounds for camp.

While walking the breadth of the grounds with Lubbock, Harrison and Wharton, Terry remarked, "This is one of the most beautiful places for a soldier camp I ever saw.

"My birthplace, Frank," Major Wharton remarked as they watched the men settling in. "I was born just up the road a few miles."

"Yes, I know," Terry answered. "Then it should mean something extra to you,"

"It does that all right. Great to be home. I've got kin here."

"Have you seen any, yet?" Lubbock asked, smoking his pipe.

"Some of my family should be here." Then he added, "Hell, I just thought of something."

"Romance?"

"A couple. Probably married by now."

"Maybe the Rangers could add some excitement here," Terry reasoned. "The kind that makes your kinfolk and girl firends kinda proud of you, John. I'll see what I can do."

After learning that Terry's Rangers were without horses, they were approached by some of the important town people who knew and were proud of Terry and Lubbock, their heroes. The town leader told them, "We don't have the best horses in the country, but by gawd they're fine thorobreds. We'd be honored to give you a few for your men."

"Well, by damnation, Mister, we'll take them," Terry replied enthusiastically. "But we'll just be borrowing them because we'll have our horses in a few days or so."

"Don't bother. Use them as long as you like." He turned around, stopped, and turned to face Terry again. He took off his hat, scratched his balding head and sheepishly looked up into Terry's eyes. "Don't suppose you could show us some of that Terry's Rangers stuff we've been hearin' about? Recken?"

Terry grinned broadly and replied enthusiastically, "Mister, you've got your self a show!"

When the Rangers received their borrowed horses from the townspeople, they mounted and gave the rebel yell. After settling down, the company commanders got their men in order and instructed them as to what to do for the night.

"Men," Harrison brought his company to order, "we're going to put on a show for the people." He looked over at Matt and Steve standing beside their mounts. "I've instructed Lieutenant Andrews and Sergeant Jorgensen to select some volunteers and lead them in the charge. Give these people the best show you can, and make them proud of us."

Most of the men could hardly restrain themselves while watching the seasoned riders in each company show off their remarkable riding skills on horses that they had borrowed a few days before. The day wore on and the Rangers partied with the local girls as they tipped the keg of beer and made themselves appear a little tipsy from drinking too much. Matt and Steve, not to be outdone, joined in.

When it came time for the Ranger volunteers to perform at the Fair in Nashville, Terry's Rangers sobered up quickly and went in proudly. Terry rode out to the center of the arena and announced the events. "Ladies and gentlemen," he yelled out in his rough bass voice. "I am Benjamin Franklin Terry, Regimental Commander of Terry's Texas Rangers. What you are about to witness this night is a series of feats performed by the Rangers.

"Behind me and beside me you see some scarecrows. Please be sure you're looking at them and not at me."

That broke any tension the audience might have had and they laughed loudly. The events were to show the local population how well the men were in marksmanship as cavalry riders.

"Our troops will line up, ride down on them and blast them to pieces."

Many of the troops took turns at showing their marksmanship by participating with the use of their carbines and Navy Sixes at the scarecrows and later at other stationary targets from horseback and away from injuring their audience.

The audience cried out for more and wanted to see more of what some called the first Wild West performances east of the Mississippi.

The local Tennesseans loved the way they strutted around as idols for them to adore. They especially loved the way they mounted their steeds and rode in competition style. Some ran alongside their horses in a fast start, jumping in and out of their saddles pony express style, twisting and turning around in the saddle while galloping at fast speeds. And then there were the clowns who caught the tail of the horse and ran behind it, or even rode facing the horse's tail. Each group of riders performed excellently and made Colonel Terry and the other officers proud of their feats. Each performance seemed to top the next as competition ran high.

To continue the festivities, fine showmanship called for some of the bosom ladies to strut out into the arena and place hats and bandanas on the ground. Several of the riders, including McTavvit and Troy, mounted their steeds, walked them to the far end of the arena and waited for O'Riley to give the go-ahead sign by bringing his arm down.

When he did, Troy spurred his mount to a full gallop, bent way down and kept his eye on the hat as he approached it. He successfully retrieved it, sat back up in the saddle and held the hat up high to the applause of the crowd. Two riders rode simultaneously down the arena from the opposite direction and performed the same act to the roar of the crowd. Company A had them standing up and applauding. Excitement filled the air.

Then it was Company B's turn. Three riders next rode in a column and retrieved colored handkerchiefs with their teeth that were set in a row. They sat up tall in their saddles and waved the handkerchiefs at the crowd as they rode the perimeter of the arena. The crowd felt the enthusiasm and never expected anything to top it.

McTavvit rode back out to the center of the arena, not to be outdone, held a fifty cent coin high in his hand, grinned and showed his white teeth for all to see that he was confident of what he was doing. When he felt the crowd understood what he was doing, he bent low and placed the coin on a dry spot. He looked up, waved his arms and rode to the starting point at the far end. He proceeded to look down the road to where O'Riley was sitting his horse and waving his hat high in the air. When he brought it down, McTavvit spurred his horse into a fast gallop, faster than ever before, eyed the coin in the center of the arena, bent real low and missed retrieving it. The crowd showed their dismay with groanings.

He rode back to the starting point, waited again for O'Riley's move and, when he saw it, rode out just as fast. He eyed the coin again, bent real low almost falling from his horse, reached out with his long lanky arm and successfully retrieved the coin.

The crowd stood up and came apart and ran into the arena. Several of Company A's rangers pulled McTavvit from his horse, lifted him up and carried him across the field on their shoulders. The women got in closer with bottles of whiskey and poured them on the Rangers' heads as they paraded around with McTavvit. McTavvit grabbed a bottle from one of the bosomed ladies, uncorked it and drank from the bottle while still being carried by the Rangers.

Several horsemen from Company B and C lined up at the end of the arena while some beautiful Tennessee ladies strutted out to the center and laid their scarves on the turf. The ladies then ran down to the other end of the arena and waited for their man to bring her scarf. The competition was on.

Scarves flew around on the ground like fish flopping and gave the men the jitters.

Terry rode out to the middle of the arena and explained what was about to take place. He sat his horse tall and straight and smiled to the delight of the ladies as he watched the scarves blow around.

"Ladies and gentlemen," he began. "It seems we have a slight breeze blowing tonight."

The audience laughed and sat tensely, waiting as he continued.

"But not to worry. Now, we have a dozen or so beautiful ladies at the other end of the arena who have just placed their scarves on the ground for these riders to pick up. The rule is simply this. Whichever scarf a rider picks up and carries to the lady at the end, she will give him the first and last dance of the evening.

"Now it seems we do have a couple of problems outside the fact that the scarves are blowing around," Terry observed.

"First problem is picking up the scarf. That's going to be easy for I've ridden with these men.

"Second problem won't be so easy," he continued. "I'm sure the riders have seen the young lady of their choice and he knows the scarf he's after. Now, they've got to match the scarf they pick up with the lady to whom it belongs. Otherwise, they'll be stuck with a different lady for the evening. Seeing the lasses first hand, either way will be a treat"

The audience roared with laughter and he ate it up with all the pride he could muster inside. "Are my riders ready?" He looked at both ends and watched the ladies fidget and the men holding back their steeds. He spurred his horse and rode to the sidelines. He pulled out his Navy, raised it in the air and fired one shot.

Each Ranger rode out, leaned in their saddles and chased a flying scarf in the arena until he caught just the right one . Once he caught it, he then finished his ride to the other end and presented it to the lady standing to receive it. Oft as not, he got the wrong lady with the wrong scarf, but enjoyed her company just the same.

This went on for several more times until all the ladies wound up with a Ranger. Although a few fistfights occurred over who got which lady, no one was disappointed that night.

The audience wanted more. The Rangers gave them some more proficient riders. Troy and Pat were among the half-dozen riders picked for the task.

Terry again rode to the center of the arena as some ladies placed a silver dollar on the turf.

"Now, ladies and gentlemen," he started out, "if you thought that was good, this next feat is even better. These Rangers are going to ride fast from opposite directions and retrieve a silver dollar these lovely ladies have placed on the ground. I can hardly see them myself. But I have confidence they can do it."

Some of the crowd yelled out, "You gonna show them how it's done?"

Lubbock rode out to Terry and suggested, "why not put Andrews and Jorgensen in?"

Terry looked over at Matt and Steve and then shook his head. "There'll be time. Let the audience wait for the best."

Lubbock rode back to the sidelines.

"To make it more interesting," Terry continued, "the winner gets all five silver dollars to spend on his gal."

Once he was certain that the men were ready, he pulled out his Navy, raised it and fired a shot.

The six men rode to the center, and with the exception of one man, they each picked up their silver dollar.

They regrouped and performed the stunt again, each time eliminating a man until only one man came in a winner, Lieutenant Pat Christian. He was a clean-shaven man, in his early twenties, standing six feet with a good moral attitude. Pat met Terry in the center of the arena to claim his prize money.

Then the crowd went wild again. They started throwing money into the arena clamoring for the riders to pick them up. Each rider showed his worthiness of the coins by riding out and picking up silver dollars from the ground at a gallop. Many a rider rode off with some spending money for the night, giving the Tennesseans a thrill.

Terry rode over to Lubbock. "Now. Let's get Lieutenant Andrews and Sergeant Jorgensen ready."

After the last rider rode away with his coins, Terry rode to the center again

"Now we come to the finality," he said with his arms high in the air as if to shush the excited crowd. "Two of the finest horse soldiers you will ever see any where. Ladies and gentlemen. It gives me great pleasure to present to you, Lieutenant Steve Andrews and Sergeant Matt Jorgensen."

Matt and Steve stepped out from the sidelines, mounted their steeds and rode around the arena in opposite directions, waving to the crowd and winking at the ladies; then met in the middle.

Terry rode back to the side lines, turned and watched as the two men readied themselves.

"Let's give them what they came for," Matt said. "I told the girls to put out three dimes in a row for each of us. No prize money this time. We ride for the hell of it. We'll pick up the dimes and ride the arena."

Having been instructed, the lasses brought out six dimes into the arena, raised them in the air, carefully placed them in two rows on the turf and then walked off.

"You get one try, friend," Matt said as they waited for the gunshot.

"Same goes for you, chum," Steve said with a smile.

The two Rangers rode to the opposite ends of the arena.

Terry rode back out to the center. "Ladies and gentlemen!" he began. "Our most proficient riders, Lieutenant Steve Andrews and Sergeant Matt Jorgensen, are going to ride at break-neck speed, lean out of their saddles and retrieve the dimes our lovely ladies have so graciously placed in the middle."

He again rode to the sidelines, turned, pulled out his Navy and fired.

The two men raced to the center of the field and each retrieved his three dimes. They continued to ride around the arena to the ovation of the crowd.

Then, out of nowhere, two buxtrosed ladies ran out into the center, laid down face up and placed a coin on their bosoms. It was a challenge unsuspected by either of the two men and a treat for the crowd to watch..

"I'll be," Matt said.

"I'm game if you are," Steve remarked and pulled down his hat.

Again, they each rode to the opposite ends of the arena, and at the roar of the crowd rode down upon the buxom ladies at a gallop, bent way down and each retrieved the coins.

When they reined up, one of the ladies ran over to Steve and pulled him down from his horse and planted a big kiss on his lips.

"What's thet for?" Matt asked.

Steve looked up and smiled. "I sorta kissed her as I picked up the coin."

Steve mounted up again and rode the arena once more with Matt. When they came to the mayor, they reined up and presented the coins to him, doffed their hats, turned and rode the arena, firing their Navies as they rode to the roar of the standing crowd who waved their arms and threw popcorn, paper and anything they could get a hold of at them.

Terry and Lubbock rode to the center of the arena and motioned for Matt and Steve to side them. While the officers dazzled the audience with their uniforms, saddles, and decorated steeds, Terry once again addressed the crowd.

"Ladies and gentlemen. Terry's Texas Rangers will now demonstrate for you a mock cavalry charge. Because of the danger involved in this, we ask that every one, especially those beautiful ladies who have been all over the field, spread out and watch from a distance.

The captains of each company rode out and introduced themselves as such and rode to the sidelines, joining the two leaders to watch. Matt and Steve rejoined their company.

Men from several companies paraded around the arena, and doffing their hats, waved to the audience. After four rides around the arena, Matt took two-dozen Company A Rangers to one end of the field while Steve took another two dozen to the other end. The horses were hot and ready to move out. Each Ranger showed great restraint, keeping his steed in line.

Other Rangers, who had horses, stood and held their reins as they faced the arena, while others sat on the opera seats of the corrals or stood on the sidelines to watch.

This time, Terry and Lubbock took the honor of firing off their Navy Sixes.

From opposite ends of the arena, Terry's Rangers rode down on each other, firing their weapons in the air. As they passed one another, they performed feats of daring. Some would fall out of their saddles as if hit. Others would jump another Ranger and knock him to the ground. Once on the ground, they would do a mock fight with their fists. Others in their saddles reined up, and without any verbal command, rode back through the lines again, firing their pistols to the utter elation of the crowd. They finished their performance with the horse soldiers on the ground, capturing their own horses and remounting them, or being picked up by a fellow soldier riding double to the other end.

Then for the finale, Terry and Lubbock rode out with the company commanders following them. The troops rode back in at both ends and joined them in the middle where Terry called out his commands.

"Troops by four." Terry and Lubbock rode in front of the troops while Harrison rode behind them.

With each company commander riding in position, and platoon sergeants in line, Terry's Texas Rangers rode in cadence, four in a group in a figure eight pattern, and then rode around the arena. The cheers from the audience were breathtaking to the troops parading in front of them and they showed their appreciation by riding with proud chests sticking out.

The Rangers had won the admiration of the local population and money to boot for each of them. All and all, it was a fine day for Terry's Rangers.

The field overflowed with farmers, ranchers, store keepers, good looking girls, bosomed ladies and drunken Rangers. It would be the last gala for them for a long time.

The next morning, Company A got the feel of a full charge on the same borrowed horses they had the night before. Matt lined them up and shouted as he rode in the middle of the line, "Trot! Gallop! Charge!"

Major Harrison looked with contempt towards the two men, but accepted thanks from Terry for helping bring in the best company in the regiment, especially with McTavvit's daredevil feats.

Terry knew Harrison's greed. But he also knew Matt and Steve's skill and mastery of the horse and the leadership of their men and it was these things that won his praise for Company A. He just let Harrison feel that he had won the credit all by his self.

CHAPTER 12

GINNY GETS A NEW HOME

On the other side of the War laid a beautiful young lady from the McBride Plantation whose only sin in this seemingly cockeyed world of hers was to be the ride to her lover in a territory filled with Yankee soldiers. Complications had set in after she was felled by a young Federal soldier's minni ball. Once attended to, she had determined that she was well enough to continue her unescorted ride to Richmond, Virginia.

Her world was turned upside down by her attending physician, Captain Henry Paterson. He was a handsome man in his thirties, married to Emma in Richmond, Virginia. His task now, outside of attending to the wounded and dying, was to send Ginny McBride back to a world of reality. For now she suffered from amnesia.

Doc knocked on the side of Ginny's tent and waited for her welcomed voice.

"If it's the doc, come on in," she said, joyfully. "If it's any one else, go away."

Throwing open the tent flap, he bent down and entered the tent. Standing before him was the most beautiful lady he had ever laid eyes on. She stood in jerry rigged Yankee clothing that would make any one look less attractive, but amazingly to him, all he could see was her beauty.

"It finally fits," she said with a smile.

"Yes. Yes, it does that alright," Doc replied, removing his hat.

"Then what's the matter?"

Doc stared a little longer, dazzled at who had entered his world. Ginny was barely twenty years of age, fifteen years younger than Doc. Her figure filled out the uniform, not in any loose fashion, and the sight was causing passion to arouse inside him.

"I said, what's wrong? Your jaw broken?" she asked, standing with her hands on her hips.

"I – I apologize, Ginny. It's so, well, only that you . . ." He became lost for words.

"I'm what? Do I look awful in this stupid uniform? After all, it wasn't my idea. My clothes were okay. A little dirty, maybe, but I'll wash them."

"No. You have to wear the uniform so that our men can identify you. You're not a prisoner, but you were mistaken once, and I don't want it repeated."

"Well?" she asked, turning, as if modeling for her client.

"Well, what?"

"Do I pass inspection?"

"Oh, yes. Yes, you do that, all right. Yes, ma'am," he answered with the accent on *ma'am*.

She put her arm through his and walked out of the tent. "Then, I suggest we take a walk. Would you like to continue our conversations, say down by the water?"

Doc replaced his hat and smartly walked arm-in-arm with her down by the riverbed.

The sun had been up for quite some time and the chill had left the air. The sound of the forest creatures quieted down at the crack of a far off rifle.

"Just one of our boys, I reckon," Doc said as they came to the edge of the river.

"How do you know?" Ginny asked. She allowed Doc to clean a place off a downed tree for her to sit.

"Don't really. Just suspect as much. Wouldn't think a Reb would be this close to fire one shot." He sat on a stump opposite her.

He took out a pipe and packed it, and then continued. "What may I call you?"

"Well, up to now, Doc, you haven't called me much of anything, except, *Miss* or *Lady.*"

Doc took a match from his pocket and struck it on the log. Putting the flame into the bowl of the pipe, he began to drag in air to light it. "Don't fit you."

"What would you like to call me?"

"No clue. What comes to your mind?"

Ginny looked out into the distance as if searching for her identity. She thought to herself, *The air is fresh. Sun is bright. The river. Well, it's running pretty like. I suppose there's fish down there.* Seeing a splash in the water and ripples forming from it, she said excitedly, "There's one. Two, maybe." Then she turned her attention back to her therapist. "What would you like to call me?"

"Well, let me see," the doc said, letting out a stream of smoke that wisped into the gentle breeze. "Start with the letter *A*. Ann, Anna, Annabelle. Nope. Not you. Sounds too much like my wife's name, *Emma.*"

Ginny's eyes widened at what she heard and she turned sideway on the tree. "*Emma's* a pretty name."

"Didn't I tell you about Emma?"

"Why should you?"

"I guess I didn't think my life was important to you. After all, we're concentrating on finding out who you are." He stood up, walked over to Ginny, and, taking her chin in his hand, turned her face towards his. "Aren't we?"

Ginny looked up and smiled. She kissed his fingertips and then slightly turned her face towards the river once more. "Beth."

Doc felt a passion throughout his body that he felt when he first saw her. His mind missed hearing what Ginny said.

"Do you like it?" Ginny asked.

Doc straightened up and looked down at the frowning Ginny.

"I said, don't you like it? You're looking mighty peculiar, Captain Paterson. What'cha thinkin'?"

"I'm sorry. I missed what you said."

"Beth," Ginny repeated.

"Beth?" Doc returned. He asked himself, *She's discovering who she is. I'm certain.* He knelt down before Ginny and placed her hand in his and said, "Beth's a beautiful name. Is it yours?"

"It is now, if you like?"

"I mean, does it sound familiar to you? Does it fit somehow?"

"I don't know. I really don't know," Ginny repeated. She stood up, turned to face him eye to eye, and replied, "Don't sound like it's me. Yet . . ." She walked down to the river's edge, picked up a pebble and skipped it across the river. For a fleeting moment, Matt's fine figure of a man, doing the same thing, skipping a stone across a river on her plantation the day she met him, appeared in her mind. But only for a second. "But yes, yes it does feel like it belongs to me. I don't know why. But it does some how." To her, she could not relate the name to her identity, but it was surely a pretty name, and the only one that fit the occasion, for she did not want to go through the entire alphabet. B's would have to do.

"Then, *Beth* it is. Short for *Elizabeth?*" he asked, confirming it.

"Yes, I like it. *Elizabeth* And you may call me, *Beth*," she replied with a smile.

One of the critical tasks of a medical officer in the Union Army is that of strategically locating a site for bringing in and discharging the wounded. A church or schoolhouse is ideal. Sometimes, just an open field would suffice. At this time, up to now, all Captain Paterson had was an empty field.

Fortuitously, a team of soldiers located a large house with a barn structure on many acres of land south of their location and commandeered them as a temporary medical center for surgeons, not knowing whether they would be fighting immediately or moving out. The owners were still occupying the property, but obligingly surrendered it for the cause, including their own services where needed. It was a constant decision that had to be made, changed, and remade in accordance with the Commander's orders, and depending on the furtherance of his strategic plans.

A group of soldiers immediately began making a clearing around it for tents. One thing about it, the Federals made certain that the hospital grounds were organized and well kept. Eventually white tents were set up in neat rows to accommodate the sick and wounded. At this time, it would be quite suitable for one Beth, for she had been wounded.

Days poured into weeks as the Yankee doctor from Virginia tenderly attended to Beth as a father to his daughter until it turned towards a bit more affection as that of a paramour. It seemed as if he was never going to win his battle, to see Beth fully recover and become whomever she was once more.

Fighting progressed on the battlefields of Tennessee and soldiers got sick. Many died. Whatever the case, the doc's services were needed more.

Beth pitched in and helped as best she could with the care and attention of the same Yankees, one of whom mistakenly shot her as a Reb. She found out quickly that she was not squeamish at the sight of blood, and learned the art of bandaging from the good doc.

He was doubly proud that his patient was becoming of use not only to his services to the sick and wounded, but to herself as a person as well. He began to see that it was good and necessary therapy.

When they both had a chance to rest, they did so together and talked, almost incessantly about the war, the wounded and dying, and again about herself. Doc wanted her to talk more about herself, to bring out her past and somehow, just maybe, strike a familiar subject where he could attach it to discovering her true identity. *There has to be a thread,* he thought, *as to who she is. And, I'm going to find it, whatever the cost.*

"You're doing a great job," Doc said, fumbling for her new name.

"Beth?" Beth asked. "Still having trouble with it?"

"Nope. No more. Just wanted to hear you say it just the right way." He looked at her, and then caught himself, looking like a young man in love. "I mean, it's a pretty name for a pretty young lass. It's you."

"Thank you, Captain." Turning from attending to a soldier, she added softly but loud enough for Doc to hear, "Now if I only had a last name."

The day was chilly but the sun had set her course to melt the snow lying courteously across the acres of a Tennessee terrain. The good-looking and gentle doctor made his rounds, checking on a few soldiers caught with the seasonal illnesses.

Doc kept his observation on Beth carefully and wisely, watching her as she kept to herself mostly, trying to find out who she was and why. He knew that, keeping her on the field of battle with only a nurse or two was not wise for her recovery.

When he saw the opportunity, he prepared Beth for a trip to Richmond along with a supply train. He carefully eyed Beth in the back corner of the medical wagon, which he had made into a comfortable setting for Beth. He fought the temptation to touch her and tenderly caress her as her beauty captivated his mind and spirit, but stay his passion he did. He knew that only time would reveal whether he could continue to imprison his thoughts before they would become reality.

Captain Paterson climbed aboard the covered medical wagon with a four-up mule team heading south from Nashville. The train consisted of three medical wagons, one ambulance and several supply wagons with a company of Yankee horsemen. Beth was made to lie in the bed of the wagon with ease and comfort, a few blankets and a quilt to keep her covered, and a down pillow for her head. She smiled at the doctor as he looked back under the canvas into the wagon at her time and again.

It was the custom for a trained volunteer soldier to move the wagon out, but this time, Doc Paterson felt it more comfortable for his patient that he should lead out a ways for he knew it would be a while before he'd see Beth again, if ever. That way he could see that she would be fit for the journey. At least, that was what he kept telling himself. He knew deep down in his gut that he was having a hard time sending her away. At the same time, however, he felt she would be safe and that he just might see her again. Only one questioned his motive, Captain John Rogers, his commander.

"Why?" he asked as he rode up to the doc.

"Why, what, John?" he answered politely, keeping the team of mules going. "We're moving our supplies to a barn just over yonder while they ride to Richmond for more."

"I figured that, Hank. Just wondering why you're driving the team."

"Oh, me leading out with this wagon? Nothing else to do. Thought it'd be good exercise. Keeping up with your command, I'm just riding a short distance to see how my patient will make it. Then I'm turning over the wagon to this young man and he's taking Beth on to Richmond with the wagon train. I wrote Emma and told her she's coming. She's kind of excited." He looked outward towards the east and said to himself, *I can only hope.*

"How's our Jane Doe coming along?"

"No change."

"Sure is a shame. Don't think Emma will mind? I mean, a beautiful young lady whom nobody knows anything about. I know my wife would spit nails if she saw her." He and several other officers had already been aware of the doc's amorous advances towards Ginny with his glances, turned up smirks whenever he caught her looking at him, and such. It was no secret around camp, but no man could blame him; she was quite beautiful, and the only female in camp, outside of a couple of nurses. "I mean, she's not just any patient. She's a female, and a very attractive one to boot."

"Can't think of anything else to do, John. She's got to be taken care of. It's lasting too damn long." He looked past John into the wilderness as if to find some type of answer. "And out here?" he continued. "Well, don't think so. Besides, Emma's not like a jealous wife. She's understanding."

"Didn't say otherwise, Hank. Got somebody in mind to continue her treatment?"

"Not hardly," Doc replied.

"I'd write in for some leave, Hank. You've got good reasons. Got to make sure your family's taken care of. I hear the Rebs are heavy in Richmond. And now, with this filly. Think it over, Hank."

Captain Rogers leaned in his saddle and looked down at a smiling and healthy Beth, yet a young girl still suffering from amnesia. "Hope you enjoy the journey, Beth. The week promises to be warm and calm."

"Thank you, John," she replied. "Hope to see you again, soon."

Captain Rogers rode off with a welcome salute to both the doc and Ginny, while Paterson whistled to his jacks to keep going.

Pulling up to the hospital area, Paterson turned the reins over to the private. He climbed back into the wagon and made sure that Beth was comfortable. "I'll see you in Richmond as soon as I can, Beth. By the time you get there, you might have recovered. Hope so. Something's got to jog your mind to who you are."

"What about what John said?" Beth asked, frowning at the doc.

"Thought about that before. Maybe. We'll see."

"I'll be all right, Capt'n," she answered, looking into his teary eyes. "You're a kind man, Capt'n Paterson. I'm sure everything will be all right."

She placed her hand on his cheek and gave him a smile of encouragement.

Doc's thoughts were to bend down and kiss her passionately, but instead he touched the back of her hand ever so gently with his lips. He smiled, turned, climbed down from the wagon and gave the driver his sign to move out.

"Giddap, mules!" the driver commanded a couple of jacks, and the wheels of the wagon rolled the company down the gutted road and across the Tennessee basin and over its hills.

Doc waved her off and told the driver, "Take care. Ride easy. You hear me?" *She's too beautiful,* he thought.

"Yes, Sir," the driver answered and drove off easy.

Doc stood to the side of the road as the other wagons moved out around him. He watched Beth's wagon as it came across the rise, dipped and disappeared as a speck into the horizon. He wondered, *will I ever see you again, my darling? Will you ever know the feeling I have for you in my heart right now?*

CHAPTER 13

BENJAMIN FRANKLIN TERRY
FLIES HIS KITE

Matt had to see Ginny, the same Ginny that Doc said good-bye to, yet neither one knew of the other's circumstance. He had to know that she hadn't left for Virginia, but he had no way to leave without deserting his regiment, and that idea began to suddenly appeal to him as he sat his horse. He figured he'd ask Steve for help and rode to where he was standing outside his tent.

"We're close by, Steve."

"Ginny?" Steve answered in a low voice. "What's on your mind?"

"I could be there and back in a few days if you covered for me," Matt suggested.

"You'd be shot for desertion," Steve countered, "and I'd be shot for lettin' ya."

"Dammit, Steve." The fog in the evenin' air caused his voice to sound louder. Fortunately, no one was stirred up by it. He brought his voice down. "I gotta go. You gonna cover for me?"

"I can't, Matt," Steve whispered, standing outside his tent with his hands on his hips. "Harrison would love to have us both shot. Besides, I'm an officer, Matt. Don't ask me to play favorites."

"What favorites," Matt asked indignantly, trying his level best to keep his voice down while still in his saddle. "Harrison won't miss me. I'm out in the field most of the day and night because of him. 'Sides, he'd love it if somethin' happened to me."

They heard Sergeant O'Riley's voice as he neared their position. Matt gave up and urged Skeeter towards the woods. Steve watched O'Riley as his rounded body approached him.

"Nice night, Sir," O'Riley said, coming to attention.

"Yes, Sergeant," Steve replied. "Jest wish the fog would lift. You can relax, O'Riley."

"You heard, Sir?" O'Riley asked, looking up and around for he had seen Matt ride out in the blanket of fog.

"Heard what, Sergeant?" Steve asked, opening his ears for an answer. He knew O'Riley always got news first before any one, but he never comprehended how he got it.

"Some of our men deserted us," O'Riley said, rolling a cold cigar around his lips.

"What?"

"Well, not exactly deserted, Sir. They sorta went across the river to visit their folks on the other side, seein' how close we were and we were stayin' here awhile."

"How many, sergeant?" Steve asked.

"Maybe a dozen or so, Sir."

"The hell you say?"

"Not to worry, though."

"Why? They gonna be back?"

"I'd bet on it, Sir," O'Riley replied, going to his at-ease position. "But I wouldn't count on it right away, Sir."

Desertion was frowned upon but at this stage of the war, it was not seriously punishable. When caught, the soldier would do detention, be locked up in the brig, or worse, do latrine duty. If they were in battle or close to battle, they were sent to the front of the line. Because of their fear of eminent death, most soldiers frowned upon deserting, and in particular of being caught.

"They take any horses, Sergeant?" Steve asked, hitting his trousers with his gloves.

"Thet's the worst of it, Sir," responded O'Riley with a sour look on his face.

"Well, Sergeant," Steve asked, gritting his teeth, "did they?"

"Yes, Sir, they sure did thet all right," O'Riley answered.

"They weren't ours."

"They knowed thet, Sir. We lost more."

"More?"

"Some, Sir. I dunno. By untying their horses, they kinda accidentally let several others go at the same time. I don't think they done it deliberately, Sir."

"Oh, thet's fine. Jest fine." Steve smashed his fist in his hand. "Anythin' else to report, Sergeant Major O'Riley?"

"No, Sir." He knew Steve was more than just angry when he heard him call him by his rank.

"Have a squad assembled and send them out to round up the horses, and the deserters," Steve ordered.

"Sir, the fog," O'Riley mentioned politely, hoping Steve would take that into consideration.

"They took the horses in the fog, Sergeant," Steve said, pivoting with nowhere to go. "They're lost in the fog as much as you would be. And by the time a squad's assembled, the fog will have lifted. Now, Sergeant. Now! Get your ass in motion and find those soldiers and bring back those damn horses!"

O'Riley moved as quickly as his rotund body would take him.

"The old man know?"

O'Riley yelled back over his shoulder, "He told me to tell ya. I wouldn't go near him, yet."

The fog lifted and Steve saw the seriousness of what had happened. A cavalry unit without horses was less than an infantry, as they were not trained to fight like infantrymen.

A good round of shouting and cursing preceded the calm. When Terry was resigned to the fact that there was nothing else anyone could do, he had the company officers and noncoms amassed in front of him.

"Give me your report, Sergeant O'Riley," Terry ordered.

"Yes, Sir. We've done gone two miles in most any directions, Colonel," O'Riley reported, "and we came up with half a dozen or so."

"Literally speaking," Terry started in, "there's no use in closing the barn door. The horses are gone. Gather up what horses stayed close to camp."

"You've got eleven hundred men, Frank," Wharton advised him again. "We owe these people fifty horses all together now. We're in worse shape than before."

"You think I don't know that, for chrissake," Terry thundered. "And we're headed for Kentucky to help Johnston. We start out without any horses, and now we owe a town fifty."

"One might think God had other plans for us," Wharton returned, lighting his cob pipe. He seemed to sometimes be loquacious at the inappropriate times. "We can't sit out the war, waiting for horses."

"John. Hear me and hear me good." Terry slapped his trousers hard and leaned into him. "And the rest of you. We started out as a cavalry unit. I don't take chance as my course. Most of you know that. We came this far with few horses. Now, we've got next to none. But that doesn't stop us, not by a long shot. Somewhere, somehow we will get our horses back, and more. And better ones."

"What are we going to do until then?" Major Harrison asked.

"I've thought about it, Tom and decided it's a good time to give the men a rest."

"What?" Wharton shouted back. "Frank, you're not thinking straight. You give these men some time off, you'll not see half of them again. And we'll have lost all the work we put into training them."

"I wholeheartedly agree with John," Harrison stepped in.

"Too many have deserted us already," Terry continued. "Hell, I know it's hard. We've been without a battle since the war began. But you saw what happened in New Orleans. Other companies started looking up at us. Called us the 'devils'."

"Yeah," Gustave Cook, a red-headed first sergeant of Company H agreed. "Some lady wanted to see our horns." He let out a rebel yell that shook the trees.

"We don't need a damn furlough, Colonel," C Company Commander spoke up loud and clear. A few others echoed him.

"If you will take it upon yourselves to watch your men," Terry continued, "I say, let them go home for a week or so. It'll do them good."

"Would you have said this had we not had this happen?" Wharton asked.

Terry walked among his officers, turned and addressed them. "You know the answer. No. But it's happened. And when the storm got the roughest, and the clouds poured down the rain, and the lightning filled the skies, you know what my name sake did?"

"Ben Franklin?" Wharton asked. "He went out and flew a kite. But, thunderation, you're no Ben Franklin and there's no storm a brewing."

"No. You're wrong, John. This is *a storm* and I'm going to fly a kite. That's just what I'm going to do. Higher than Ben ever did."

O'Riley, who was standing a ways away, was joined by a few other heads as he turned and looked to the sky. He asked, "Now, why do you suppose he wants to fly a kite?"

"Mr. Franklin put a key on the other end of it, O'Riley," Steve informed him.

"What in heavens name for, may I ask, Sir?"

"To show that he could harness a bolt of lightning, my good man," Steve answered.

"And did he, now?"

"He did. And so will our Commander."

O'Riley removed his hat, scratched his head and stared at Steve with one eye.

"You know I'm with you, Frank," Wharton said. "What's your plan?"

"Gentlemen," Terry continued, "the South gave me eleven hundred men to fight in this war. God will give me the horses. At this juncture, it's time to show our faith in Him and our courage and strength in ourselves."

Wharton waited and watched with the other men as Terry took his time to let them know what his plans were. "Where are we headed, Frank?"

"What would Mr. Franklin do, John, if he were in this predicament? I'll tell you. He'd not sit on his laurels and let the clouds roll by. No, by thunder. He would not. I'm going to ride to Bowling Green and get us some horses."

Wharton looked at Terry, liked what he heard from Terry and said, "You heard him, men." He walked out into the midst of the company commanders. "Get a crew of wranglers ready. We're moving out at dawn."

"You're staying, John, to look after things," Terry said.

Terry looked at his men and grit his teeth. "For now, ask any man here if he wants to go on furlough, and let him. Others can see that their gear is clean. Or if he has a horse and can ride, he can go with me."

Steve and other officers set about and rounded up a dozen men who could act as wranglers.

Matt rode back into camp and got caught up in the scuttlebutt that took place that day.

"My chance, Steve," he said, landing his back side on the ground beside a tree while he ate from his tin plate.

"You've got a horse, Matt. You should join up with the Commander in the morning and ride with him. He could use you."

"What if I jest deserted with the rest?"

"You're not thet kind."

"Then give Skeeter to some other Ranger who'd ride with the Colonel."

"You're willing to do thet?"

"Any thin' to get to Ginny."

"Let me work on it."

In the morning, the wranglers quickly rigged up a wagon, hitched up two horses to it, rode out and lined up with Terry. Those who did not have horses, took turns and rode in the wagon while others walked along side. They set their path towards Bowling Green.

"When the dust cleared from Terry's small squad of wranglers, Steve and the other officers instructed their men about the furlough.

"Because some idiots ran off to see their mommies," Steve began talking to his men, "we lost some good horses. Now you have to get out there and find one for yourself, if you can. If you don't and you'd like a furlough, report back to me."

The men let out a cheer that could be heard throughout the woods. Indeed. Matt sensed what was happening when he heard the shouts as he was not too distant inside the woods, riding patrol.

"How long, Lieutenant?" one of the men asked.

"I don't know," Steve replied. "Several days, a week, maybe more. However long it takes to find a horse. Or however long it takes for Terry to return with horses. Some of you who live close by, if you have a horse at home and would like to use it, by all means, we'll pay you for it."

"None of us live close by, Sir," a reply came from the ranks. "Those men who do have already done gone."

"Well, let me put it this way. If you come across a horse, a good horse, and you bring it back with you, we'll pay you for it, providing it weren't stolen. Get a slip of paper showin' you paid for it in good money."

"What if we find our own horse, Sir?" A high-pitched voice trilled the air.

"Well, sonny," Sergeant O'Riley interrupted. "You ride him back and we'll make him a present for ye."

The men laughed with O'Riley, but then quieted down when they saw the serious look on Steve's face as he walked up and stood directly in front of them..

"Men," Steve addressed them, "we're in a war."

"The hell we are," another voice shrilled. "We ain't seen the enemy, yet."

"We'll be seein' battle any day now. We lost horses. Now answer me this. How the hell are we goin' to fight without horses?"

He looked at the stunned expressions on their faces. Some showed doubt. Most showed trust. "We're not. Terry took a squad of men and he promised to bring us back some horses. I believe him.

"You can take some time off, or you can check out your gear. Do something useful with your time. O'Riley will check you out. Sergeant, take over."

Steve caught sight of a young horse soldier walking back and forth in the clearing talking to himself. Steve excused himself from Harrison and called over to O'Riley to send him to find out what his problem was.

"He's damned mad, Sir," O'Riley reported. "Said he joined our unit to fight the Yankees and he'll stay here and fight them if he has to *walk* with us."

"Send him in here, O'Riliey."

In a few moments, O'Riley introduced the young man to Steve. "Sir, this is Private Daniel Thurman from Waco, Texas."

Steve eyed the young lad up and down and figured he was at least seventeen, if that. "You're willing to fight if you had to walk with us?"

"Yes, Sir."

"Well, at the moment, Private, we've no enemy around to fight." Then Steve thought about what Matt said the night before. "But let me ask you. If I gave you a fine horse, one of the best in the outfit, would you be willing to catch up with our Commander?"

The young man's eyes lit up and he immediately responded, "Yes, Sir!"

"Then wait here," Steve said, and walked outside to await Matt's arrival.

Matt was at Major Harrison's post when O'Riley caught sight of him. He dismounted, knocked at the door of the tent and waited for Harrison to answer him.

"He's not wanting visitors at the present," O'Riley shouted at Matt as he rode up to him.

Steve walked over to him. "Simmer down, Sergeant," Steve ordered, "and keep your voice down."

Matt stopped and stood at attention.

"Follow me, Sergeant." Steve walked away towards the Private he had just left.

"Private Thurman."

"Yes, Sir," Thurman obeyed and stood at attention.

"What's this all about, Sir?" Matt asked, looking at Thurman.

"At ease, gentlemen," Steve addressed the two men. He had a slight smirk on his face that caused Matt no little alarm, wondering what was going on.

"Sergeant Jorgensen," Steve said militarily. "This young man needs a horse. He's an excellent horse soldier from Waco and an expert marksman. The Colonel needs him to help bring horses back from Bowling Green. I'm volunteering him your horse."

"Did I hear you right, Sir. Skeeter . . ."

"Attention, Sergeant," Steve ordered.

"You are hereby ordered to surrender your horse voluntarily to Private Thurman."

Knowing what Steve was up to, Matt pretended to get angry, looked at Steve, gritted his teeth, tightened his lips and said nothing, but stood at attention as ordered.

"Yes, Sir!"

"Take off, Private," Steve ordered Thurman.

"You don't mind, Matt?" Thurman asked.

Matt remained at attention, hemmed and hawed and then said, "Take care of him, son. When we get our horses, I expect to get him back."

Thurman threw himself into the saddle, spurred Skeeter into a canter and rode off to join up with Terry.

"For your benevolent offer, we are sending you on a furlough until we can round you up another mount."

"Furlough?" Matt asked.

"Well, wherever Ginny is. Git!"

Stunned at what just took place, Matt's face lit up like a roman candle.

"One question, ol' man," Matt queried.

Steve turned with his hands behind his back and looked at Matt. Then it hit him at the same time.

"How?"

"You don't have a horse, chum," Steve noted.

"Yep, ol' buddy," Matt returned. "What good is a furlough without a horse?"

"Well, now, as I see it, thet's your problem. I can't answer everything for ya." Steve turned and walked away.

Indeed, Matt began his trek that morning to the McBride's plantation on foot. Early the next morning and after many tiring hours of hoofing it, he hitched a ride on the back of a wagon for a great deal of the distance. He lay in the hay and fell fast asleep.

He had to finish the last ten miles or so on foot. With rest and some food, he made the extra miles seem like yards with the excitement and expectation of seeing his Ginny soon.

"Sergeant!" Major Harrison yelled as he stood outside his tent, watching Private Thurman riding Skeeter.

O'Riley ran to the tent on the double and saluted his officer. "Yes, Sir!"

"That horse. That belongs to Sergeant Jorgensen."

"Use to, Sir." O'Riley waited for his returned salute which Harrison took his time giving.

"What's that Private doing with it?"

"Sergeant Jorgensen volunteered it to the Private, Sir because he's an excellent rider and could help out our Commander, Sir."

"Why did Jorgensen give him his?" He bit the end off a fresh cigar and spit it to the wind. "Where the hell is he?"

"He's on a furlough, Sir."

"He what?" The Major fumed, brought out a match and struck it on the side of the tent post. "Tell Lieutenant Andrews to get his fat ass over here! On the double, Sergeant!"

"Yes, Sir!" Sergeant O'Riley saluted, turned and ran towards the Lieutenant's tent. On the way, he noticed Steve walking towards him and stopped him.

"Beg your pardon, Lieutenant, but Major Harrison asked me to find you."

Steve returned O'Riley's salute. "You found me, Sergeant."

Steve took his time walking to Harrison's tent. Stepping inside, he removed his hat and addressed his commander. "You wanted to see me, Major?"

"Where's Sergeant Jorgensen?" He twirled his cigar around in his mouth like a kid with a lollypop.

"I sorta told him he could have a few days off as furlough. Like Terry told us."

"He said any rider without a horse. He had a horse."

"Yes Sir, but Private Thurman didn't and he's such a good rider, he'd be better with the Commander. And, I didn't think you'd want Jorgensen to accompany the Commander to Bowling Green. Know what I mean, Sir?"

"No. Just what the hell do you mean?"

"Well, the Colonel takes a mighty good likin' to Sergeant Jorgensen, didn't think you'd like thet."

Harrison turned, put his hands behind his back and played with his fingers. Then he turned and asked, "Saddle and all?"

"Saddle and all."

"Where'd he go?"

"Sir, he's got a girl across the Tennessee about fifty miles up and figured he'd see her and come right back. By then we should have horses and he'd join up with us."

"I know about his girl. We all have girls, but you don't see any of the rest of us whining." Harrison pivoted and slammed his cigar into the ground. "And he gave up his best quarter horse for a few days pleasure. The idiot."

"Yes, Sir. I mean, no, Sir. Well, Sir, he's not exactly an idiot, just a Sergeant in love with a girl."

"How long's it been?"

"Since he's seen her . . .? Oh, I see what you mean. Months, I suppose, Sir."

"I am not in sympathy with any horny Yankee who'd give up his best horse for a filly, I don't care who she is."

Steve heard the word "Yankee" and flinched.

"Don't think I don't know what side he's on. I wouldn't turn my back on him one bit. If I could prove it, I'd have him shot.

"When he comes back, and if he comes back, you make damn sure he sees me. I don't appreciate this."

"Yes, Sir," Steve returned.

"We don't want wimps in our company. We're better off without him. And if I find out he went over to the other side, I'll personally hunt him down and kill the bastard." He paced back and forth with each angry word. He looked up at Steve still standing there. "You got a job to do, Mister. Do it!"

"Yes, Sir!"

Steve saluted, turned and walked briskly out of the tent as quickly as he entered it. "I'll be a son-of-a-one-eyed-kicking mule."

"I heard that remark, Lieutenant," Harrison said, following him to the opening of the tent. He stared at Steve's back who was sensing he was going to get chewed out. "And I couldn't agree with you more. Now get the hell out of my sight."

Steve did just that and tried his best to stay out of the Major's way for the next few days as he continued training his men in the fine art of shooting. He wondered to himself now if what Harrison said about Matt could be true. He had some doubts before, but now his doubts were growing, and he had to live with the fact that he gave Matt a way out.

At the same time, he envied every moment Matt was away from camp . . . on a furlough, fearing at the same time, that he would never return.

CHAPTER 14

A RETURN TO THE MCBRIDE PLANTATION

It took Matt three days, hitching a ride on a wagon, and walking the rest of the way, but he reached the ridge road leading to the plantation just after sunup on day four. There was a fog across the roadway that led into the woods, but he could still see the plantation off in the distance. When he got closer, he stopped and rested to give a good look.

Everything I ever wanted is right there, he said to himself. He bent down, picked up a pebble in the road and threw it hard into the woods for good luck. He was back at the McBride Plantation where he left a hundred weeks or so ago, it seemed; an awfully long time. It was here where he met his first slaves, worked as their master, and made friends with them, listening to their singing and witnessing their way of living.

Naomi was a house nigger that had taken over the duties when the well-loved house nigger, Bertha was killed by Sin. She and other Negro slaves met Matt at the main house. Matt sensed a fear in them from the look in their faces.

"Where's Ginny?" Matt asked, looking around the plantation for signs of her or her father.

"Mister Jim," Naomi yelled out nervously.

Matt ran down the road that led to the house. He stopped when he saw Jim running out in his stocking feet while putting on his boots.

"Matt!" Jim cried out. "Is that you, man?" He looked at the happy Confederate horse soldier and smiled. "Of course it's you. Matt, it's good to see you, son." He leaned up against the tree that had stood for years in the front yard and finished putting on his boots. "Won't you come on in? It's good to see you." He stomped his boots on and then led Matt to the porch. He abruptly stopped, turned around and asked, "Where's your horse?"

"Lent him out." He looked around for Ginny, feeling that how Naomi acted was a cause for concern. "They let me come home for a few days until they could get some more horses."

When the two men climbed the steps to the house, Matt summoned for Ginny, but no one answered.

Sylvia came out, wiping her hands on her apron. She was a young lady Jim had met at a dance before Matt left and had married her while Matt was away. "Hello, Matt," she said with a half smile. She was happy to see Matt again, but knew he would not be pleased with what he was to find out.

Matt stopped, looked at her and wrapped his arms around her. "Sylvia."

She broke from his embrace and shook hands with him.

"You can call her, *Mrs. McBride,*" Jim added" "Sylvia and I were married just after Ginny left."

"Well, congratulations, Mrs. McBride. Jim." He looked with a puzzled look at Jim. "Kinda sudden like."

"We were going to wait, but just couldn't," Jim answered.

Matt looked past the couple. Going further in, he yelled again, "Ginny! Honey! I'm home. It's me, honey . . . Matt." Still there was no answer. He walked further into the house while Jim followed him. "Ginny, darlin'."

Then he turned to Jim, and asked, "Where is she, Jim?" A sense of alarm filled his eyes, and his brow furrowed into a look of fear. "Where is she, Jim?" he yelled. "Where is she?" A cold chill filled Matt's body. He cried out again, "Ginny!" and ran through the house.

Jim returned to the front part of the house and waited for Matt to finish his search. Matt disappeared upstairs into her bedroom, then came out and ran down the stairs.

"Where is she, Jim?" he yelled. Then his yelling stopped as he looked out into the distant woods. His yelling turned to tears that he could not contain.

He walked towards the door where Jim tried to embrace him once more. Matt shrugged him away and walked past him to the edge of the porch. The eeriness of the low-lying fog drifted over the land as if to hide her presence forever. He stepped off the porch and out into the mist and stood at the end of the road, alone. It was Matt's moment of solitude.

Old slaves known to Matt came out of their cabins. Among them was a family he had helped get together in marriage, Hezekiah and Nancy, together with their two children, Nathaniel and Joel. Hezekiah was the first black man Matt saw when he saved him from a whipping.

Jim and Sylvia walked down the road and joined Matt. "She's disappeared, Matt," Jim said softly with his head bowed.

Matt looked out into the empty woods and asked, "What's happened, Jim?"

The three of them stood in silence for what seemed an eternity.

"So cold." Matt said shivering. "She's out there somewhere."

Hezekiah walked up to him and placed his strong hand on his shoulder. Then Matt allowed Jim and Hezekiah to encompass him with their great arms as they led him back to the house. Sylvia followed.

The rest of the day went by like minutes as Jim explained the best he could to Matt without breaking apart himself. Matt sat and listened but heard very little of what Jim had to say.

Sleep came hard for Matt that night, but weariness wore him down and sleep overcame him.

The sun shone through the trees, lighting the morning and burning away the fog. Naomi thought a hot cup of coffee would help Matt once he awakened fully and began to think straight. She put the pot on, filled it with coffee grounds and eggshells, and brought it to a boil. When she figured it was hot enough, she removed it from the stove, poured Matt a cup of coffee and served it to him. She did the same for Jim and Sylvia.

Matt sat and composed himself for a while. No one spoke.

"Mister Matt," Naomi said softly, breaking the tension. "I'm the one who helped heal ya when you got your head bashed in. 'Member?"

Matt sat still and then reached out his hand to touch her.

She looked at it and then over to her husband, Zeb.

"Naomi, honey," Zeb said softly but strongly, "you knows how he's feelin'. Takes his hand, woman. You takes his hand and you calms him down. You takes it. Hear?"

Naomi took a hold of Matt's hand and held it while Matt held hers. The two felt a special sense of feeling between them flow through their veins, for now it was Naomi's turn to comfort Matt as he had comforted her before in the loss of Bertha, McBride's first house nigger. They said nothing.

Looking in Zeb's dark eyes, Matt blinked as if to say it was going to be all right.

He looked back at Jim, released his grip on Naomi's hand, rose and walked towards the doorway. "Why did she have to leave here?"

"She got your letter, Matt," Sylvia repeated what Jim had told him the night before.

Jim got up and walked over to Matt. "She knew you were going to Old Virginia and she wanted to be there first to see you ride in, resplendent in your fancy new uniform. She told me over and over again just how it would be. She knew how your commander would parade his soldiers in and show you all off to the locals. She was so, so proud, Matt. So proud."

"But we didn't go to Virginia, Jim," Matt responded without looking back. "We never went to Virginia."

"We thought you had," Jim said. "We didn't receive any more word from you, so we figured you were on your way."

"Some other big General took us from goin' to New Orleans and brought us to Nashville. I'm supposed to be in camp right now," Matt said, still looking into the fog.

"I was wondering," Sylvia surmised, looking at Matt through teary eyes.

"I should 'ave written her that I wasn't goin', but too much was goin' on," Matt continued. "Figured I'd get here and surprise her."

"She had already left, Matt," Jim said, joining Matt's stare out into the woods. "She was so excited after getting your post, she wanted to get her family ready for your big march in. I was to go as soon as I could join them." Jim turned and looked at Matt. "There would have been no way for me to have gotten her back until she done reached Virginia."

Matt felt his blood boil inside as he stood there, thinking about his Ginny out there somewhere, perhaps dead.

Jim bowed his head, walked out on the lawn and sat in one of the two big chairs that was positioned under the tree. "Why did we leave Richmond in the first place, Matt? Our family's rich with textile and cotton from other plantations. Was it only a silly dream of ours."

He reminisced about reading in a copy of the 1858 Richmond Gazette an article that set the wheels in motion where " . . . Senator James Henry Hammond of South Carolina replied to Senator William H. Seward of New York:

Without the firing of a gun, without drawing a sword, should they [Northerners] make war upon us [Southerners], we could bring the whole world to our feet. What would happen if no cotton was furnished for three years? England would topple headlong and carry the whole civilized world with her. No, you dare not make war on cotton! No power on earth dares make war upon it. Cotton is King.

"It's not like what I envisioned, Matt," Jim said. "A gun was fired, and many more afterwards and many more to come."

Matt rested his hand on Jim's shoulder. "I've not fired mine once in this damn war."

Jim turned towards Matt and stood up. "Son. It kinda looks like you're gonna have to."

Matt turned and caught Naomi's eye and said, "I know'd you patched me up, and you took good care of Ginny, too." He looked over at Hezekiah. "And I saved your scrawny little butt the first day I rode in here, Hezi." He walked over to the children and to Nancy. He held them close to him and said, "And I brought you together with Hezi here, and got you all legaled up and married so you could have more kids, and a good place to raise them."

Matt smiled and rubbed the kids' heads. He looked at Nancy's belly and said, "You've got another one in the basket, I see, Nancy. Good."

Jim straightened up, took out his pipe and lit it while he listened to Matt. He began puffing on his pipe, and like times before, let Matt have his say.

"Here I stand as a Confederate soldier supposed to fight so thet we can keep you as our damn slaves. At least, thet's what I'm led to believe I'm fightin' for."

"That and the Confederacy, Matt," Jim said. "That and the Confederacy."

"All thet hokum simply means to me is thet if we keep slaves, we'll have a rich Confederacy. Well, I don't want any more slaves. Never did. And as far as the Confederacy goes, all I want is my Ginny."

"And I, Matt," Jim agreed. "And I."

The slaves were hearing the same argument made by Matt so many times before while trying to work with them when he was their boss. Now he stood in front of them, a soldier, ostensibly as their defender, their savior and they stood listening with mixed emotions. *Which way would they turn when the wind blew after the war?* Matt asked himself.

"Nancy," Matt asked, "are you free right now?"

Nancy held onto her kids and answered him back. "I sees where you is goin', Mister Matt," she replied, putting her arm around Hezekiah. "Yes, Mister Matt. I be free. I be free 'cause you set me free when you lets me marry mah man and give me my kids back. I be free as free as I eber wants ta be." She said this, knowing that before Matt came along, her marriage to Hezekiah was a sham marriage, as they lived surreptitiously together with her children being known as bastards among the white folk. However, the black folk knew otherwise.

"Good," Matt said, smiling a little better. Then he looked sternly at Hezekiah. "And Hezi, are you free?"

"Free as I eber wants to be, Mister Matt," Hezekiah answered.

"You got your family."

Then he looked at Naomi and Zeb. "And you, Naomi. Zeb. Are you free?"

"Yes sah, Mister Matt," Naomi responded. "We be free as birds."

Turning to Jim, Matt rephrased his question, "Then, Jim, I ask you, what the hell . . . jest what the hell am I fightin' for? To keep our slaves, or to free 'em?"

Jim stood there smoking his pipe. Biting down on the stem, he started clapping his hands. "Good job, Matt. Good job."

"And your answer, Jim?" Matt asked again.

"For the Confederacy, Matt," Jim replied once more with the same answer. "For the gawddam Confederacy."

"And Jim," Matt continued. "Jest what the hell is this Confederacy I keep hearin' about?"

"I believe Ginny said it best, Matt," Jim answered. "The bureaucracy. Big important people. A flag, perhaps. Money, of course. And, definitely a cause."

"And, land, Matt," Sylvia added. "This is our land, and we aim to keep it."

"A portion of this great country." Jim stretched his arm upwards and made a sweeping gesture with his pipe in his hand. "Certainly." Then he placed the pipe back in his mouth and took a drag. He exhaled the smoke and said, "I don't know, Matt. It could be all of these and more. When we win this war, and by thunder we will win, you will certainly know by then what the hell the Confederacy is all about."

"And I, sir," Matt said defiantly, "am a soldier fightin' for this Confederacy, am I not?" Matt never revealed to Jim that he was really from Montana, a territory, which was for the most part, made up of sympathizers for the Confederacy, although Matt and his family were not raised with such loyalties. They had separated themselves long ago from the gold. They were cattle people. Matt had let Jim believe he was from Wyoming, Yankee territory.

Jim knew Matt's turmoil in selecting which side to fight on. As for him, he was a man who owned slaves for a living. Now, the deciding issue of loyalties as to which side who was on appeared as a giant wall between them, and Matt knew that Ginny was all Southern.

Jim stood up and approached Matt. He relit his pipe, which gave him a moment to reflect on Matt's question. It was a moment of hesitancy, which ate at Jim's stomach as he sensed Matt was not yet truly loyal to the South. He drew a breath, clenched his teeth and said, "She's out there, son. I don't know where. But we've not heard from her or about her, and . . . I hope she's still alive. I have no other course than to think that."

"If she's not, then I killed her?" Matt asked, looking sternly into Jim's eyes.

"No, son," Jim said, putting his arm on Matt's shoulder. "If she's dead, then love killed her. Just like with Juliet, and Cleopatra, and thousands like them. She rode the wind to get to her true love. To you, certainly. And for the Confederacy, and for her dream home in Virginia."

"And I killed her and her dream," Matt restated, hanging his head down.

"We do strange things when we're in love, Matt," Sylvia said.

"I couldn't stop her from going to Virginia," Jim continued. "Heaven knows I tried."

"What am I suppose to do, Jim?" Matt asked, trying to hold back his tears.

"What would she have done, Matt," Sylvia asked," if it had been you who had died on a battle field, reaching out for her?"

Matt kept looking into Sylvia's eyes as if to find an answer.

"What would she have done, Matt?"

Matt shrugged his shoulders, and answered meekly, "I don't know, Sylvia. "I don't know."

"She would have gone on with her life, Matt," Jim explained. "Ginny was not a weakling. Not by any stretch of the imagination. And had you been killed in battle, she would have taken up where you both left off. Nothing would have stopped her."

"I think she would have married Richard T. Sullivan of Virginia," Matt surmised humorously, smiling a bit with his eyes to seemingly relieve his anger.

"I don't have a clue as to who or what Richard T. Sullivan of Virginia is," Sylvia interrupted, looking curiously at the two men.

"Oh, it's a fictitious person she made up when she got mad at me one day," Matt added.

"Then, Matt, if that fictitious person became a part of her life again, yes . . . yes, I firmly believe she would have married . . . *Richard T. Sullivan of Virginia*." Jim laughed and Matt joined in with him.

"You see, Matt," Jim said. "She had dreams of settling down in Virginia with the man she loved, a real live Richard T. Sullivan of Richmond, Virginia, our Capitol. She envisioned her palatial home situated on a beautiful hill overlooking Virginia's Shockoe Valley where she could be the lady of the county, and her husband a fine, upstanding person of grandeur and knowledge, and perhaps of military status.

"When you never came back, and she learned that you enlisted in the Confederacy, she fell deeper in love with you than ever, because she saw in you her dream coming true," he continued. "And, when she heard your regiment was headed for Old Virginia, she knew her dream was coming true. Nothing could have kept her from finding you, and sharing that moment of you riding in a full military parade into Richmond. You were her fulfillment. *You* were her Richard T. Sullivan of Virginia."

Matt turned around and saw the McBride's slaves, standing all around. Humming began among them, and then they joined together in singing their favorite, "She's Gonna Rise Up and Gits Down Her Old False Teeth". Jim joined in, blending in with his bass voice. Eventually Matt joined in with them.

It was the spiritual that Hezekiah gave a tune to with his banjo the day Bertha, the House Negro, was murdered by Sin Crouch. Her last words were for getting her false teeth in heaven when she died so that she could properly eat her food again.

"Get me a horse, Jim," Matt said softly. "I'm gonna find her."

Jim took his cob pipe and emptied it by knocking the bowl against the tree limb. He turned to his slaves and said, "Find Matt something to eat, Naomi, and then pack him some food to take with him."

He turned to Matt and put his arm around him. "Eat some and get some rest first. If she's still alive, you'll find her."

Matt's thoughts were heavy on finding Ginny, but after a few minutes, he was sound asleep. A few hours were all Matt needed to regain his strength.

When he sopped up his plate of eggs and biscuits, he downed his coffee, joined Jim and Sylvia and the three walked out the front door. "She's out there, Jim, and she's still alive. I feel it."

Jim had Hezekiah saddle the best Tennessee gelding for Matt. "His name is Skeeter, Matt," Jim said, as he presented him to Matt. "Ginny told me how you liked that name, so she chose it. Take him with our blessings."

He held Matt firmly by the shoulders and continued, "I hope you find her, Matt. But, whether you find her or not, win the war for her. Will you do that for us, son?"

Matt took the reins from Hezekiah and mounted Skeeter as proud as if it were the horse his dad gave him for a birthday present some years earlier.

"Fits real good, Jim," Matt said, sitting tall and straight in the saddle. "For Ginny, I'll ride to hell and back."

"Youse look like a statue, Mistah Matt," Naomi said, smiling from ear to ear.

"He oughta," Hezekiah said, standing proud beside him, holding onto Skeeter's bridle. "He's gonna be some day. Jest watch an' see."

"Then turn loose ob him, and let him ride on," Nancy said, rubbing her pregnant belly.

"Bring Miss Ginny back, Suh," Hezekiah mustered out with tears. "Do thet, Mr. Matt. Ride on! And may de Lord Jesus bless ya."

And ride on he did. Waving back, he let the cold Tennessee breeze blow his cape up and over his shoulders. Spurring

Skeeter on, he disappeared over the ridge from whence he came, and was quickly out of site of the McBride Plantation.

Matt spent several more days in the saddle looking for Ginny with no success. He rode outside Federal campfires to watch and listen for any news that might shed light on her disappearance. He heard about a young Yankee boy having shot a young girl dressed like a man, but never learned of her fate. He knew it had to be her. At times, he was shot at and he rode like the wind to stay alive. He never found out who shot at him or why. He was only interested in staying alive to find Ginny. He lost contact with the soldiers who had talked about the shooting of a girl, yet watched and listened at other campfires. He never found any more about her.

It was a gray, cold morning when Matt awoke and gave up the search as a lone and desperate man. His clothes had become dull and tattered from the bushes and tree limbs. He sported a beard that he became accustomed to and he was in bad need of a bath.

Ginny, darlin', he said to the wind as he limply sat his horse, *you'll always be mine, my darlin'. You'll always be mine.* He rode back towards the last known position of camp for his regiment, hoping to find them there or their whereabouts.

CHAPTER 15

A REASON TO KEEP ON LIVING

Terry and the horse wranglers returned with over three hundred and fifty of the finest Kentucky horse stock that General Albert Sidney Johnston could muster up for them. The sight was thrilling for John Lubbock and the Rangers as they piled out from every hole they had buried themselves in to stay warm while waiting for their return. Shouts and gunfire echoed and reverberated through the woods.

Terry not only felt he had flown Benjamin Franklin's kite but that he had successfully captured the lightning which Franklin discovered and harnessed it in horses.

"I've never seen horses like these," Wharton commented as he watched the horse-master and the chief groom put gear on a Kentucky thoroughbred selected for Lubbock. "Where's mine? he asked, looking around.

"I have one picked out for you, too, Major," the horse-master answered. He came back quickly with a chestnut stallion. "I saw you eyeing this one when we came in, and rightly so. He's a bit wild and has a temper, but I know you can handle him well."

"You've chosen well, John," Terry answered.

"Good lines. Great looking stallion," Lubbock agreed.

"And you, Frank. And you, too, John." Lubbock referred to Wharton.

Terry Lubbock had already mounted up by the time the horse-master returned. Wharton stepped up into the saddle, looked towards the grounds, and with Lubbock, rode easy for it was their first ride on their new horses. After each of them felt comfortable with his mount, they spurred their horses into a canter and then into a lope.

"Look at thet," O'Riley commented to his men while watching his commanders ride. "I've never seen better riding in me life."

And he wasn't exaggerating, for the three officers were now in their forte.

"What should I do with your other horses, Sir?" O'Riley asked as Terry rode by.

Terry reined up and walked his stallion over to O'Riley. "How many horses did the city loan us that ran away?" he asked.

"About fifty, Sir, if me memory doesn't fail me."

"Then pick out fifty and give them back. Tell them . . . no, ask them if this will atone for the loss of their nags that ran away and pay for the damages to their city which our men caused."

O'Riley walked towards the horses, stopped, turned and looked at the Colonel. "You heard, did you, now, Sir?"

Terry nodded and rode out to catch up with Lubbock and Wharton. The three of them continued their ride around the perimeter getting use to their new mounts like children with brand new toys. Of course, Terry had the advantage, having ridden his horse back from Kentucky.

This treat did indeed make up for the damages his men did to the fair city while drinking their beverages and engaging in fisticuffs over their women as the city had never seen. The guerillas in Terry's regiment, idled far too long, had shown gallantry in their side ventures, and the women loved their newly found devils *with horns*.

It was early November when Terry's Rangers received their horses from the Confederacy.

The regiment, also, officially received its title from General Johnston, the *Texas 8th Cavalry*. Terry, Lubbock, Wharton and Harrison had been elected by the company commanders to their official military ranks at Nashville with Terry becoming the Colonel and Lubbock the Lieutenant Colonel. Wharton was promoted to Major and Harrison was elected Field Officer. Harrison felt very proud and deserving at receiving his new rank, though he reserved some rivalry for himself against Wharton.

"Gentlemen," Colonel Terry addressed his regiment as he rode to the center of their company, joining Wharton, and Harrison. "I salute you. We are no longer guerillas."

The Rangers shouted and fired their weapons in the air with enthusiasm and excitement. It was their day of victory. Terry waited until the shouting and the shooting subsided.

Matt rode closer to his regiment checking closely any gunfire that he had heard.

"We are the Texas 8th Cavalry," Terry continued. "Not because we asked for it, and not because we weren't first. It just took this long to get our commission as an official cavalry."

"And it don't make any sense," a red-headed Ranger piped in. "We have nothin' thet says Texas 8th on 'em."

"I'm not too keen on that, either, son," Terry answered him. "As far as I'm concerned, we're the first." He looked at the men and paused long enough to reflect their feelings about their new name.

"I don't like the name," Terry made note. "Even though it is our official name."

"I think we should stick with our well-earned name, *Rangers'*, Wharton suggested. "We've been carrying it around loosely long enough."

The men yelled out again in favor, some firing their arms.

O'Riley rubbed his nose and grinned, knowing full well what Wharton was getting at. It came.

"Terry's Rangers!" Harrison yelled out.

"No," Terry corrected him. "Terry's Texas Rangers."

Once more, the regiment, including the officers and Terry and Lubbock themselves, fired their Navy Sixes, shotguns and carbines, whichever was the handiest, and threw out the loudest rebel yell they could.

The ground quaked and the trees shook their leaves to the ground. The day was one for festivities.

At an officers' meeting that afternoon, it was Colonel Terry's order that the men wear the name *Terry's Texas Rangers* encircled with stars on their caps and a lone silver star pinned on it which stood for Texas.

"But we still have no uniforms, Sir," Steve threw in.

"No, Lieutenant," Terry answered. "We don't. What do you, or any of you suggest."

"Well," Steve spoke up again, "we're all wearin' our own, sort of so to speak."

"Captain Walker of G Company wears a leather shirt and a big sombrero," Terry said with a smile at Walker. "And, I may add, for your size, it fits you. And I don't think you're too concerned about uniforms. Are you, John?"

"Thanks, Colonel," Walker threw back at him. "Not one bit."

"But, I hear what you men are saying," Terry answered. "How can anyone distinguish us from anyone else out there 'ceptin' our pins?"

"And them do make good targets, Sir," Steve added.

Lieutenant Pat Christian stood up and joined in. "You proved that at Manassas, Sir. And since I'm up, beg your pardon, Colonel."

"Yes, Lieutenant?"

"Sir, why don't we finish makin' our own uniforms? Most of us have already. Like John's leather outfit, of course."

"Now we're getting some place," Terry agreed.

"Well, we've been called the *Devil's Rangers*, no disrespect to you, Sir," Steve suggested. "We've sorta added red as our colors already with our red shirts."

"Then, why not trim our collars, pockets, and cuffs with dark epaulettes so the red will stand out?" Christian added.

"Anything further?" Terry asked.

"Just a stripe of red on our leggin's, Sir," Christian said with a broad smile. "We'll be one hell of a good-lookin' outfit."

The men enthusiastically agreed with a rebel yell.

"Well," Terry joined in, "hop to it! See that every man is dressed accordingly as quickly as possible. I want us to look dapper in that parade in front of President Davis." He stopped for a moment, looked the men over and added, "I see we've got stars put on everything, including guns and holsters. I like that. Shows creativity."

"Another thing, Colonel," Steve stepped in. "What about our new flag?"

"Our new flag? Well by golly," Terry said, "it seems to me that it's time for us to unveil her. Bring the flag out, O'Riley."

O'Riley unbuttoned his blouse, pulled out the flag and presented it to Terry. "I've had it on me person all the time, Sir."

Terry unfurled her and showed her to the Rangers. "A couple of our ladies from Hempstead, Texas did a good job sewing it together. We'll fly her proudly."

The flag had the same blue background but the star from the first flag was gone. Inside a circle was a red St. Andrews cross with twelve stars and the words *Terry's Texas Rangers* ini gold stitching arched around them. On the opposite side of the circle were the words, "We Conquer or Die"

"But," Harrison retorted, "we got rid of the single star." He seemed to be the only one not in favor of the design

"We have the star on our hats," Terry reminded him. "The extra stars in the cross are for the Confederate States of America."

"Beg your pardon, Colonel," Harrison stormed in again. "We have thirteen states and there are only twelve stars. Seems to me that we need to add one each time a state is added to the Confederacy."

"And we shall, Tom."

"Then why not add the star now?"

"Because, some of us feel that one of the states is not entirely a Confederate state."

"Georgia?" Harrison came back. "It's just as confederate as her adjoining states."

Wharton kept silent, watching and waiting to see what was going to happen.

"It's made up of a lot of Federals," Terry said with tight lips. "And because it is, we did not add a star." He looked at the

193

rest of the men. "Any of you officers concur with Major Harrison?"

Then, with Wharton, the rest of the officers gave their hearty disapproval in unison. "No, Sir." He watched the pride in Terry as he took the flag, felt the fine velvet material and looked the flag over.

"Note our slogan," Terry brought it to their attention. "We *Conquer or Die.* We came up with that slogan simply because we will conquer. Or . . . we will die. And that includes me as well as every officer under me."

A sense of pride swelled up inside the men as they listened intently to their leader as he included himself and his subordinates into the rank of brave soldiers. Terry's eyes focused not only on the horse soldiers, but also on their leaders.

He added, "Our regiment will not be made up of cowards. Each and every one of you was handpicked. And, gentlemen, by the Almighty's help, we will conquer."

The company officers and their aids stood in rank with their men.

"Hoist her up, Captain Christian." Pat earned himself another rank that day.

Pat took the flag outside, and with O'Riley's help, mounted her on a pole, stuck the pole into the ground and hoisted the new flag high in the air while the men saluted her and sang *The Texas Ranger War Song* to the tune of *The Bonnie Blue Flag.* She was Terry's Texas Rangers' battle flag, and they flew her with pride.

The whole event made them feel like they had more camaraderie with one another. With all of the excitement and enthusiasm of all the rest, even Harrison felt the pride they all shared.

"Gentlemen!" Terry got their attention once more and the shouting and hoopla quieted down. "We've got horses. Only three hundred. But they're the best. Major Harrison will select who will have a mount, and instruct you to choose your horses and groom them well."

When Terry finished, Lubbock took over. "Take charge, Major Harrison." The two Colonels walked back to their headquarters together.

Harrison mounted his steed and rode to the center where he addressed the men.

"Your commanding officers have been instructed as to how you will get your new horses. After that, you will have one last furlough in town. Do not, I repeat. Do not tear the town down . . . again"

"Men," O'Riley started in as he sat his new horse in the circle of A Company, showing her off with a little pride. "This is a horse. My horse. He's the finest Blue Grass thoroughbred . . ."

". . .Confederate money can buy . . ." the entire company joined in.

O'Riley rubbed his face, squinted and spit tobacco juice on the ground. "Now, some of youse will be issued a fine Kentucky thoroughbred. You will ride 'im, or he will ride you." He looked at all the men. Some realized they were not chosen to receive a horse. Rubbing his chin, he continued. "The rest of youses be the caretakers. You'll have your turns when your turns come."

He rode the width of the company in front of him at a slow walk with his quirt in his right hand. "You might wanna consider your selves as horse-doctors, cause thet's what ye be most of the time. Thet's why ye'll need more than one of youse to take a horse. You might not like it one bit, but youse has to do it.

"You'll spend days and nights keepin' your horse healthy when you your selves will be sicker than a horse." He laughed at what he had said and continued. "Get it? And I'll be there to help youses, with me horse-master and chief groomer beside me.

"Your horse is your second best friend. Your guns is your best. Bein' without a horse in battle, you can still fight with your guns. But if youse has to send your horse to a reserve camp at the rear, you'll be regrettin' it for you'll be fightin' on your feet."

"What are we to do in battle, Sarge," a young horse soldier, sitting in front asked, "if our horse gets killed in battle?"

O'Riley wiped his mouth with his bandana and squinted at the soldier. "Now, did I not tells ya thet you best hope thet didn't happen? Didn't I?"

"He brings up another point, Sergeant," Steve's deep voice sounded over O'Riley's ears. "Your horse is nothin' more than a weapon for you to use." He stepped forward and addressed the men. "You're in battle for one reason. To kill your enemy. How you do it is your own business. But your horse is used to get you there and get you safely back."

"How would you know, Sir?" another horse soldier asked Steve. "You ain't seen battle either."

"Good question. No. I haven't. Not in war, but I've been in skirmishes where I've had to kill a man who was trying to kill me, and I had my horse taken away from me. I know first hand how important a horse is, now. Had I known then, I wouldn't have had him taken from me."

He looked at the soldier, and then into the eyes of the rest of the men. "You ride your horse to win. Sometimes you'll kill your horse yourself by spurring him on until he falls. I've seen most of you ride. Some of you are great. Some good. Most of you can fall off in battle because you're too soft on your animal. Don't be. It's your life or his. Think on it. He's not a pet.

"Sergeant Jorgensen and I've been assigned to train you, and thet's just what we've been tryin' to do. You're good at pickin' up ladies' hankies and stayin' on, but what if your horse dies under you?" He looked at the soldier who posed the last question. "What would you do, Red?"

"Steal another horse. You taught us thet."

"And don't forget it. Steal it, but not from your fellow horse soldier, unless he's dead. You'll either find one standin' around, or get one from the enemy. Shoot him for it."

Steve paused and looked at the men sternly. "I don't want any of you out on the field of battle without a horse. If you can't find one, your brother better pick you up. Understand me?"

In unison they all answered, "Yes, Sir."

"Carry on, Sergeant," Steve ordered and walked back. He stopped and turned to listen as O'Riley addressed the men.

"Thanks you, Sir," O'Riley replied. "Like the good Lieutenant says, you spur your horse 'til he can't go no further and then youse steal the enemy's horse. Keep the cavalry strong, men, no matter the cost. Any questions?"

"I'd like to add one, Sergeant," the horse-master said, rising to his feet and walking out in center."

"And it's about time, too. Go ahead."

"It's been a long time since many of you have ridden a horse all day. Most of you haven't ridden a horse in battle. Some of you have. I've been with you. But some of you need to know this.

"Sure, he's not your pet. But take good care of him like he was. Your horse depends on you. You're his master, not the other way around. Feed and tend to him properly. We have hay now because we're in Nashville. Out there on the field, your horses eat and drink what they can. Get them clean water when you can. Care for them, and don't let them eat wild weeds thet can clog 'em and hurt 'em. When you have a problem with your horse, let me know about it."

"Thet's it, Sergeant?" O'Riley asked as the horse-master turned and walked back.

"What about you?" another horse soldier asked O'Riley.

"What about me?" O'Riley looked at his body and knew readily that the soldier was referring to his weight. "Humph. Good question. Jest remember not to eat too much. It'll slow the animal down, even with McClellans."

McClellans were lightweight military saddles that the Rangers hadn't adapted to yet. They had rather have their own saddles, but now they had to adjust to the McClellans.

"You'll need to ride bareback," the same soldier remarked and closed his mouth as quickly as he had opened it. A laugh started through the ranks but just as quickly, subsided.

O'Riley rode it off with a "humph!" Then he continued, "McClellans weigh less than your old saddles. Yes. Thet they do. And if you lose your horse, get your good saddle back. Be rememberin' thet.

"Now, girlies," O'Riley started in on them again. "Do any of you remember what a horse looks like? Can any of youse remember how to ride one?" he asked again. "Well, those who do, go get one."

The men rose and scrambled fast and furiously to get a horse, each one afraid he was going to be left out.

"Now, mount him and ride him," O'Riley shouted. "Any of youse stays on might get to keep 'im."

Steve took his mount and tied him to a hitching rail then stood and waited for the fun to start.

And, start it did. He, O'Riley and the horse-master knew that some of the men had not been accustomed to riding as they so ably claimed, and so they stood with their arms crossed and leaned against the hitching rail and watched.

First of all was the clumsy untying of the horse and then watching the horse run off. They watched another as his horse reared up and scared the young rider. When a rider-to-be calmed a horse down, he seemed to be all right, until he reached down for his saddle, or started cinching the girth. Some how, the horse just knew he wasn't going to be saddled and ran away.

The bridle was the hard part, for the young stallion knew whether or not the horse soldier had any savvy with tack equipment. If he did, that was fine, but if he didn't, the young man would play havoc and most times not get the bit in the horse's mouth. Again, the horse would pull back, and if successful, run away

Finally, the test of the rider was getting on the horse, most of which had never been ridden. These were called *green horses* or *gree-broke horses*. Runaways would ride into the cook's wagon, clanging pots and pans and mess-kettles, kicking them high in the air with their hooves.

There was jerking and scrabbling of the horses, jingling and rattling of equipment. The horses turned every which way, bumping into each other, biting and kicking other horses and in some cases their own riders. The boys would bang their horses into patent sheet-iron stoves, the kinds they had seen advertised in the illustrated papers and sold by the settlers of Alexandria, which were about as useful as a piano or a folding bed on the prairie.

"Do I hear someone cussin'?" O'Riley's husky voice competed loudly against the disturbing ruckus.

"I knowed we should have shoveled the manure before we tried to mount these beasts," one of the men swore through his teeth as he sat in the middle of a dung field.

"Somebody give me a hand with this saddle," another would yell out. Some knew it would take at least two people to saddle one of the critters.

Even once the saddle was on, some of the blankets slipped and hung loose, causing the saddle to slip back on the rump of the horse, while another hung upside down under the horse's belly.

"Stay loose," O'Riley yelled out. "Watch your damn spurs, son. Oh, no!"

The young lad clasped his legs tight around the horse's thighs he was riding, but forgot he was wearing spurs. They dug into his horse and caused him to buck until the boy was high in the air and back on the ground, looking up at the sky.

"Oh, son, you never ever want to spur a green horse. When was the last time you rode a horse?"

The boy looked up at the Sarge and over at his runaway horse and answered, "Never did, Sarge."

"Never?" O'Riley threw his quirt down. He looked at Steve with other horsemen who had gathered around, having the time of their lives, watching the carnival.

"Close up!" O'Riley yelled out to no avail.

After awhile, however, the men and boys found their way about riding their four-legged equipment and began to enjoy themselves. O'Riley smiled, rubbed his mouth with his bandana and sighed.

After things settled down and the horse soldiers were adjusted to their newly acquired equines, Terry consented to a parade through Nashville, which was way overdue. The Tennesseans were proud of Terry's Texas Rangers and watched as Colonels Terry and Lubbock led the rest of the regiment with their Captains in front of each company. This was their regiment. Each of their caps was decorated with a printed star and *Terry's Texas Rangers* around it. To the side of this was a small brass star, which represented the state of Texas.

Terry and Lubbock rode to the side, and positioned their mounts so that they could receive the salute the men gave as they rode by.

Three hundred horsemen rode together on their Blue Grass horses and the rest of the men marched behind while the musicians played the *Bonnie Blue Flag*. The regiment marched to her chords and sang the new words to the pride of the Colonels.

We are a band of brothers from home and kindred fair
The glory of old Texas in southern border war
For like a fiery billow we dash upon the foe
And well the music of our carbines
the Yankee troopers know

"I like the words, Frank," Lubbock returned with pride.

"So do I, John. So do I."

"There's several choruses," John replied. "It is my understanding that one of our own musicians penned the words."

"Well, make sure he gets an extra chevron," Terry added. He smiled as the musicians seemingly played louder.

Then, when the parade reached its zenith, the men rode into the Fair's arena. Terry and Lubbock rode to the far end and sat their mounts while they watched their men perform their trick riding once again to the thrill of the people, and especially to their lady friends. The Rangers thought a great deal of Terry and Lubbock, as though they were invincible. The two Colonels had earned their respect as expert leaders.

They all knew this would be the last hurrah for a while and so the whole town joined in the merriment and most all got drunk. Most all except one, Matt Jorgensen, for he was still riding towards camp.

CHAPTER 16

A REGIMENTAL HERO

Steve had led Company A into some skirmishes with the Union army, but no major battle yet.

The Union Army had set themselves up six miles east of Mammoth Cave. However, Colonel Terry had no idea yet of the strength in number of his enemy.

When Matt found the road that led to the Rangers' camp, he found himself behind the lines of the Union Army. It was then that Matt realized that he had the advantage of discovering for himself the number of Union soldiers and he knew Colonel Terry would be in need of this information. Matt's intent now was to get on with his life for his safety and for the sake of Ginny, and to quit shielding himself by merely playing soldier.

He rode low and easy around Federal campfires and sized up their numbers and strength. Having no writing instrument, he memorized the numbers in his head and totaled them up later.

It was now a question of determining whether he would live or die for Ginny and for the cause of the Confederacy. He had come to the realization that he was a Confederate soldier fighting for the same causes, which Ginny would have fought. He would fight his damndest even if it meant getting killed in a war he once thought was stupid.

Matt reached the first line of scrimmage and saw that Terry's Rangers were fighting a squadron of Union soldiers ferreting out Terry's strengths and weaknesses. He knew it was not a full-scale battle because the bulk of the Yankee brigade was behind him. When he found a clearing, he knew he had to ride swifter than lightning, faster than he had ever ridden before. He considered himself the best and his new steed would prove his worth. Skeeter gave his all as he carried Matt straight through the enemy line.

Matt rode without fear, hoping that his ride across the lines would create confusion among the rank and that the enemy would take a second look before firing at him because he came from the rear. It seemed to be one of the longest rides Matt ever took, but it worked.

It caught Steve's attention when he saw a lone horse soldier riding hard towards him with light gunfire directed at the rider. Behind the rider, he saw several Yankee horse soldiers taking pursuit of him from out of nowhere.

With dust from their hooves and more gunfire, the rider appeared doomed to meet his Maker. He rode like the Devil was riding beside him through the thick gathering of confused horsemen. He continued riding through a small band of Yankee horsemen with their backs to him, as they fought the Rangers. Galloping at full speed, Matt drew his shotgun from its scabbard and fired at the troops in front of him, emptying both chambers in rapid succession. He brought three soldiers down with the buckshot before they realized he was the enemy.

Seeing it was Matt, Steve alerted his company of the immediate situation and rode to help. "A Company" followed Steve's command and rode behind him. Steve took aim with his Navy and shot a soldier who was taking a bead on Matt.

Matt turned in his saddle to see the man go down, then looked at Steve as he approached him and gave him a *thank-you* salute at the tip of his hat.

"Matt!" Steve shouted with a face-filled grin.

"Yep!" Matt yelled out as he kept riding. "Brought some damn Yankees in with me. Can you take them off my back?" He placed his shotgun back on his saddle horn. Jumping a hedge, he rode hell bent for leather towards safety. Steve and the other horse soldiers continued chasing the Yankees.

"Who the hell is thet soldier?" Major Harrison yelled out over the noise of the gunfire.

"Makes no never mind who he is, Major," Colonel Terry yelled out with his saber unsheathed. "Give him protection."

While other companies of Rangers rode out to join Steve, the Federals turned and ran. Steve's company watched their enemy hightail it, and with the relief soldiers, reined up, turned and rode back to camp.

Matt reined his steed and waited for Steve to catch up. When he did, Matt yelled out to him so that all could hear, "Sir, you were right. They have three thousand men headed our way." He hoped that if Terry or any of the other officers were around, his reporting in military style would impress the officers and possibly help clear up why he had been gone so long.

Steve looked puzzled, but he knew this information was evidently true because it was coming from his friend. He caught onto Matt's gesture at barking his find, and after gulping down the bad news, he yelled out, "Good work, Sergeant. Side me." He spun Buddy around and the two rode towards Colonel Terry's headquarters.

Terry sat on his white stallion and waited for Steve. Before they could reach Terry, Major Harrison rode and intercepted them. "What the hell was that all about, mister?" he asked Steve.

"Sir," Steve said, saluting the major. "On my orders, Sergeant Jorgensen went behind enemy lines as a scout to bring back information as to their strength. He tells me that they have three thousand . . ." He gulped again and with a look of consternation said, "three thousand . . . troops headed our way."

"You did what?" Harrison was furious with an order that he was not privy to. "Where the hell did you get approval for such an act?"

"During his furlough, Sir," Steve came back quickly. "We discussed that since he was going across the Tennessee, he might meet up with the enemy. I told him to avoid them at all cost, and if he got the opportunity, bring back some information about them."

"You're saying he was scouting out information for us?"

"Yes, Sir," Steve replied. He caught Terry and Lubbock listening and continued. "Like our brave Colonels did in Richmond, Sir. Hell, if he could tell us how many were grouped together, I thought it'd be to our advantage, Sir."

"You're covering up for this man, Lieutenant," Harrison came back sharply but quietly as he knew Terry was within ear shot of their conversation. "I'll deal with both of you later."

"Are you sure of your count, Sergeant?" Harrison asked Matt directly.

Matt nodded and answered, "Yes, Sir. I counted at least three thousand and then some."

"Ride with me up to the Colonel and report to him your findings, Sergeant."

The three men cantered up the hill to where Terry sat his steed.

It was hard for Harrison to restrain himself, feeling proud for the moment, knowing that Terry had to be appreciative of the information Matt had supplied him. After all, Terry knew now that he had been on that special mission.

"Sir," Harrison reported to Terry. "Sergeant Jorgensen just returned from the enemy side and reported that there are some three-thousand troops on their way to do battle with us."

"I heard. Sergeant Jorgensen?" Terry asked. "Who gave you authority to go on the other side of the Tennessee?"

"Furlough, Sir." Matt answered.

"What furlough?"

"The one I was given when I lost my horse, Sir."

"Lost your horse, hell," Harrison interrupted and then caught himself in an embarrassing moment.

"You were saying, Major?"

"He gave up his horse so another private could ride as a wrangler for you," Harrison grunted, pointing a finger at Matt.

"Admirable." Then he recognized that it was his star Ranger. "You're Sergeant Jorgensen. Matt. Couldn't tell behind that beard. I heard you gave up your horse to Private Daniel Thurman. I remember him riding your fine animal." He looked at Matt and continued. "You gave up your stallion to another. What did you hope to gain out of it, Sergeant?"

"Jorgensen, Sir," Matt responded. "A furlough to see my girl."

"Oh. She lives around here?"

"No, Sir. Over the Tennessee some miles."

"A day's journey?" Terry continued. "Three? By the looks of your beard, you must have been gone quite a spell."

"Ten days, Sir."

"She must have been some girl," Harrison butted in.

"I think she got killed, Sir." Matt added.

"You think?" Harrison cried back at Matt. "What do you mean, *you think?*"

"It's rumored that some Yankee soldier boy shot her, mistaking her for one of us. I reckon."

Terry looked apologetically at Matt and offered his concern.

"But you don't know this for a fact." Harrison said, fidgeting with his jacket pocket for a cigar, but not taking one out.

"No need for sarcasm, Major," Terry sounded off.

Matt gritted his teeth and gave Harrison a look that would have killed a coyote.

"You say three thousand troops?" Terry asked. "Must be Willich's German Brigade." Terry looked around at his broken division. Without giving Harrison a glance, he said, "With this man's bravery, riding ability, and marksmanship, why isn't he a lieutenant, Major?"

"Beg your pardon, Sir," Matt said, drawing a breath. "Sergeant O'Riley wanted to, but he found out I'm from Tennessee, and said you only take Texians, Sir."

Terry grabbed a cigar from Harrison's vest and bit off the end. "Well, son. I mean that. I want only the best, and I want Texians, However, I'm from Kentucky, and now I'm a Texian. Major Harrison here is from Mississippi and now he's a Texian. As I see it, you're from Tennessee and now you're a Texian, too. And a damn good riding Texian, I may add. We need men like you to help lead our outfit. A Company can stand a third lieutenant. Hell, my whole division could stand a hundred like you." He lit up his cigar and added, "See to it, Major."

Harrison reluctantly and with resentment in his eyes agreed. "Yes, Sir!"

Terry looked at the two men and smiled. "Look around you. We haven't got many officers at all in A Company. No captains, not by any bush tail, and God knows we need one."

He turned and walked away without looking back, but said in passing, "And shave off that gawd awful beard.

"And Tom, when you've finished, come to my tent."

"Yes, Colonel," Harrison replied.

Terry and Lubbock returned to their headquarters to map out their strategy with the information that Matt brought to them.

Matt became a lieutenant that day and shaved off his beard, took a bath and got into some clean clothes. He saw the new battle flag waving and smiled at it. It didn't take much for the two lieutenants to later relax against a tree for a breather. Matt looked around and saw more horses than ever in camp. They were not the ordinary kind. These looked to be good stout horses.

"Terry brought them?" he asked, taking out a cigar from his shirt pocket.

"What are you looking at, friend?"

"Horses."

"General Johnston got 'em for us."

"How?"

"Devil be damned if I know. He jest got 'em and let me tell ya, they are all Kentucky's finest. Said so himself."

"Whooey!"

"What you so damn excited about? You've got a good lookin' stallion."

"The best. Name's Skeeter. Which reminds me. About my saddle."

"In my tent. Kept it for you."

"Good. This one ain't me." He pointed to his saddle, lit his cigar, blew a smoke ring and laid back. "What do a lieutenant do?" Matt asked.

"Give orders, chum," Steve answered. "Give orders, and make sure they're carried out."

"Seems to me to be a lot of work."

"We have men under us who make our work easy for us. For instance," Steve grabbed him by his hand, pulled him up, and with their horses in tow, took Matt to the nearby Sergeant and introduced him to his new rank. "Sergeant O'Riley," Steve said.

"Sergeant Jorgensen, as I live and breath now," O'Riley answered with a frown, wondering what was happening with all the *order* gibberish he had been listening to from a distance. "And what would be bringin' ye back so soon into our lovely company?" It was a sarcastic remark and he was ready to follow it up, had Steve not interrupted him.

"Sergeant, Lieutenant Jorgensen is our third lieutenant, now."

Sergeant O'Riley cringed, threw his hat down on the ground, and kicked a stone a mile for good luck. Picking up his hat and putting it back on his head, he stood at attention and said, "Yes, Sir!" He had already been training all of "A Company" in horsemanship and now knew that Matt was going to ride the men harder. And he did.

"Glad you're happy to have me back on board, Sergeant," Matt said lightly to O'Riley and left him to simmer by himself.

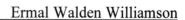

CHAPTER 17

JIMMY

December 8, 1861.

There often comes a time in a man's life, more than a man would like to admit, when something appears to be what it isn't. The burning, crazy yearning to find his girl alive, well and back in his arms again, was what drove Matt incessantly towards his unknown destiny day in and day out. She was dead according to all the stories he had found out about her, but he refused to succumb to any reality of its truth. He pushed on to find her at each and every opportunity.

A seasoned officer, Major Thomas Harrison had served under Colonel Jefferson Davis' 1st Mississippi Rifles at the beginning of the Mexican War. He knew the smell of battle, but for some unknown reason, he made a decision in the eyes of his men, that December day in Jimtown, that caused the men to resent him more than ever.

Matt and Steve were with Harrison when he took two companies on a scouting expedition and spread them thin. They found a company of Federal infantrymen on their side of the Green River and Harrison gave the command to halt.

Matt watched Harrison as he eyed the Federals crouch into position, bring their rifles up at an angle with their bayonets and wait for them. They didn't make an advance; they just waited. Matt and Steve held their mounts back, waiting for Harrison's command to charge.

Matt watched Harrison as he looked towards the second line. It stood erect behind the first row and together waited with raised bayonets for the Rangers' charge.

Matt and Steve continued to wait for Harrison's order as the Major conferred with one General Patrick Ronayne Cleburne, Commander of the Confederate infantry. His sobriquet was *Stonewall Jackson of the West*. He was the Brigade Commander of the 2nd Brigade of the Kentucky Army. His stature was long and tall, a fortyish gentleman from Cork County, Ireland ostensibly born on St. Patrick's Day, and sported a full head of black hair and a good size beard. Unfortunately Harrison and Cleburne did not discuss the situation with other officers, and because Cleburne had previously fought with the British military, and successfully, Harrison chose to listen to his advice.

"You're a politician first, a soldier second," Cleburne suggested to Harrison. "Your goal in this war is political. Looking at this skirmish, I'd advise you to forget it. This is not a good fight for you."

"It's a skirmish, Ronayne," Harrison answered. Cleburne preferred to be called by his middle name. "It's not that big a deal. My men are ready."

"Precisely, Tom," Cleburne returned. "If you win it, you've got a small feather in your cap. If you get killed, nothing more will be said for your corpse."

"I'm not afraid to fight."

"Then go for it. And leave me out of it."

"What's your plan?" Harrison asked dejectedly.

"Hell, part of my infantry can take them out without me and you getting involved. That's leadership."

Cleburne turned around, the General he was, looked over a map stretched out on his desk, and murmured ever so softly, "*Get along with your own business and leave me to mine.*"

Without turning around, his eyes focused sternly on Harrison, "Question is, are you ready to die?" He humphed, "I'm not." He turned around and said matter-of-factly, "I'll tell you this. I will be ready to die for the South when my time comes, not before.

"Now, look, Tom. You want a fight where you can be the victor, not the victim. If you want to be a hero and make governor, you'd best be listenin' to me. You come back wounded without a limb, forget it. Voters don't cast their votes for a part of a man."

"You figure it's that close?" Harrison questioned.

"I know it's that close."

"But what if I don't get another chance? What if the war gets over with real fast like?"

Cleburne took two cigars out of his vest pocket, gave Harrison one and took one himself. "You'll get a better chance. This war's gonna last far beyond Christmas. Hell, I haven't had my first battle yet, and I'm as anxious as you. It only takes one charge. One gawddam charge with you out there in front of your men. Do as I do. Just stay out of harm's way."

Harrison lit the General's cigar and then his own, watching Cleburne's eyes as they seemingly burned into his.

Cleburne concluded, "I wouldn't touch this one, if I were you."

Cleburne's chance came later, and he proved his theory right when he fought at Shiloh with four men to his one in one of the fiercest battles and came out a hero and one of the greatest field commanders of the Confederacy.

It appeared to the two Lieutenants, however, that Harrison was having second thoughts as he looked all around and apparently saw nothing but Yankee soldiers pointing their rifles in the direction of his men. Matt kept Skeeter calmed down for knew he was ready to ride and ride fast at the given command. He kept his eyes peeled towards the Federals and at the same time watched carefully for Harrison's decision.

"What are we waiting for?" Matt cried over to Steve. "We have over two hundred men. For crissake, let's get on with it." This was his first battle, and both Matt and Steve felt an easy victory at hand.

Harrison turned and motioned for his men to follow him in a withdrawal. "Sound *Recall!*" he barked.

Embittered as they were, Matt and Steve led their men somberly back to camp.

Matt stayed in his saddle once they reached camp and looked again through the thickets at what might have been his first victory.

"We were within their reach, Matt," Steve said, gritting his teeth. "We could have run them over, and with shotguns and breech-loaders, we could have won the battle in no time."

"Hell, and it were only a small skirmish," O'Riley remarked, riding past the two men. "It wouldn't have involved much bloodshed at all, most using Spencers. Would've done me proud, not to mention 'Molly'." He referred to his Model 1851 lightweight Navy that he carried before the War. Many of his men used the newer .44 caliber, Model 1860, or the .36 caliber Model 1851 Navy. However light they both were, it was still cumbersome to a lot of the volunteer horse soldiers new to its use, and it was evident with the many lop-eared horses at the beginning. But, O'Riley never traded up. Like others who were partial to their old trusty side arms, O'Riley was to Molly, his ever-polished Navy.

The two companies returned to Johnston's Brigade and met up with the rest of the Rangers.

CHAPTER 18

SHOTGUNS AT CLOSE RANGE

"**I**'ve got an idea how we can get our company's confidence back, Steve," Matt said in a quiet voice with a cigar dangling between his lips.

"How?"

"Remember when I galloped back into camp with the Federals on my tail?"

"You want me to tell you what a hero's welcome was all about again?"

"No. No. But, I was thinkin'. Back there I got three of them bastards in front of me because I had my shotgun and could shoot at close range. We've got to instill this skill in the rest. What d'ya say?"

"Go on."

"The key, the way I see it, is for us to get within striking distance. I figure fifteen yards at most."

"Fifteen yards?" Steve dropped his jaw and slid down the bark of the tree to the ground. "In battle? We'd get slaughtered."

"We won't if we rode up close to them at full gallop."

"And get shot up while doin' it."

"Not necessarily. We've done a good job of trainin' our men to ride like thunder. Well, we take them one notch further."

"Teach them to use shotguns at fifteen yards? I suspect they already know thet."

"Or less," Matt retorted, taking a draw from his cigar. He flicked the butt out into the meadow and sat down next to Steve. "The hard part is to get them to ride into the enemy at a full gallop firing pistols at first and then using shotguns at close range."

"It'll never work."

"Think it won't?"

"Maybe." Steve scratched his chin and looked over at Matt whose eyes were intently staring at him. "Go on."

"Thet's it. We go back to Green River, ride hard and bent low so they don't see our faces. We rise up in our saddles, and ride fast into the enemy with our Navy's blasting away. When we get close enough, we change over to shotguns. I can just see their faces now."

"Whose? Our men or the Federals?"

"Both, I reckon. The enthusiasm for our own men knowing thet they're going to do this, and the fear of the Federals when they see us galloping down their throats."

Steve thought again and said, "Worth a try. Let's run it past Jimmy first thing in the morning and see what he thinks." Jimmy was a name the men tagged onto Harrison for having them retreat when they wanted to fight.

Harrison had his second cup of coffee by the time Matt and Steve caught him outside his tent the next morning.

"Got something on your mind, gentlemen?" he asked when he saw them traipsing up the hill to his tent.

"How'd you guess, Major?

"I can smell trouble a mile away. What is it?"

"Well, Sir," Steve opened up as he was the first lieutenant with seniority over Matt. "Matt here has come up with a scheme I think is worth considering."

Harrison looked at Matt, took the last swig from his cup and spit it out. "Damn coffee grounds. Well?"

"Shotguns at full gallop!" Matt blurted it out without hesitation and waited for Jimmy's reaction. "We go back."

Harrison's eyes widened and he leaned in towards Matt. "What?"

214

"I figure fifteen yards at the most, Major. Use eighteen and twenty-two buckshot in each of the double barrels."

"You crazy?" Harrison shouted back at him. "Up 'til now, I thought you were prima donnas. Now I sure as hell know you're outta your gawdam minds. Shotguns at fifteen yards at full gallop." He turned and walked away. "It's never been done."

"The Revolutionary used them close up," Matt rebutted. "Thet much I found out from Colonel Terry when he pinned me. Now I'm suggesting we do the same. We can scatter the hell out of the Federals, make them run for their gawd fearin' lives. Think about it, Major."

Harrison remembered what Cleburne said about the skirmish. He stopped, turned and said disgustingly, "I won't have it; but Jorgensen, you can take a patrol out and scout the river area. Don't come back until you have something to report. And you, Andrews, get back to your men. Give them some close-order drills. I want to see them spiffed up better than last time. Give you a chance to test your theory on haystacks. Get your men to gallop in and shoot the hell out of them at fifteen yards. See how they fare out."

Matt stepped forward, but was stopped by Steve. "Thet's your answer, Sir?"

"No. Those are my orders." Harrison turned and walked away in a brisk military style.

Matt followed Steve back to their tents. "Close order drill," Matt said in disgust. "Hell, all he thinks of is marching in some damn parade somewheres."

"Do what Jimmy wants, Matt."

"He wants to work my butt off because he hates me." Matt smacked Steve on the shoulder and walked ahead towards the company, grabbing Skeeter as he went.

"I need volunteers," Matt said to the men working at cleaning their guns and tack. "We're goin' back to the river. Who'll go?"

"Who's leading?" Troy asked, disgruntling. "Jimmy?"

"I am. Want to go with me?"

"What're we gonna do?" Troy continued. "We've already embarrassed ourselves."

"Trust me on this one, Troy," Matt said, walking through their midst. "You with me?"

"Oh, what the hell. Beats boredom." Troy packed his cleaning gear in his saddlebag and grabbed hold of his reins.

Matt and Steve had their men well trained, alert and quick for action with their horses saddled most of the time. Matt had more volunteers than he needed and selected twenty of whom he considered the best.

The Rangers were in their saddles and riding before Steve gathered his men for drill. He watched the patrol as it headed north towards Green River and disappeared into the thicket of trees.

Matt rode with pride that morning, knowing that he was about to put a new idea into the mind of horse soldiers. He also knew he was going against orders, but he felt, under the conditions, it had to be done. He reasoned with himself that he should have gone over the Major's head to Terry himself; feeling that he was Terry's favorite son and Terry favored the use of shotguns over carbines.

A two-hour's ride into their patrol brought them close to the river's edge where they spotted a Yankee campfire on the other side. They quickly ducked under cover of the trees and thickets to keep from being detected. Matt surveyed their situation with Doc, a veteran of Terry's first battle before they were Rangers. He appeared to be in his late forties.

"I make out a company of some hundred men or more. How do you see it?" Matt asked.

Doc slapped back his answer, leaning south in his saddle "Close, unless some are walking around back. Got to consider thet. What's your plan, Sir?"

"Glad you asked, Sergeant." He wiped his lips with the back of his gloved hand. "Sure could go for a chaw right about now."

"You nervous, Sir?" McTavvit asked from behind him, offering him a chaw of tobacco.

"Damned right. Ain't you?" He took the chaw and thew it into his mouth, grinned a little and looked towards the Federals. "You got your shotguns primed and ready, Private?"

"Always, Sir."

"Rest of you?"

"Loaded, Sir."

Matt took his shotgun, broke its chamber to make sure it was loaded and flipped it shut. "Here's the plan. I've been ordered to scout the area. Thet's all. I figure we need a victory to make us feel like men again. How do you feel?"

"You're fixin' us to charge 'em?" Doc asked, standing firm with his legs planted in the soft dirt. "I don't like it."

"Why not?" Matt asked.

"We're to report what we see. We're not ordered to fight any."

"I picked you, Doc, because you're older and wiser. But I also know you're a pretty brave man. I've watched you. You're not afraid now. What's your thinkin'?"

"You get us killed, for what?"

"Thet's your thinkin'?" Matt returned. "Take your mount and ride on back. I won't hold it agin' you. Tell Jimmy what we've seen. And you can tell him this, too. Tell him we licked the hell out of 'em and we're comin' back as a patrol unit in one piece."

"You don't know thet, Sir," Doc retorted. "There could be twenty more around the trees."

"If they are, they've got their pants down." Matt spun around towards the other three men. "Any one here wants to head on back with Doc, go ahead. We're wastin' time."

No man moved.

"Let's hear the Lieutenant out," McTavvit said softly, hoping his high-pitched voice wouldn't carry across the river.

"Thanks, Private," Matt said, reaching for his makings but bringing his empty hand back down. "This is the shallowest crossing, thet's why they're camped here. I figured they're waitin' for the rest of their company. Federals are too cautious some times."

"More like scairt all the time, you mean," one of the other riders piped up with a laugh.

Matt gave a slight grin. "We only have this one chance."

"I'll not ride back alone," Doc said. "If the rest stay, I'll ride with you."

"I didn't have any doubts." Matt took his hat off and wiped the insides with his bandana. "I don't want any of you killed, but we're in this war to win it." With a nervous grin, he added, "Then we can go home to our girls." That was a cliché that he found the other officers used to keep the men in positive attitudes. The men also knew it was just a rib, and not necessarily true.

"When we leave here and hit the river, we'll ride in at a fast trot. We'll be bent low in our saddles. At a given time, when I yell out, fires up and spur the hell out of your horses. Fire your Navy's, and when you get to see their scared faces, change over to your shotguns. You can't afford to miss.

"You got extra shells, use them. We'll ride in a line right through them to a clearing, turn, reload and ride back.

"Need some, Sir?" McTavvit asked, taking some shells from his saddlebag and handing them to Matt.

"We're figurin' to get ourselfs killed," another young soldier jested. "But, what a hell of a way to go."

"Yeah," Matt said with shortness of breath, giving the young man a stern look. "I figure thet we'll get their undivided attention once in the camp and they'll put their back sides to us. When you run out of buckshot and someone's in your way, clobber them or run 'em over. Again, ride to the clearing, reload, turn and give them a second dose. Then, get the hell out of there. Ride for home. Don't wait for my command."

"Jest what're you tryin' to prove, Sir," Doc said, giving Matt's reins to him.

"If we succeed, I figure the Major will get his confidence back with us, Doc. Shotguns at close range." Matt mounted up and the rest followed him.

They walked their horses to the clearing and mounted them. At Matt's command, they spurred their steeds onward and rode hard and fast across the river on the best Kentucky stock money could buy. Matt was right, the river was shallow. The sand was hard and gave their horses sure footing. The Rangers rode low in their saddles, then with Matt, they rose up and gave their rebel yell and charged the camp in a single line formation. Before the Federals could get to their rifles, Matt and his men had stirred enough confusion that caused them to scatter and run for shelter.

The Rangers fired their shotguns at close range at the fleeing soldiers, hitting many with buckshot. One Ranger reported later that he saw a nose fly off at one place, and an ear at another. The shotguns were effective. The sight was horrendous for the scampering soldiers and caused them to run faster. Some of them turned and used their Navy's while others found rifles and prepared to return fire, but the Rangers were out of range.

The riders turned their mounts, reloaded their shotguns and rode to meet their opponents again who were firing their Henry repeaters and rifles in rapid succession while running at the same time towards tree shelter. The Rangers were trained in carrying a spare shotgun belt around their saddle horn as well as an extra pistol or two in their waist sash, and use them they did. Matt knew his horse would head for the clearing at lightning speed, so he put the reins in his teeth and used his Navy in one hand and the shotgun in the other.

The Federals got out from behind the trees into battle positions. Again, some stood erect while others knelt and fired at the hoard of rushing devils coming straight towards them. They saw the flash of the Rangers' shotguns and Navy's, fired one volley wildly and fled on foot for their lives. Some lost their lives. Others were wounded. Most were scared, confused, embarrassed and running.

Matt was correct when he said they would ride away unscathed, for none of the Rangers were injured. By the time the Federals were again fully armed and firing at them, Matt's patrol was back across the river and into the woods. They realized their safety would be short lived if they stopped, so they rode through the trees, branches and brushes without fear of being impaled, scarred or marred.

They were back at camp before noon with tired and lathered horses. The Rangers' hearts were beating with pride as they rode in. They were exuberant in their victory and could hardly restrain their excitement that showed on their faces.

Steve and a few of his men rode to greet them, and when they heard shots being fired in their direction, took off through the woods to chase a few ensuing fighters on horseback. In minutes they returned.

"Get any?" Matt asked as he sat sideways in his saddle, enjoying a chaw. The men stayed in their saddles with him.

"Not a one. They all skedaddled for home. They'll think twice next time." He sided Matt and asked, "How'd it go out there?"

"Got to make my report to Jimmy." Matt flipped his leg back over the saddle horn and let Skeeter walk towards Jimmy's tent. "We used shotguns up to their faces, Steve. Rode right into the enemy and scattered them like wildfire."

"It was crazy, Sir," Doc added. "But I have to admit, it worked."

"What if it hadn't?" Harrison asked after he heard the report. "What if all of you were killed in that skirmish? What the hell good would it have done?" He paced the tent floor with a cigar in hand and an angry voice thundering expletives. "I ordered you strictly to scout the area. You were to report back to me with what you found. It would have been my decision whether or not we should have attacked. You could have caused our whole outfit to be wiped out."

"You didn't think it could work, Sir," Matt answered, standing at attention. "I had to prove thet it could. Right now, many of our men now have their confidence restored as Rangers."

"You had to prove nothing. Your job is to train our men. You could have proved it on the training grounds with your men. Ever think about that?"

"Beg your pardon, Sir, but it's not the same," Matt added. "We've been shooting at haystacks 'til we're sick of haystacks. They don't fight back. It's like trying to hit the broad side of a barn."

"You think you could do that?" Harrison asked with his cigar stuck between his teeth.

"We had to confront the enemy with it first."

"It was our decision, Sir" Doc said, standing outside the tent. "We heard him out and thought it was a good plan."

"You had to. You were under his command."

"He gave us the choice to come back to camp, Sir. We honored thet. We chose to stay with him."

Harrison paced the ground with his hands behind his back.

"It was a victory, Major," Steve reminded him. "You get the credit. Think how the old man is goin' to like it."

And like it, he did.

"By gawd!" he exclaimed. "Now that's fighting. Guts, men! Guts! You can tell me that story a hundred times and I won't tire of it." He turned to the Major and pounded his fist in his hand. "Make damn sure our men are trained for shotguns at full gallop. By Georgia peach, we're making history. By damnation!"

"See to it, Lieutenants," Harrison ordered.

Although he was hesitant in carrying out the order, Harrison obeyed his commander as a true officer.

Matt and Steve turned and headed enthusiastically down the hill, but before they were out of earshot, they heard Terry say to Harrison, "Am I a judge of officer material or what?" And he added, "You're a damn good field officer, Tom."

They turned and saw Harrison cringe and walk away. "I don't think he likes us, Matt," Steve said with a grin.

"Who the hell cares?"

CHAPTER 19

THE FIRST FALLEN BRAZORIAN SABER

Camped along the Green River near Munfordville, Union Commander, Colonel August Willich led the construction of the Louisville & Nashville Railroad pontoon bridge, which spanned the Green River. The purpose of the bridge was for the passage of Federal trains and artillery.

To prevent any surprise attacks by General Braxton Bragg's Brigade while constructing the bridge, Willich had launched two companies of his famed 32nd Indiana Volunteer Infantry Regiment, consisting mostly of Prussian veterans, across the river. These were the companies that Matt's patrol hit, partially destroying the Louisville & Nashville Railroad Bridge over the Green River.

Watsonville, December 17, 1861

When the bridge was finally completed, four more companies of Willich's 32nd Infantry marched over rocky ground through the fog across the bridge towards Munfordville determined to avenge the destruction of his fine work. When they spotted Terry's Rangers through the woods, they took cover behind every forage, haystack in the cornfields and along the railroad embankment.

Aside from the moon hiding its face behind some snow clouds creating eerie shadows throughout the darkness of the area, several Confederate campfires lit up Rowlett Station on that December night as the Federals camped close by.

Matt and Steve sensed that what Terry had feared about the Union soldiers was about to happen as fog laid low on that December morning.

Just before dawn, bullets flew through the air and the noise of nearly three thousand Union soldiers throughout the woods made the Rangers strike camp and mount up.

With their horses already saddled, the horse soldiers were in them and in formation. Terry's Texas Rangers were ready to ride in their first real battle. Terry chose to take his regiment through the middle, acting like a wedge to the Federals.

The fog lifted early and Willich's German Brigade waited for Terry's counter charge.

Colonel Terry looked every bit the professional soldier President Jefferson Davis would have commissioned had Terry made it to Virginia. Mounted on his white stallion, he led the charge while Lieutenant Colonel Lubbock, slumped in the saddle, rode by his side on the sorrel.

"John," Terry brought Lubbock's attention to him.

"What?" Lubbock answered weakly.

"You're looking peaked. Kinda down and out in the mouth. Anything wrong?"

Lubbock straightened up in his saddle. "Just a stomach ache. It'll go away."

It got worse as the day went on. Lubbock had the sweats and Terry was getting more concerned, but let it be.

Company A was readied in line waiting for Harrison's order. This time Harrison again brought the full company into charging position. Matt rode his horse proud among Company A. "Remember what we did in our first patrol, men. We're gonna be twice as good. You with me?"

Harrison heard Matt. He grit his teeth but said nothing.

There wasn't one voice that was not in accord with Matt's challenge. Steve quickly lined up beside Matt and the first lieutenant. Squadron sergeants readied their men. Pride had set in and strengthened every horse soldier. They lined up across from the Federals and waited for Harrison's command. Lieutenant Pat Christian's infantry lined up behind and alongside the cavalry unit. No more shots came from the other side.

Tension mounted as Harrison eyed both lines of Willich's forces. He saw that the first line of defense had prepared their bayonets to lift his riders off their horses. They expected to halt the horse soldiers in twenty steps of their two lines of savage bayonets. The butts of their rifles were wedged into the ground. Some kept their bayonets standing out at right angles while others kept them straighter. The infantrymen in the rear lines extended their bayonets between the heads of the men of the first line. They waited for the charge.

Harrison gave the command but Company A, sensing the command, had already begun their ride with lightning speed, each man giving out a rebel yell that shook the ears and pricked the heart of every Federal soldier with fear.

Willich's 32nd Indiana Infantry faced the fury of the pistols and shotguns in a kneel and parry formation as the Rangers rode low in their saddles, came up and blasted away with their Navy's. Then at close range they switched to their shotguns, first one barrel then the other into the Union lines at fifteen yards and rode right through them.

"Where'd those gawdam devils come from?" one Federal soldier yelled out just before a shotgun blast blew his arm off. The blast fragmented his comrades' bodies next to him, causing many to drop their rifles and run for cover.

The Rangers charged again and again as before with Matt. They jumped fences and hedges with determination to get the job done right. It was with this fierce bravery in a few short minutes at Rowlett Station that the Rangers became called, "Terry's Devils". These devils charged with such enthusiastic zeal that they caused the Federals to stagger from shock and run at the outbursts of their shotguns. It was in vain that Willich's trained infantrymen threw themselves into groups defending themselves. Matt heard repeatedly the command coming from their ranks, "guard against the cavalry". The Rangers fought with such fierce bravery that they recovered their confidence as many Union soldiers fell under their devilish charge.

Then it happened. Matt witnessed a kneeling Union soldier parry his bayonet into Terry's horse causing Terry to fall.

Matt turned and fired his Navy at one of three soldiers who was quickly on top of Terry, slamming him to the ground. But before he could get off a second round, one of the soldiers shot Terry in the head as he lay on the ground. Terry's saber fell limp from his hand. Matt had no time to save him, but aimed and fired at the one who had shot Terry. That soldier fell across Terry's lifeless body.

Steve caught the third troop with his shotgun as the man numbered in with those who ran away. It was a swift, yet hard fight for Terry's Rangers. With their leader gone, the Rangers' spirit went all out for revenge. Matt felt this shared vengeance strong in his blood, as well as did Steve. It was more so for Matt now, for his vendetta was also for Ginny's untimely and unnecessary death. He never wanted to forget it. They rode their horses at full gallop and chased the Federals across the bridge where many fell or jumped into the Green River. Matt was truly a Confederate horse soldier.

In minutes the battle was over. Neither side won, but because of the devilish way Terry's Rangers fought, the Union Army lost one-hundred and sixty three men that day, with over two hundred more wounded. The Battle Flag of Terry's Texas Rangers fell and was never recovered. The Rangers suspected a soldier of the Willich's 34th Illinois possibly retrieved it soon after the battle as a souvenir.

The sun was still above the horizon when a couple of Rangers drove a wagon with three wounded Federal soldiers in it to the center of the bridge.

"Got three of your wounded here," Doc said as he pulled up.

The Ranger riding with him was Chaplain Robert Franklin Bunting, a stout man with gray sideburns and a beard. "Our medical staff tended to them," Bunting said somberly." "Can't say the same for a lot of the others. Sorry."

A Federal officer, accompanied by four soldiers, walked over to the wagon. He was a young man who looked aged perhaps because of the war. His uniform was torn and muddied, but he wore it as if it were new.

"Thank you, Sir," he replied and saluted the Chaplain.

The soldiers hopped up into the wagon and brought the men out on litters, anticipating their officer's command.

The officer then looked over at Terry's body lying on the cold ground. "He's your Commanding Officer?" he asked.

"Yes, Sir," Bunting replied, climbing out of the wagon with Doc. "Colonel Benjamin Franklin Terry."

"Kinda thought it was. I saw him fall."

Captain Willich, who had been watching nearby, rode over to the wagon.

"Our Commanding Officer, Captain Willich, Sir." The officer stood at attention and saluted him as he approached them.

Willich looked tall and untouched, sitting on his white mount. "I recognize the uniform, Chaplain. Thank you for bringing my men back."

"With your permission, Sir." Bunting saluted Willich and received the return salute.

"You have it, Chaplain. Soldiers, give them a hand."

"With your permission, Captain Willich," Matt said as he and Steve walked their horses onto the bridge. "We can take it from here." They both saluted Willich.

"Do your job, son." Willich returned their salute and sat his horse.

The two Lieutenants looked down at Terry's body on the bridge and rode over to it.

"One shot in the head," Bunting noted.

"His killer is dead," Matt added. "Piled up on one of those heaps, I reckon."

They dismounted, and with Doc's help, carried Terry's body to the wagon.

Willich nodded approval as well as a sense of condolence towards Matt.

Bunting and Doc climbed back into the wagon, turned the horses and rode back. Matt and Steve stayed behind.

Willich and the other officer took their sabers out, placed each in front of their chins and saluted.

"Your men put up a brave fight," Willich said.

"And yours," Matt returned.

Matt's interest was also in looking for the Union soldiers he had killed. Steve sided him.

Dismounting, Matt gave his reins to Steve to hold while he walked over to take a closer look at the soldiers. The one who had shot Terry in the head had been thrown off his body carelessly by the Rangers, and was lying disjointed in the road. He was a man who looked to be in his thirties with a neatly trimmed beard. He might have been a grocer, or a banker. He had a clean expression about his face. He was not the man Matt was instinctively seeking, a boy who might have been the one who shot Ginny.

Matt walked over to the body that Steve brought down whose face looked up into the sky as if he were praying. He had been gunshot in the stomach from Steve's shotgun. He was a younger man, but still not the man Matt wanted to find.

He walked over to the third man, a boy barely sixteen if a day older. His face showed little sign of ever having been shaved. His hair was blond sticking out of his Union cap and his eyes were blue, looking up. He was someone's precious son who signed up perhaps giving a false age. Matt knew his kind. To him, this could have been the boy who shot his Ginny. He looked to be honest, young, and scared. That would have fit the description given to him by Jim who had talked to the Commander of the Federal unit camped in Tennessee. It was a young lad whom the Commander gave detention to for shooting a woman. It mattered little that she wore clothes like that of a Rebel. To Matt, the boy had a peaceful look upon his face as if to say, "I'm sorry. I hope this settles it." The bullet that killed him was in the middle of his forehead. He had died instantly, his eyes wide open.

Steve watched Matt bow his head and walk away, kicking at a rock in the road. He handed Matt back his reins and gave a look around once more to make certain they were out of harm's way.

They mounted their steeds and caught up with their wagon, leaving the Federals to continue the clean up. Matt looked down at

Terry's still body in the wagon, his saber laid across his chest. His cape covered his face.

The Regimental Chaplain Robert Franklin Bunting officiated the burial of Colonel Terry with six other Confederate cavalrymen later that day. One of them was Terry's younger brother, Colonel Frank Terry who commanded Company H. A hurriedly made Bonnie Blue draped Terry's pine coffin with his saber lying on top. Prior to sending Terry's body home by train to Nashville, and later to Houston to lie in state, Bunting had the Bonnie Blue removed and properly folded. After everyone had left, he took Terry's saber, and placed it with the flag inside his tent. Terry was the first of the *Brazorian sabers* to perish.

The intent of the Rangers now was simply to get out of Watsonville before Willich had a change of mind.

CHAPTER 20

THE SECOND FALLEN
BRAZORIAN SABER

The Rangers continued to march further south with Johnston's Brigade on their way through Kentucky, bivouacking deep in the woods without fire for fear of being attacked. The first night was silent, for the men were still feeling the loss of their leader. And they watched the ailing Lubbock cradle his stomach and lose color.

Steve left his tent that night and met Matt lying on his bunk inside his tent.

"How d'ya feel, friend?" he asked Matt as he offered him a cigar.

"About the battle? Pretty damn good." He lit his cigar and blew the smoke straight up.

"Too bad about Terry."

"Yeah." Matt threw out absently, thinking to himself about the great man. *Why him?* He asked himself, watching the smoke waft into the air and disappear into the night. Terry had become Matt's idol as a leader, a soldier, and a horseman. He was the type like his dad, hard as nails but gentle, as a man should be.

"Great man," Steve added. Looking at Matt, who was staring into space, he asked, "Whatcha thinkin' 'bout?"

"Oh," Matt responded, then took another drag. "Short stuff will be on top of us like slop to a hog now thet Terry's out of the way."

"'Sorta 'fraid you might be right." Steve found himself a cigar from his shirt pocket. Taking a light from Matt's match, he continued. "Major Wharton's called a meeting for us."

"What about?"

"We're supposed to elect John Lubbock as our new commander. It's the rule of the Rangers, and us officers have to carry it out."

"You seen Lubbock?" Matt asked.

"I know. What d'ya make of it, friend?"

"He's been heavin' a lot. Kinda afraid he's got camp fever. He's got the symptoms."

Steve nodded and left the tent. A while later, after thinking heavy about Lubbock, Matt flipped his cigar out the tent, rolled over and fell fast asleep.

And so it was done, rather solemnly and quietly, but directly. The next day, Lieutenant Colonel John Lubbock became Colonel and Commander of Terry's Texas Rangers.

As Matt and Steve walked back to their tents after chow while the sun set, Matt suggested "Of course, Lubbock had to be the successor to Terry, regardless of whether he's sick or not."

"No question. But how the hell is he going to lead us with him having camp fever?" Steve asked, lighting his cigar. "He's gone to sickbay. Pretty bad off."

"Is it typhoid?" Matt asked. "Have you heard?"

"No word on it, but you know it has to be. They're gettin' him ready to take to the hospital in Bowlin' Green." Steve kept talking as if to the wind, for Matt's mind was still on the loss of Benjamin Franklin Terry.

"Hell, he'd better get well," Steve kept on. "We don't have too many good officers who can lead this regiment. Major Wharton's temporarily in charge while he's gone."

Steve looked over in Harrison's direction.

"I see our friend knows about his being passed up." Matt pointed to Harrison relieving himself by a tree and holding onto a branch tightly as if in anger. The two men kept walking.

Steve smiled, and then looked at Matt for a serious moment. "Again, I'm sorry to hear about Ginny."

"Thanks." Matt turned and looked away. "All my fault. She was rushin' to meet us in Virginia. She didn't know I wouldn't be coming. Had I not posted her a letter, she'd still be with us today." He looked back at Steve. "She rode out and got shot on my account."

"Blaming yourself won't bring her back, Matt," Steve said, trying to comfort him. After a quiet moment, he continued, "God's watching over her, wherever she is." He stopped and looked up into the empty night sky.

"Never heard you to be religious like, Steve." Matt stopped and looked up into the sky with him.

"Growin' up in the South, chum," Steve said, "one gets to be religious every mornin' and twice as much in the evenin'. And you can't hang around those damn niggers without their singin' gettin' you a little religious."

Matt took out a cigar, lit it and let the smoke out slowly. He looked up at the stars again and saw one shooting across the skies. "Yeah. I remember them back on her plantation. Singin' and singin'. They must have found a special somethin' no one else found, cause I always seen a smile on their faces and music in their hearts." He smiled. "Hell, I enjoyed it so much I even found myself singin' right along with 'em. That is, when I knew the words." He remembered Bertha's song. "I'm gonna rise up, and git down my ol' false teeth," he sang. Then he dragged on the cigar a last time and flung the butt to the wind. "They could dance, too. Sure wish Pa and Lucas could've seen 'em. Might've made our lives a little easier, enjoyin' it like they seem to do."

When winter set her full blast into the Rangers' Kentucky camp that January, '62, many of the Rangers could not resist the cold elements. And, due to imperfect medical knowledge and discipline, camp sanitation among the Confederates in Bowling Green and throughout Kentucky was terrible. Epidemic outbreaks began early and continued throughout the winter. Many brave, strong and courageous Rangers died with measles, respiratory infections or from camp fever; typhoid. Throughout Kentucky and Tennessee, local homes opened their doors to the sick because of inadequately staffed hospitals. When feasible, the sick and wounded were transported by rail to hospitals at Nashville. It was estimated that ten soldiers to one died of sickness and mistreatment than died in battle. What Rangers did make it, had become seasoned horse soldiers, and were again ready for battle.

On 9 January, the day after being elected the Commander of Terry's Texas Rangers and only three weeks after Colonel Terry was killed, Colonel Lubbock left the regiment at Nashville due to typhoid fever and joined Colonel Terry.

Chaplain Bunting laid Lubbock to rest with his eulogy. Afterwards, and as with Terry before, he took Lubbock's saber and placed it appropriately with the Bonnie Blue respectfully folded in a box in his tent alongside Terry's. He was the second of the Brazorian sabers to ride to their final glory.

Majors Wharton and Harrison called a meeting at their headquarters with the company officers two days after Lubbock's demise.

"Gentlemen," Wharton said forthright and without hesitation, Colonel Lubbock is dead. It's our loss, Heaven's gain."

Harrison interrupted and said, "Colonel John Lubbock suggested Major Wharton to be your next commander. Under protocol, as before, it has to be with your vote as well." His voice belied himself about wanting Wharton elected over him.

The officers followed through with electing Major John Austin Wharton officially as their Colonel in charge of Terry's Texas Rangers over Harrison.

Major Harrison shook Wharton's hand and added, "We've been prepared for it." He spoke for the rest of the officers and horse soldiers and made the vote unanimous. "We accept your leadership, Colonel Wharton." It was a humbling moment for Harrison, which did not go unnoticed by Terry's Rangers, primarily by Matt and Steve, and of course, O'Riley.

It was that quick. Young Colonel John Austin Wharton was elected by the Company Commanders to take charge of the Texas 8th Cavalry, Terry's Texas Rangers.

Because of Wharton's promotion, Harrison felt dejected and even worse whenever Matt and Steve were in his presence. Somehow, he seemed to feel that they had become an anathema to him in every way. He became more and more cognizant of his small stature when sized up next to their six-foot plus frames. He felt like a man of inadequacies and had to prove himself fit to command solely by the power of his rank.

Colonel Wharton looked around at the officers and stood straight and firm, confident in spite of his feeling weak. "I thank you all for your vote in electing me your leader. We have come a long way in a few months. We shall continue to stride for what Colonels Terry and Lubbock so gallantly strove for, victory. Gallant Victory!

"Our Colonels did not die in vain. We will not let it be so." He looked past the officers as if into eternity, and continued. "One day, it is still my hope, we will march in front of President Jefferson Davis in full regalia and prove that we are the best damn cavalry that ever existed.

Harrison bit his lip, but he was loyal to the honor and discipline as a true officer, and he considered himself top drawer for leadership as well in this category. He thought, *"My turn will come."*

EPILOGUE

Great concern shadowed Major John Austin Wharton's health, however. Ten days later, the Regimental chaplain (and de facto war correspondent) Robert Franklin Bunting made note in his column to the Houston Tri-Weekly Telegraph about Wharton's condition. Another week passed, and Bunting corrected it, writing that he had recovered and was doing an excellent job.

Dusting the snow from his hat, Matt sat on a felled tree, took pencil in hand and wrote:

2 February 1862

Dear Ginny.

I'm still in Tennessee. The winter is cold. Bitterly cold. Eighty-four Rangers died before January ended. Only five from battle. Seems we're plagued with a really bad winter. We have less than half the men prepared for duty.
Colonel Terry's gone. So is Colonel Lubbock. Brave men, both. The Brazorian Sabers. We're still calling ourselves, Terry's Texas Rangers. God I admired Colonel Terry! Did you know he was a rich man? He was wealthy. But none of it went with him. Only his fame and his glory. Colonel Wharton is now in command. I suppose he'll prove to be a good leader. He was in command of Company B.
Whatever happens, I suppose now I have to sorta live up to Terry's legend. Don't you worry, darling, Steve and I will keep his name alive as long as this War lasts.

They tell me a young girl was shot by a blue boy who had no sense. Somewhere close by. I suppose that's why I keep coming back here, fighting and trying to figure all this out. I can't believe it was you who he could have shot. But if it was, I know you're still alive, darling. I feel it. I feel it as if you were sitting here on this stupid log with me right now.

He paused, looked around, and seeing no one, he continued.

Maybe you are.
I love you so, darling. And I miss you so very much.

Your Matt

POST SCRIPT

A monument commemorating the value of Terry's Texas Rangers (8th Regiment Texas Cavalry C. S. A.) was unveiled on June 26, 1907 at the south entrance to the Texas State Capitol in Austin, Texas.

In Memoriam of

Colonel Benjamin Franklin Terry

By W. M. Gilleland 4 January 1862

The war steed is champing his bit with disdain,
And wild is the flash of his eye
As he waves to the wind his dark, flowing mane,
Stars, neighs, while the scouts and bugler's refrain
Proclaim the battle is nigh.

Charge! Charge! And the Ranger flies on his steed
Bold Terry! The fearless and the brave;
His troops on his trail are moving with speed
And each has crowned his name with a deed
That story or song will engrave!

He swept to the field with an eye of delight,
At the head of his brave, chosen band,

As a meteor's course, 'mid the storms of the night,
So splendidly shone his form in the fight,
And sunk down with a glory as grand.

He fought for the land of his kindred and birth,
Not for fame – though his laurels are won;
His thoughts had a higher, a holier worth
Than the trumpet's acclaim which tells to earth
"Of the man!" not the deeds he has done.

The lightning that burst on the warrior's head,
From the foe that outnumbered his band
Deterred not his course, as thro' columns he sped –
And left on his pathway the dying and dead,
That yielded their breath to his band.

The thunders of battle are hush'd on the plain,
And the wild cry of carnage is o'er,
Dark vultures are gazing from high at the slain,
And the earth drank the flood from the dark purple vein
That thrilled to life's passions before.

But tear-drops of grief dim the eyes of the brave,
For their lion in death is laid low,
Then banners in sable above him they wave,
And muffle their drums in his march to the grave,
To the music and language of woe.

The Magnolia City laments for the dead,
Through streets his gay banner he born
To a far distant land – but low lies his head,
Yet columns shall rise on the fields where he bled,
And freemen his memory adore.

O calm in the tomb is the conqueror's rest!
For his labors of life are well done,
And though quenched is the light of his generous breast,
With heroes immortal his spirit is blest,
Who e'er death have the victory won.

"Who is B. F. Terry? A visionary, entrepreneur, friend and patriot who gave his life for his country and the freedom of its people." *None but Texians, A History of Terry's Texas Rangers",* Jeffrey Dixon Murrah

We Conquer or Die
by James Pierpont

The war drum is beating, prepare for the fight,
The stern bigot Northman exults in his might.
Gird on your bright weapons your foemen are nigh,
And this be our watchword, "We conquer or die!"
And this be our watchword, "We conquer or die!"

The trumpet is sounding from mountain to shore,
Your swords and your lances must slumber no more,
Fling forth to the sunlight your banner on high,
Inscribed with the watchword: "We conquer or die!"
Inscribed with the watchword: "We conquer or die!"

March on to the battlefield, there to do or dare,
With shoulder to shoulder all danger to share,
And let your proud watchword ring up to the sky,
Till the blue arch re-echoes, "We conquer or die!"
Till the blue arch re-echoes, "We conquer or die!"

Press forward undaunted, nor think of retreat,
The enemy's host on the threshold to meet,
Strike firm, till the foeman before you shall fly,
Appalled by the watchword, "We conquer or die!"
Appalled by the watchword, "We conquer or die!"

Go forth in the pathway our forefathers trod,
We too fight for Freedom, our Captain is God,
Their blood in our veins, with their honors we vie,
Their's too, was the watchword, "We conquer or die!"
Their's too, was the watchword, "We conquer or die!"

We strike for the South-Mountain, Valley, and Plain,

For the South we will conquer, again and again,
Her day of salvation and triumph is nigh,
Our's then be the watchword, "We conquer or die!"
Our's then be the watchword, "We conquer or die!"

An excerpt from the next thrilling story in the Brazos series

THE LAST BULLET

PROLOGUE

5 February 1862

A mind is a powerful instrument especially for a horse soldier with time on his hand and near the home of his sweetheart in Tennessee, but because of the War he was restrained from seeing her.

Matt Jorgensen, a cowboy on the run from Montana, was caught up in a desolate part of the country in a War he felt was none of his business. But because of the awkwardness of the situation, he had a choice to accept this calling or be killed as a spy. He opted for the lesser of the two evils.

When he had the an uncanny opportunity to slip away on a furlough and ride to the side of his girl, Ginny McBride, he took it, only to find out that he was too late. She had already saddled up and rode to Richmond, Virginia to see him in his entire splendor, riding in a parade in front of President Jefferson Davis.

Through the grapevine, he found out that she had never reached Virginia, but instead was shot by a young Federal horse soldier and presumed dead. . This news swelled with anger inside his chest for the Federal soldiers camped on the other side of the stretch of woods in a place called Shiloh. But because he could not find evidence of this in any form, he adopted the strong possibility that she was still alive. With this burning sense of feeling inside him, he sought to find her at every opportunity.

After his first futile attempt, he returned to his unit determined to fight the army that was responsible for her being shot; the Federals. With this determination, he found himself to be a leader of men and thus began the stories of the *Devil's Rangers,* Terry's Texas Rangers. He and Steve shaped the Rangers into the Cavalry unit they were meant to be, using their own techniques, some new and some that were used in the Revolutionary War.

The Rangers found their two trainers to be like Romulus and Remus of old; a cut of the wild, and as hungry as devouring wolves. Matt now had a cause and a purpose for fighting, and it rubbed off onto Steve. At times, Steve found himself a little concerned at Matt's determined attitude with wanting to kill. It was almost a blood-thirst revenge for Ginny.

"If you're trying to commit suicide, go ahead," Steve confronted him one day when Matt never let up on his men. "But don't expect me to go with ya."

"Steve," Matt gritted his teeth. "Suck it in."

Steve had heard many times when Matt would call out like this to show his anger. "You can't take it out on the men, Matt." He sucked in his stomach and spurred his gelding out to meet his group of men. Didn't Jesus say, "Let the dead bury the dead?"

"She's not dead!" Matt belted out.

Matt found himself again with pen in hand, one of many times, writing to the wind, hoping beyond hope that Ginny would somehow some way read his mail, although for all the ones he wrote, he never mailed any of them.

"Writing to Ginny again," Steve Andrews said, walking up behind him.

Steve was a six-footer, slightly shorter than Matt, one hundred-seventy pounds of good muscle, and a handsome soldier in his early twenties, same as Matt.

It began to rain and hard drops caused Matt to fold his letter up and stuff it inside his shirt pocket.

"Want I should mail it for ya, friend?"

"I can mail it if I've a mind ta," Matt returned.

"But you don't. You never do. You don't even know where she is." Steve turned up his collar.

Matt gave him a deaf ear and took his slicker down from a tree branch and slipped it on. He walked towards the chow wagon where the other horse soldiers were lined up for the evening meal. Steve sided him.

"Oh, I know how you're feeling, but some how, some way you're going to have to let go. You know thet, too. Don't cha? "

Matt remained silent while Steve continued with his tirade.

"How long I've knowed ya now? Coupla years at least. Yep. And all this time my sister, you know, Brenda, she's sweet on ya, I knows."

When they reached the wagon, Matt grabbed a tin plate and stood in line.

"Go ahead of us, Sir." One of the soldiers paved a way for the two officers with the sweep of his hand.

Matt and Steve did as suggested and took their filled plates to a dry spot covered by a tarp held by two tree branches. Steve continued.

"She's not getting any younger, and she needs some kids. When this War gets over, and it will, we're goin' back to her. What cha gonna tell her? Thet you're still in love with some ghost.?

Matt bit his lip, but kept eating, shaking the rain from his slicker.

The rain came down harder that night and Matt and Steve found themselves dry in Matt's tent. Steve's tirade never slacked up, just like the rain. The harder the rain hit against the sides of the tent, the more Steve talked, and louder.

Finally, Matt rolled over, pulled his hat over his eyes and fell asleep.

"I'm not going out in thet rain to get into my tent," Steve suggested to Matt as he pulled the flap back and looked out over the water-soaked fields. Not a soul stirred outside and the chow wagon was just opening.

Steve looked at Matt's letter sticking out of his shirt pocket. He leaned over and tried to ease it out. With the exception of a few grumbles from Matt's mouth, he was successful with retrieving it.

He shook off some of the rain from it, opened it and began reading it.

Dear Ginny.

It's been gaw-awful this past week with rain coming down off and on. Cold. But I hear we're going out again soon.

I feel you close to me, sweetheart. More and more. I know you're somewhere safe and warm. Don't know where. But I know God will bring us back together. My buddy Steve is coming, so I'll close for now and talk atcha later.

"Geez, he's got it bad," Steve said under his breath. He looked back at Matt and slipped the letter back into his pocket. "If only you felt the same for Brenda, friend."

"Shut up and get some sleep," Matt said, shifting his body to his side.

Steve smiled and pulled a blanket around him as he stretched out on a dry spot on the ground. "Can I say one more thing? Jest one more thing?"

Matt grumbled but said nothing.

"As much as you've written Ginny, I've been writing Brenda about ya."

Brenda was Steve's sister and a school teacher in Nagadoches, Texas. She was a couple of years Steve's senior, and a handsome catch for any cowboy. Steve liked Matt a lot and figured he would make a good husband for her. So every time he had a chance, he would try to do a match making with the two.

" Wanna know somethin'?" Steve asked.

Matt made no sign.

"She thinks you're fallin' for her. Uh huh. She told me so. Wanna see what she wrote me?"

Matt sat up with a click of his .36 as he drew it and pointed the barrel at Steve. "Gonna put it to rest, friend?"

Steve's eyes widened and he slipped back into his blanket without a word.

Matt eased up on the hammer and put his pistol away. Before he laid his head down, he heard Steve say one last time, "She can't wait to see ya again. Soon."

Matt humphed, laid his head down and went fast to sleep. Within a while, Steve followed suit.

Both men sensed the rains would keep coming and the War would rest awhile. Major Thomas Harrison had other plans for such a season, which would not be to the liking of either Matt or Steve. He was a short-statured man with a Napoleonic attitude for leadership. He was also an admirer of Brigadier General Pierre Gustave Toutant Beauregard who towered him by about five inches or so, but was a great follower of Napoleon's war tactics.

Harrison's plans were not yet fulfilled, for he thought the War would have been short and in his favor for running for governor of Texas. Now he was in the thick of battle, which was not to his liking. Watching his comrades fall in battle had paid its toll in Harrison's soul and fear gripped him to where the bottle became his constant companion.

To make up for his stature and his fear as a battlefield leader, he looked for avenues of escape. One avenue was his delight in disciplining, at his convenience, two men he both envied and hated at the same time. He watched for months how Terry's Rangers respected the two lieutenants as heroes. He enjoyed the fact that he had authority over them and he laid plans to exercise this authority as far as he could.

The rains continued to come down hard and the chill factor dropped. His plan was for Matt and Steve to torture their men to drill in inclement weather to where they would come to hate and despise them. After all, he felt this was a lull in the War with the hard rains and he could take advantage of this period to get satisfaction against his nemeses, Matt and Steve.

What he did not expect was that his best laid plans could up and fall apart and bite him on his calloused posterior. He was not the bravest of men to come up against Matt and Steve with such a plan, but he knew he could get away with it. He uncorked his courage to carry out his scheme, and when he emptied it, he opened another and laid on his cot waiting for the moment to summon the two men for extra duty.

ARTICLES, BOOKS and WEB SITES

Years of research and study goes into the making of a novel, keeping with historical accuracies, even of the minute kind. I want to acknowledge the following authors and internet sites, which have helped me in this endeavor.

"Causes of the Civil War"
http://members.aol.com/jfepperson/causes.html

"Americas Civil War"
http://www.thehistorynet.com/AmericasCivilWar/articles/1997/0 997_text.htm

http://www.crt.state.la.us/crt/tourism/civilwar/generals.ht m

"Ad for Runaway Slaves, Feb. 10, 1864"
http://jefferson.village.virginia.edu/vcdh/fellows/runaway.html

"Letter from Juliana Dorsey to General Cocke"

"Letter from Nelia W. of Edge Hill plantation"
http://jefferson.village.virginia.edu/vcdh/fellows/women1.html

http://www.ninetyone.canby.k12.or.us/Classrooms/wigow sky/civilwar/civilwar.htm

http://www.civilwarhome.com/ftsumter.htm

"Document of slave life"

http://www.campus.ccsd.k12.co.us/ss/SONY/psbeta2/slavpho2.htm

"A poster asking for the return of a runaway slave"
http://www.campus.ccsd.k12.co.us/ss/SONY/psbeta2/shriver.htm

"Cotton Gin" by a student in Mr. Munzel's 8th grade Social Studies class of 99
http://www.pausd.paloalto.ca.us/jls/virtualmuseum/ushistory/cotton/

"Gin Helped Expand Cotton Industry",
http://www.concentric.net/~Pgarber/gin.html

"The Online Archive of Terry's Texas Rangers

Sharing & preserving the history of the 8th Texas Cavalry Regiment, 1861-1865 http://www.terrystexasrangers.org/

"Notable Notes about the Terry's Texas Rangers"
http://www.tyler.net/stark/notable.htm

"Eighth Texas Cavalry"
http://www.tsha.utexas.edu/handbook/online/articles/view/EE/qke2.html

"Horse Artillery of Terry's Texas Rangers 8th Texas Cavalry" http://home.flash.net/~porterjh/whitesbattery/

"AEC Cemetery #2 – Slave Cemetery"
http://www.roanetn.com/slave/part6.htm

"East Tennessee's Mountain War"
http://www.state.tn.s/environment/hist/PathDivided/east_tn.htm

http://www.hrticket.com/top/1,1419,N-HRTicket-History-X!ArticleDetail-6598,00.html

Steven A. Bridges huskyfan@ix.netcom.com

Terry's Texas Rangers
http://www.terrystexasrangers.org/library/bibliography.html

Chronological Order of Events Leading
to the Battle of Corinth
October 3rd and 4th, 1862 , By Hugh Horton

Corinth 1861-1865 By Margaret Greene Rogers

http://www.terrystexasrangers.org/library/southern_bivou
ac/v1n3.html Annette Wetzel

Ranger Chaplain Robert F. Bunting 8th Cavalry
http://www.interment.net/data/us/tx/brazoria/sandypoint/sandypoi
nt.htm

"History of the Tenth New York Cavalry" Captain Van-
derbilt

http://www2.cr.nps.gov/abpp/battles/ky004.htm

http://www.bufordsboys.com/McClellanSaddle.htm

http://www.nonebuttexians.com/Texians.pdf

http://www.civilwarhome.com/shilohdescription.htm

http://www.civilwarhome.com/civilwarcavalry.htm

http://www.nytimes.com/learning/general/onthisday/bday/
0427.html

http://library.thinkquest.org/3055/graphics/people/beaureg
ard.html

http://americancivilwar.com/campaigns/Stones_River_Ca
mpaign_Map.html

"The Atlas of the Civil War" by James M. McPherson

"Green Ones and Black Ones"
The Most Common Field Pieces of the Civil War
By James Morgan

The Civil War Society's "Encyclopedia of the Civil War
and Mark M. Boatner's "Civil War Dictionary."

http://www.civilwarhome.com/potpourr.htm

"None But Texians", A History of Terry's Texas Rangers, Jeffrey D. Murrah http://www.nonebuttexians.com/Texians.pdf

http://www.civilwar.org/historyclassroom/hc_stonesriverh ist.htm

Ranger Chaplain Robert F. Burning's account in a contemporary newspaper, 1861

http://home.neo.rr.com/ohiocav/rangers.htm

The Handbook of Texas Online", Thomas W. Cutrer http://www.tsha.utexas.edu/handbook/online/articles/view/EE/qk e2.html

Texas Rangers Libraryhttp://www.terrystexasrangers.org/library/official_reports/1 862_"04_12.html

Goldman, Pauline Scott, ed. "Letters From Three Members of Terry's Texas Rangers 1861-1865." Unpublished M. A. thesis, University of Texas, 1930.

http://www.keathleywebs.com/terrysrangers/terry1.htm

http://www.civilwarhome.com/hillatchickamauga.htm

http://www.nostalgiaville.com/travel/Tennessee/Warren/ warren.htm

http://blueandgraytrail.com/date/August_21

http://en.wikipedia.org/wiki/History_of_African_America ns_in_the_Civil_War

The Army Of The Cumberland" (Chapter VII) By Henry M. Cist, Brevet Brigadier-General U. S. V.; A. A. G. On The Staff Of Major General Rosecrans, And The Staff Of Major-General Thomas; Secretary Of The Society Of The, Army Of The Cumberland

http://www.civilwarhome.com/advancetomurfreesboro.htm

http://members.tripod.com/~douglk/nathan_bedford_forre st/Nathan_Bedford_Forrest.htm

http://www.civilwarhome.com/stones.htm

http://www.civilwarhome.come/stones.htm

http://www.civilwarhome.com/CMHmurfreesboro.htm

http://www.cr.nps.gov/hps/abpp/battles/tn006.htm

http://www.cr.nps.gov/hps/abpp/battles/tn006.htm

http://www.ngeorgia.com/people/forrest.html

http://education.yahoo.com/reference/encyclopedia/entry/ ForrestN

http://www.ngeorgia.com/people/forrest.html

http://www.tsha.utexas.edu/handbook/online/articles/WW /fwh4.html

http://www.gthcenter.org/collections/mscrpt/W-Z/wharto n.htm

http://www.answers.com/topic/john-a-wharton

http://www.terrystexasrangers.org/biographical_notes/h/h arrison_t.html

http://faculty.washington.edu/kendo/terrys.html

http://www.b17.com/mosb/generals/harrisont.htm

http://www.keathleywebs.com/terrysrangers/terry3.htm

http://www.terrystexasrangers.org/histories/fitzhugh/terry s_texas_rangers.html#1

http://www.tsha.utexas.edu/publications/journals/shq/online/v019/n3/article_5.html

http://www.tsha.utexas.edu/handbook/online/articles/LL/flu2.html

http://www.texasranger.org/dispatch/19/BR-%20Albert_Sidney_Johnston/Johnston.htm

http://en.wikipedia.org/wiki/Nathan_Bedford_Forrest

http://www.indianainthecivilwar.com/hoosier/crittend.htm

Kate Scurry Terrell, "Terry's Texas Rangers," in *A Comprehensive History of Texas, 1685 to 1897*, ed. by Dudley G. Wooten (2 vols.; Dallas: William G. Scarff, 1898), Vol. II, p. 682;

Clarence R. Wharton, *History of Fort Bend County* (San Antonio: The Naylor Company, 1939), p. 169.

http://www.city-data.com/picfilesc/picc13414.php

http://www.thc.state.tx.us/publications/brochures/CivilWar.pdf

http://www.thc.state.tx.us/heritagetourism/htcivilwar.html

http://www.liendo.org/

http://www.thc.state.tx.us/publications/brochures/CivilWar.pdf

"John A. Wharton: The Forgotten General", Paul R.Scott, http://www.terrystexasrangers.org/biographies/submitted/wharton.html

http://www.tsha.utexas.edu/handbook/online/articles/BB/kbb5.html

http://www.tsha.utexas.edu/handbook/online/articles/HH/fhaaf.html

http://www.rosecity.net/genealogy/bledsoe/fam/fam00060.html.

http://www.cemetery.state.tx.us/pub/user_form.asp?step=1&pers_id=69

http://www.tsha.utexas.edu/handbook/online/articles/WW/fwh4.html

http://www.tsha.utexas.edu/handbook/online/articles/MM/fmu15.html

http://www.terrystexasrangers.org/histories/scott_thesis.html

Eighth Texas Cavalry Regiment, CSA By Paul Robert Scott

The University of Texas at Arlington July 1977

Our Trust Is in the God of Battles: The Civil War Letters of Robert Franklin Bunting, Chaplain, Terry's Texas Rangers: R. F. Bunting, Thomas W. Cutrer Hardcover, 2006 University of Tennessee Press
http://en.wikipedia.org/wiki/Albert_Sidney_Johnston
http://www.terrystexasrangers.org/biographies/submitted/wharton.html

http://en.wikipedia.org/wiki/Fort_Monroe%2C_Virginia

http://www.edinburgh-tattoo.co.uk/tattoo-experience/fact.html

http://en.wikipedia.org/wiki/Battle_of_Murfreesboro

http://www.historynet.com/magazines/american_civil_war/3032626.html

An article on Murfreesboro written by Michael Haskew and originally appeared in the January 1997 issue of *America's Civil War* magazine.

http://www.civilwarhome.com/kniffinstonesriver.htm

http://www.answers.com/topic/battle-of-stones-river

http://www.civilwarhome.com/CMHmurfreesboro.htm

http://www.southerntradewind.net/1stgacavalry.html

http://www.georgiaencyclopedia.org/nge/Article.jsp?id=h-2211

http://home.earthlink.net/~larsrbl/CW/Romepage.htm

From the journal of Kate Cumming, Confederate nurse, July 30, 1863: http://romegeorgia.com/history.html

http://en.wikipedia.org/wiki/Rome,_GA

Cornelius C. Platter Civil War Diary, 1864 - 1865 Pages 1 – 6 Author: Platter, Cornelius C.

http://dlg.galileo.usg.edu/hargrett/platter/001.php

hhttp://www.cgsc.army.mil/carl/resources/csi/Robertson3/robertson3.asp

And last, but certainly not the least, I want to thank the many Civil War re-enactors I have met and talked with at many events, and especially to those from Terry's Texas Rangers.

Photo by
Phillip Ritchie
Red Roof Studios
Costa Mesa, CA

Photo by
Phillip Ritchie
Red Roof Studios
Costa Mesa, CA

Photo by
Phillip Ritchie
Red Roof Studios
Costa Mesa, CA

Photo by
Phillip Ritchie
Red Roof Studios
Costa Mesa, CA

Photo by
Phillip Ritchie
Red Roof Studios
Costa Mesa, CA

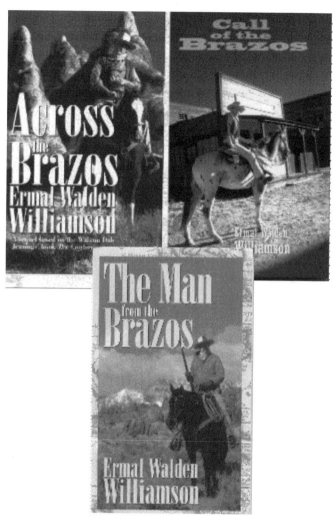

If you enjoyed Ermal's Civil War novel, you might want to order the next novel
Book two in the saga – "The Last Bullet" - $17.95
And the first three copies in the Brazos Series.
"Across the Brazos - $19.95
"The Man from the Brazos" - $16.95
"Call of the Brazos" - $16.95
Prices include shipping and handling
Ermal Walden Williamson
521 W. Atlantic St.
Branson, MO 65616
www.ermal.com
duke@ermal.com
417-598-0088